THE
WIFE
IN THE
PHOTO

BOOKS BY EMILY SHINER

The Hotel

THE
WIFE
IN THE
PHOTO

EMILY SHINER

Bookouture

Published by Bookouture in 2023

An imprint of Storyfire Ltd.
Carmelite House
50 Victoria Embankment
London EC4Y 0DZ

www.bookouture.com

ISBN: 978-1-83790-386-3
eBook ISBN: 978-1-83790-385-6

For Claire
You make the world a better plac

THE
WIFE
IN THE
PHOTO

EMILY SHINER

bookouture

Published by Bookouture in 2023

An imprint of Storyfire Ltd.
Carmelite House
50 Victoria Embankment
London EC4Y 0DZ

www.bookouture.com

ISBN: 978-1-83790-386-3
eBook ISBN: 978-1-83790-385-6

For Claire
You make the world a better place.

PROLOGUE

Loud voices float out of the windows of the Warners' craftsman home, disrupting the quiet that settled on the neighborhood after the afternoon storm. Even though the worst of the storm has passed, there's still a thick mist hanging in the air. It wraps around the house like a blanket, cocooning the people inside. Water drips from the deck railing, pooling on the stairs. The wood is slick, dark and dangerous, the gorgeous home almost glowing in the haze. The living room lights are all turned on, shining like beacons through the windows.

Moonlight filters down from behind slow-moving rain clouds, the light sometimes dappling the professionally manicured front lawn, the clouds sometimes casting the entire house in shadow. Two years ago, the Warners' daughter, Jessica, threw a baseball through the kitchen window, but that's long been repaired, all the glass perfectly shiny and transparent thanks to the washing crew that comes by once a month in the summer and fall.

Freshly spread mulch in the front garden lays in wet

mounds and lumps, protecting the plants and beautifying the garden. While the Warners have lived in the house since Jessica was a little girl, the yard was never filled with plastic toys and broken dolls. The HOA wouldn't like it, but they would keep it neat anyway. Orderly. It's perfect, just like the family inside.

A chorus of late-summer crickets pauses their music when a door slams. Then another. Loud footsteps echo out of the windows.

Raised voices again.

The crickets don't make a sound.

On sunny days the blue of the house can almost blend in with the rest of the sky. The white bargeboard is only decorative, but Lola Warner always wanted a home that looked like something from a storybook, and whatever Lola wanted, Lola got.

For a while anyway.

When a pizza delivery car drives into the cul-de-sac to turn back around, the voices inside the house stop for a moment, then continue, louder than before.

The front door slams open, then shut.

There's a loud shout and a response. Someone swears, the language used crude as to be hurtful. In the quiet storybook neighborhood, and in this beautiful house, the foul language is so out of place it's almost comical. The next-door neighbors always watch movies at night, and since getting surround sound, they can't hear a thing.

They don't have any idea what's going on next door. They have no clue Lola is standing out on the deck, her thin arms wrapped tightly around her body like a hug. She didn't know it was going to be so cool outside, and if she had, she might have worn a jacket. But really, the only thing going through her mind at the time had been to *getoutsidegetaway.*

Sometimes you just need some fresh air to think clearly. But the air isn't fresh; it's thick, a cousin to the fog that clings to the side of a mountain after a storm. She feels it in her throat and swallows hard, reaching up to touch the skin on her throat as she does.

Her pulse beats hard under her fingertips.

How in the world did it come to this?

It's funny, almost, to her. The way things can change so quickly; how many secrets can be hidden behind the flawless front door. She chose that shade of red, wanting it to look bright and inviting, but in the murky light from the moon it just looks garish.

She laughs.

The person standing opposite her doesn't.

Lola takes another step back, then another. Reaching behind her for support, her hand finds the top railing. She clutches it. The wet wood is cold, but she doesn't let it go. When they'd had the deck enlarged so they could all sit outside in nice weather, she'd been so worried it was going to be too small, but now it feels huge, an oversized parody of a southern porch.

The person coming toward her is still yelling. Letting go of the railing, she reaches up and claps her hands over her ears. Pressing down hard enough, she can hear her heartbeat.

It's fast. Like she ran a marathon.

She takes a step back.

Then another.

Even huge, the deck isn't big enough for the two of them. She's Alice in Wonderland, everything around her both too large and too small at the same time. She feels space expand and contract around her, pressing down on her chest, making it diffi-cult for her to catch her breath.

Another step back.

Here she can feel the edge of the stair and she toes at it, her bare feet chilled. No, scratch that. Every part of her is chilled. She fears she'll never get warm, not when she thinks about the terrible things that were just said to her, not when she feels how prickly her throat feels from yelling in response.

And then her foot slips.

For one long moment, during which she tries her best to simultaneously grab for the railing, throw herself forward for the safety of the deck, and think about all the things she wanted to do with her life when she was a little girl, Lola seems to hang there, suspended. From the outside, she's still moving. In her mind, though, she's caught in time and in place, floating, like a fly trapped in amber.

And then she's falling.

Down the stairs, her body twisting as she gains momentum, gravity, that heartless bitch, yanking her down to the ground. She gasps at the snap of a rib. Her shoulder bangs hard into the corner of one step and for just a moment she has a final thought, one clear line running through her mind.

I'm going to be okay. People fall from three stories up and survive. This is nothing—

All thought stops. Lola's hair spreads out around her like a halo.

It should be poetic. It *would* be poetic, but it's so trite, so overused. There's nothing poetic about death, nothing attractive about the way a body looks when it has gasped out its last breath and drawn nothing in.

Look at her. Like an angel.

Lola Warner wasn't an angel. Nobody would have claimed she was. She was a good person, sure, but not an *angel*.

She looks like she's sleeping.

But she's not sleeping. There's nothing calm about her face, about the way her brow is furrowed, and her head is turned so far to the side that the tendons in her neck snap out, stretching the skin tight.

You can't be calm when you see your death coming and there's nothing you can do to stop it.

She looks so peaceful.

She's not.

She looks alive.

She's dead.

Lola is dead, sprawled on the ground, the heavy mist that's been falling all evening picking up again and covering her body, her face, her hair, in fine drops. It looks like a bridal veil, the water slowly collecting in the hollow of her neck, her collarbone, the small depression right along her jaw.

She doesn't move.

The deck steps leading down from the house to the walkway are slick, the railing wet, everything dripping, soaking, chilled to the bone.

Everything is wet. Cold. Nothing moves.

Except for the person at the top of the stairs.

ONE

EVAN

My vision blurs as I put the glass down on the kitchen counter. I know I need to stop drinking, but I don't think I can. Everyone is watching me, and I turn slowly, making sure I don't trip over my own two feet, that my shoes don't catch on the tile, that I don't accidentally pitch forward and fall down.

No, I shouldn't have been drinking this much, I can admit that. I'm man enough to admit that.

But drinking like this is the only thing that's making it possible for me to get through the quiet of the evening without snapping at anyone. Even with people in my house trying to take care of me, the last thing I want is quiet. I need noise, need something to take my mind off what's been going on. Without it, I feel ungrounded, a ship unmoored, lost at sea.

And I can only imagine how it is for my daughter. Jessica is too young to lose her mother, especially like this.

Nobody should lose their mother like this.

While I'm drawing comfort from having other people in the

house to make noise and remind me that life isn't over for me yet, she's upstairs, hiding in her room.

It's the only way she seems to be able to live with me. She hides from me, her face turned away from me when we're in the same room. Even if I can see her, I can't read her mind, can't tell what's going on in her heart. She's broken inside, and of course she is.

She just lost her mother. If she wasn't broken, if she wasn't falling to pieces and crying every moment thoughts of Lola come to her, I'd wonder what was wrong with her.

"Evan." Mike Maroni, the detective who I'd almost consider a friend from work, puts his hand on my shoulder to steady me. I want to push it off and show him and the rest of the guys in the kitchen that I can stand on my own two feet, but I'm afraid that pushing his hand off me will cause me to lose my balance.

Turning my head to look at him makes the room spin. I close my eyes and take a deep breath, fighting the heavy feeling in my stomach. *I've had too much to drink.*

I can't fall over in front of the guys from work. They need to see me being strong even though I just lost the love of my life.

"Mike. I'm fine. I just need to get to bed." Whiskey swirls in my stomach and his face swims in front of me. It's a bad sign when my vision is blurry, but what would people really expect from me right now? Lola's been in the ground three days and she's not coming back. Anyone else in my position would be drinking too, I just know it, and I'm not going to apologize for it.

"I'll get you to bed." He sighs. "Just... you need to lay off the bottle. Jessica needs you right now, and you're going to have trouble taking care of her if you're always drinking." He nods to another guy, Lance, who grabs the whiskey by the neck and takes it to the sink.

I don't have to watch him to know what he's doing. The glugging sound the whiskey makes as it pours from the bottle down the drain is loud in the silence of the room. For a moment I wonder if Jessica can hear it, then I shake my head.

Of course she can't. She's locked in her room, probably with headphones in, probably crying on her bed or maybe talking to her best friend, Britt. She doesn't care that the only thing helping tether me to this world is being poured down the sink right now.

"I can get to bed on my own." Now I do shrug his hand off my shoulder. The ground spins a little bit, the custom tile Lola had ordered swimming a little before my eyes, and I close them for a moment to stop the movement. "Seriously, I appreciate you guys all coming by but there's no need to babysit me. I'm a big boy."

Mike presses a glass of water into my hand. "Can you make it up the stairs?"

I want to be offended at his question. Hell, I want to scream at the man for even asking that, but that's a great way to have HR think that I shouldn't come back to work right now. It's probably pushing it with me starting up again in a few days, but I need to be out of the house. Jessica and I need our normal routine back.

Or as normal as we're going to be able to make it without Lola around.

"Of course." Giving him what I hope is a charming grin, I drain the water and hand him the glass. "You guys can let yourselves out. Lock the bottom lock on your way."

Without giving them a chance to respond, I walk carefully across the kitchen, making sure to focus when I put each foot down on the floor. The floor tries to move, tries to drop away from me as I walk, but I refuse to face-plant right here in front of everyone, and to keep that from happening, I need to be deliberate in my steps.

When I reach the stairs, I sigh, sagging against them, grabbing the banister and using it to pull me up each step, one at a time.

One more.

Then another.

Almost there.

Behind me, I hear the sounds of the guys cleaning up the kitchen. It's kind of them to want to do that for me when I can barely get dinner on the table myself. They all think it's because I'm missing my wife so badly. They think I can barely function without Lola, that not having her in my life makes it difficult for me to even breathe.

If they knew the type of person I really am then they wouldn't be down there picking up the kitchen and taking care of me.

That's why I have to be careful. Lance poured my whiskey down the drain to help me, and I didn't fight it because I want to be able to think straight.

I need to make sure I don't slip up and tell anyone the truth.

TWO

ARIEL

SUNDAY, AUGUST 27

It's unnaturally cold out tonight and my breath puffs out in a little cloud when I exhale. Shifting in my seat, I rub my hands up and down my arms, trying to keep warm. Yes, I could turn on the heat and warm up that way, but any sound, any light, any*thing* could draw attention to me.

And that's the last thing I want.

A chill tears through me and I shiver again, pulling the spare blanket I keep on the passenger seat into my lap. My coffee has long gone cold, but I still take a sip of it, closing my eyes as I imagine the caffeine running through my veins.

The first time I was here watching the house, I didn't need caffeine to keep me awake. I'd been on the edge of my seat the entire time, my nerves so tense that any little sound made me feel like I was coming out of my skin.

I'm still focused of course. Now, though, I've been here so many times that it feels familiar. I know the sounds this street makes, the way some neighbors fly down the street and loop the cul-de-sac, windows open, '90s rap pouring through them.

Others take their time, inching along the road to their driveways like insects, terrified to cause an accident.

I know how long it takes Evan and Jessica to make it up to their rooms and turn on the lights upstairs. I've seen how quickly she flies up the stairs from the sidewalk to the oversized front deck and how Evan takes them slowly, like an exhausted old man.

Whatever he's carrying is weighing him down. There's sadness in this house; I can feel it just from looking at it. I don't know the full extent of what happened here, but I'm going to find out.

Lola deserves that much.

A slamming door makes me sit up in excitement. Without looking, I fumble the travel cup back into the cupholder and lean forward. Squint against the dark to try to see better. My heart pounds and I take a deep breath to try to calm down. Every nerve of my body is on high alert, ready for what's coming next.

The Warners' house is lit up tonight. Jessica always turns on as many lights as possible. It's like she's trying to keep back any shadows that might come for her in the dark. I'd know she's home even if I hadn't seen her get dropped off by a friend. They'd arrived in a little red car, the brakes screeching as they'd stopped in front of the house. The two girls had sat there for a moment, but they'd had their windows up and I couldn't hear what they'd been saying.

Not that it really matters in the long run, does it? I can imagine what Jessica would say to someone.

I don't want to go in there.

Don't make me be alone with my dad.

My head swims so I close my eyes, open them again. I have to stay focused.

I'm ready to make my move, to show up at the front door and accuse Evan, but it's not time yet. No, although that would be satisfying, it would also be dangerous. It's best that I wait until I'm able to get inside the house. From there, I'll be able to take care of things.

For now, the only option I have is to sit and wait. I'm terrible at that, however. Terrible at taking my time when I know full well someone needs my help. Jessica needs me. I'm here for her.

The upstairs lights all click off, one by one. I sit for ten more minutes, just waiting. If there's a scream, or if I think she's in trouble, I'll throw the plan out the window.

Nothing happens.

Finally, half-relieved and half-disappointed, I turn the key, start the car. The engine rumbles to life and I immediately crank up the heat, needing something that will help keep my fingers from feeling like they're going to freeze off. The weather is supposed to be a lot warmer but right now I'm chilled, thanks to an unseasonable cold front.

I'm about to shift into drive when movement catches my eye. Something in my periphery moves and it makes me freeze. Hair on the back of my neck stands up and I slowly turn, my eyes scanning the Warner house.

And then I see it.

Jessica's window slides all the way open, her room softly lit from within. I freeze, my breath in my throat as I watch her. She's so beautiful, isn't she? Too young for what happened to her, too young to have to deal with losing her mom and living with just a father. I watch for a moment as she adjusts the window, allowing a stream of cool air into her room.

For a moment, I'm confident she's going to climb out and slip down the roof, dropping carefully to the grass, then turn and run down the street. I freeze, my hands tight on the wheel, waiting for her to do something stupid, something I'll have to stop to keep her safe.

But she doesn't. The window remains cracked, the light inside turns off. She just wanted some fresh air.

"I hope you locked your door, Jessica. Someone hurt your mom. I just don't know what really happened." I whisper the words to myself then finally shift into drive. Eleven o'clock is past when I like to go to bed, and it's been a long night of sitting here. I'm exhausted. I need more sleep than I've been getting, but until I can be sure Jessica isn't in danger, I'll be back here again in a few days.

Too many nights in a row and someone will notice my car sitting here. Too many nights and I'll have to worry about a well-meaning neighbor calling the police. But I'll be parked on the main road tomorrow, watching to make sure Jessica gets to school safely. School has just recently started back up and nobody will pay attention to my car on the main road.

I pass a black Mini Cooper on the way out. It loops around the cul-de-sac, moving slowly, then follows me from the neighborhood. My breathing hitches and I stare in my rearview mirror, trying to see who's driving the car.

It's not the first time I've seen it in the neighborhood.

Is someone onto me?

At the main road I turn to the right. The Mini Cooper turns left, and I exhale. Adrenaline courses through my body, better than any amount of caffeine. Each night I'm here I feel like I push my luck.

It's time to put my plan into action. All of the pieces are in place and I'm ready.

THREE

LOLA'S DIARY

WEDNESDAY, JUNE 28

He's so distant recently.

Maybe it's work. I knew when I married Evan that his job would be stressful, that there would be long nights when he might not make it home. Or nights when he'd come home and pour himself a drink before pouring himself into bed.

We've had plenty of those: nights where I would lie awake next to him, listening to him breathe, wondering what had happened at work that could be so upsetting he would rather willingly embrace the oblivion whiskey had to offer than turn to me for help.

So it's not like I don't know what it's like to have Evan be quiet, to have him draw into himself. We've gone through that off and on for years. When he was an officer on the streets it was because he had to deal with a bad accident, a mugging gone wrong, or an overdose. Then he worked his way upstairs and now he mostly deals with interpersonal problems within the force. Those can be bad though; I know they can.

But this silence is different. It feels heavy, significant, like all the other silences that grew between us in our marriage were just practice, just *beginner silences*, and now we're facing the real thing and... it's exhausting.

Because it's not just his silence that has me a bit worried, if I'm being honest.

It's the way his lips quirk up when he checks his phone. It's how he keeps it on him all the time, never giving me the chance to type in the password—our anniversary—just to check, just to *make sure*.

Not that I would, right? But I might think about it.

He comes home from late meetings and gets right in the shower. We haven't... oh God, this feels terrible to admit... we haven't been intimate in months, and even though I want him more than anything, want him to pull me into his arms to hold me, it's not reciprocated.

And I don't know what to do about it.

Jessica hasn't noticed, or at least I don't think she has. She's too wrapped up in school, in spending time with Britt, in being a fourteen-year-old girl who's just trying to fit in. While I don't think her best friend is a great influence on her, I'm just happy she's happy.

At least someone in the house is.

I have to stop thinking like that. Things seem bad now, but this is tale as old as time. If Evan is finding... comfort somewhere else, I'll find out about it. I'll help him remember the vows we made.

He loves Jessica. He loves me, I know he does. If he's having an affair, then we can get through this. I want to stand by him. I want to remind him why we got married, why we started a family together. I've always been his rock—he's told me so many times that I have to believe it—and I'm going to continue to be his rock.

He loves me.

I'm going to remind him of that.

I know how to make him smile.

Yes, there might be someone else right now, some threat to my marriage, to our family, but she won't last. She's a fling, a distraction, nothing more.

We're everything to Evan. Me—and Jessica.

I hate knowing I'm not the first woman to deal with this and certainly not the last. But we're going to be a success story. I love Evan. He's worth fighting for.

Is he perfect? No.

But I want to fix this. The question is: does he?

FOUR

EVAN

MONDAY, AUGUST 28

It hits me as I'm driving to work.

My coffee in the cup holder next to me sloshes around, some of the brew almost spilling out of the hole in the top of the lid, but that's not what I'm focused on.

I need help.

Things like this always come to me too late, always when other people have already caught on to just how much trouble I'm really in. Having a teenage daughter is hard enough. Having one without a mom there to guide her and make sure she doesn't make stupid decisions is even harder. Just the thought of trying to navigate everything that Jessica is going to start going through without someone there to help is enough to make me want to scream.

And they say police have the hardest job.

Being a father and trying to keep up with chores in the house may just be harder than what I do at work.

Last night I noticed just how terrible it had gotten around the place. I saw how the laundry had turned into tall teetering piles that made me want to hold my breath as I walked past in hopes they wouldn't fall over.

It all just fell apart so *quickly*.

And if that wasn't bad enough, I saw the expression on Jessica's face when she looked down at her plate of macaroni and cheese for dinner. Again.

She didn't say anything, but I felt her judgement loud and clear. That's the thing about teenagers—they don't need to verbally express their disappointment for everyone to know how they're feeling. Instead, it oozes out of them, creating an aura around them, something so physical that it feels like you should be able to reach out and touch it.

I know Jessica is unhappy with me. We dance around each other like two people paired together in gym class dance lessons. We both know the motions we're supposed to make—or we thought that we did—but without Lola there to make sure we don't step on each other's feet, that seems to be all we do.

I sigh as I pull into the parking lot and glance at the time, wincing at how early I am. Surely my daughter is going to notice that I keep leaving for work just a bit earlier every morning. It's not that I don't love her. It's just that looking at her right now, when she reminds me so much of her mother, is difficult.

When Lola was alive, there was a buffer. There was something there, a calming presence, her protecting the two of us from each other as we bounced around in the house. But she's no longer there, and instead of bouncing around harmlessly, the two of us careen and slam into each other.

We're going to break each other if we're not careful.

The building towers over me, over the entire parking lot, and I look up at it as I walk toward the front door. Made from large pieces of cut rock, it was designed to be formidable, to make people think twice about just stopping in, and it does just that. Only a few cars are in the lot, all dispatchers, I'd assume. I look for a Mini Cooper, exhaling hard when I see it's not there, then look back up at the building itself. The windows are large but most of them dark, and I realize with surprise that I'm actually early enough to be one of the first people in this morning.

That's not something that's happened in a very long time and I have to dig in my pocket for the key to unlock the front door. From there, it's the simple matter of keying in my personal code to turn off the alarm before closing the door behind me and locking it so nobody can sneak in.

The only floor that has any light streaming from the windows is the third. How the dispatchers managed to get that floor—the one with the biggest kitchenette, with the gym on it, for God's sake—is beyond me, but they practically live up there. It's their space, the place they all feel totally comfortable hanging out and working, and nobody is really allowed to come there unless they're hitting the gym.

Except for me. I was allowed there, up until I wasn't. Even though I should feel confident walking onto that floor and talking to whoever I want to, the third floor is one I avoid now. In the elevator I press the button for the fourth, praying nobody will want to go down from the third before I get into my office.

It isn't until I'm down the hall and through my door that I feel like I can relax. Up here, nobody can bother me. Sure, my assistant will get here soon and will start buzzing around, flitting in and out of my door when she has something she needs to talk to me about, but I'm not going to have to worry about anyone else making it in here to interrupt me.

Up here, I can pretend that none of this nasty business with Lola ever happened. Her picture is still on my desk, right where everyone would expect a loving spouse to have a picture of his family. In it, the three of us are at the beach, Jessica already sunburned, her nose freckled and starting to peel a little, matching grins on all of our faces.

It's the last trip we took together before it all fell apart. Just looking at it should be enough to bring me to tears, should be enough to make me feel terrible about everything that happened. Instead, though, the growing pit in my stomach makes me take a sip of my coffee. Of course I miss my wife.

Of course my daughter misses her mom.

I miss how easy it was in the house when Lola was still alive, and that's something I'm going to need help with. I need someone to help me make it easy again, to take some of the pressure off me, to make it feel like Jessica and I aren't strangers living in the same 2,000 square feet.

Someone who can have a hot meal on the table when I get home from work, who can make sure Jessica has a nice snack after school that will encourage her to sit down and do her homework. I need someone who will be there to do the dishes, the laundry, the cleaning.

They need to be there when Jessica and I need them, willing to get down and dirty to clean up our messes, and willing to run any errands I ask them to, just to take them off my plate.

It sounds like I need a new wife, but I can only imagine the gossip were I to tip into bed with someone new this soon after losing Lola.

No, not a wife. Something close though. Something that wouldn't make anyone bat their eyes, something that will allow me to actually move on with my life again after losing my wife.

My thoughts drift to the third floor, but I rein them in.

Not a wife.

A housekeeper. That's what I was thinking about on the way in to the office this morning. A housekeeper would be appropriate. That's something nobody can fault me for wanting.

And it's someone I should be able to keep at a distance so nobody ever finds out what I've done.

FIVE

I'm ripped away from the report I'm reading when Miriam leans her head in my door, her gray hair perfectly pulled back into a tight bun at the base of her neck. I've wondered before how she keeps every strand in place, how she prevents them all from flying away by the end of the day, but that's not something to ask your assistant.

Women like their secrets. I know this by now.

"Evan, I'm popping out to lunch. Would you like me to grab you anything?" Her steely gray eyes cut into me, and I find myself wondering again just how old she is. She's mentioned before that she has a grandchild. I have no idea how many children she has; unlike me, she doesn't keep any photos of her family in her little office.

That's fine. Some people really like keeping their personal life private at work, especially considering the type of people who might want to come into my office to talk to me and who will walk right by her desk.

"Nothing for me, thanks." I hesitate, leaning back in my chair and stretching my arms over my head. My phone has been going off all morning, most of it little things I can easily handle without getting up from my leather chair, and my back is a bit sore. "Although, Miriam, do you have a moment?"

She pauses, and it's obvious she was ready to get straight into the elevator to go to lunch, but nods, fully stepping into my office. This morning she's in a dark suit with low heels that look like they came from the '70s. And they probably did.

Miriam is always appropriate: she never dresses in a way she shouldn't; never speaks out of turn. Not like some of the dispatchers. Not like...

I drag my thoughts back to the present and the woman staring at me. "I think Jessica and I need help." It feels strange to admit that, especially to someone I don't really know outside of how quickly she can make copies and that she's good at filing, but Miriam and I have worked together for a long time.

She's probably one of the people who knows me the best. It's impossible to work with someone for as long as the two of us have been together and not know what's going on with the other person. Even when I don't tell her I'm having a bad day, I'm sure she can tell. Miriam has been a constant for me here at the department for years and she's absolutely the right person to ask for help. From time to time, I've felt guilty that she knows everything about me and I don't know about her personal life, but she seems to like it that way.

She exhales softly and nods. "I've been worried about you. And about Jessica. You two need help, rattling around in that house all alone." Silently, she crosses my rug and then sits down across from me at my desk. When she leans forward, I catch a glimpse of a necklace with a blue stone right at her collarbone.

"I don't want people to worry," I begin, but she cuts me off.

"How could we not? You and that sweet daughter of yours all alone in that great big house? I've been wondering if you're eating enough, if she's getting enough sun, if the house is clean."

"Jessica is fine," I lie, but again Miriam cuts me off. This is so out of character for how she usually is at the office that I stare at her, my mouth falling open a little bit.

"Jessica is not fine and neither are you. You lost Lola... what? Only three weeks ago?"

When I nod, she continues. "Nobody expects you two to be fine, but that doesn't mean you can't take steps to get help. It's okay to ask for help, Evan; I hope you know that, no matter how much you might want to try to handle it all on your own. You can hire someone. You should think about it."

She's right and she's reading my mind. It's nicer than I'd like to admit to have someone looking out for me right now. Since the funeral, I've been the one taking care of Jessica—the only one taking care of her. She's been a handful, which is to be expected, but it's really nice right now to let someone worry about me.

Of course, this is the heart of Virginia, and people have brought over casseroles. They've offered to run errands for me, to mow my lawn, but I've turned them all down. The last thing I want is people sniffing around where it happened, where Lola died. I also hate the idea of anyone thinking that I'm weak and that I can't handle my daughter and my house on my own.

But hiring someone for help is different. That's not charity. That's a job, and they'll be an employee of the house. It's someone you can write off on your taxes, someone you can prove you really need.

It's different than Bob the neighbor coming over to mow your lawn out of pity.

"That is what I've been thinking about," I say, mentally snapping back to the conversation at hand. "I think Jessica and I need help. A housekeeper. Someone to run errands, keep the place in order, all of that. I was hoping you might know someone."

She nods slowly, tapping her chin with one finger. "That's

smart. The last thing you want is to open your doors and let someone in your house you can't trust."

I agree but I don't say that. Instead, I wait. That's what I'm used to doing—waiting until I get the information I want from people. They always come through, and right now I have to hope Miriam isn't the exception.

"You know, I think I have someone you can talk to." She smiles at me, and I feel the tension drain out of my shoulders. "She's great; we met at a church outreach program. About your age, I'd wager, hard worker, willing to do whatever it takes to get the job done. And I think she was a chef for a bit, or worked as a line cook or something. You might be able to get her on board with cooking."

A cook. A cleaner. Someone to come into the house and make my life better. Nobody will bat an eye at this, especially when the recommendation comes from someone like Miriam. I knew asking my assistant was the best option. As great as she is at taking care of things in the office, I knew she had to be good at finding the person I need to keep my house from feeling like it's going to collapse in on us.

"She sounds perfect," I say. "How do I get in touch with her?"

SIX

ARIEL

TUESDAY, AUGUST 29

I refuse to let my nerves get the best of me. Even though part of me wants to run from this imposing building, get back in my car, and head out of town, I won't do that. I'm here for a job, and it's probably the most important one I'll ever have.

This is what I've been working toward, and there's no way I'm going to back out now, no matter how scared I might be. Yanking on the door handle, I swing the front door of the office building open and stride in, holding my head up high like I know what I'm doing. On the inside, though, I'm shaking. I honestly can't believe what I'm about to do, but then I remember this isn't about me.

It's about Lola.

"Can I help you?" The girl sitting at the front desk is pretty in a small-town sort of way. Her button nose and small mouth are offset by large brown eyes, which she's outlined with liner. When I don't answer immediately, she tilts her head and taps one finger on the desk between the two of us to get my attention.

"I'm here to see Evan Warner." I say his name causally, like it isn't one that I've cursed daily for the past few months. It comes out *Wahh-nahh*, and the girl stares at me a moment longer before breaking into a smile.

"Of course, right. He's on the fourth floor. Does he know you're coming?" Her hand hovers over a phone like she's ready to ring up and let him know I'm standing here, and I nod.

"Yes. He knows. He called me."

"Oh, great. Then you can go on up." She flicks her wrist behind me, and I turn to see the elevator there. I hadn't noticed it.

What else have I missed?

When I don't move, she repeats herself. "Fourth floor of course."

"Of course."

"You'll have to tell his assistant who you are. That's Miriam. But if you're on his calendar then she'll let you through." She grins at me like it's some secret joke the two of us have, that I might not really be on his calendar, that I'm here to... what?

"Miriam. Got it." Her name flows easily from my lips not just because I'm no longer as nervous as I was a moment ago, but because we've met before.

It's hard to keep my stomach from flipping as the elevator ascends. I close my eyes until I hear the cheery ding above my head. The doors open silently, and I step out into the small office, the carpet muffling my footsteps as I walk up to the only desk in the room.

"Miriam, hi. Good to see you." The words spill from my lips, and I blush. It's just that I'm suddenly, inexplicably nervous. In every moment leading up to this, I've been confident, I've had no doubts that I'm doing the right thing, and now suddenly I feel sick, like I should run and hide, like this is a terrible idea. But then I remember who I'm doing it for, and I plant my feet on the carpet, staring at the woman sitting in front of me.

She takes a moment to answer, finishing typing whatever she was working on before looking up at me, her mouth pursed before she starts to smile. "Ariel, you made it! How are you?"

"Good. I'm good." Relief washes over me. I'm doing this. Everything I've done, all the long nights watching him and Jessica, all the time I spent trying to decide how to handle what he did to Lola, and it's finally happening. "How are you?"

"Oh, working." She laughs, putting me even more at ease. "You're here right on time though, which is great. Chief Warner will appreciate that. He likes it when people are punctual."

"Well, that's me." I clear my throat and look around the lobby. Miriam has the only desk in here. On the other side of the room is a little coffee station with a few mugs waiting to be filled. There's a bookshelf and two plush seats for people to use while waiting to see the chief. I look at all of this but don't really pay attention to it.

I'm only interested in Evan. He's right behind the closed door on the other side of Miriam's office. It's stupid, but it's almost like I can feel him there, like I know he's *right there.*

"Looks like he's off his call." Miriam points to the phone on her desk, one with lots of clear buttons on it that will, I guess, light up when in use. "Let me take you on in there."

"Thanks." My mouth is suddenly dry, and I swallow hard. Some water right now would be great, just to help me clear my throat a little bit. I'm parched but before I can ask her for something to drink, she speaks again.

"Follow me." She stands, planting her hands on her desk and pushing herself out of her seat like her body has conformed to it, like it's difficult to move. I wait, respectfully, my hands clasped in front of me. Her brain is sharp, but her body moves slowly. To be fair, though, I don't care how slow she goes.

All that matters is her taking me in to see Evan.

Hopefully he won't be able to tell how much I'm sweating. When Miriam turns and leads the way across the office, I risk dropping my nose to my armpit and taking a quick sniff.

I'm fine. Nothing bad there. Just the sweet smell of lavender and roses. What I wouldn't give for my deodorant to be named something powerful like *Thunder Ice*, and not *Floral Fields*, but that's on me. I'll just shop in the men's section next time, gender roles be damned.

But first, I have to meet Evan. I have to get him on my side, convince him that he and his daughter need my help. I have to prove to him that I can not only help him but make his life a thousand times better.

And then I'm going to ruin him.

SEVEN

LOLA'S DIARY

SATURDAY, JULY 1

He put his phone down.

Jessica needed him outside to look at something. I don't know what it was—a good mom would—but the only thing I could focus on was his phone.

He'd been drinking, *again*, and that has to be the only reason he put his phone down on the counter instead of slipping it into his pocket. I watched the scene, watched as he rolled his eyes and huffed a sigh before heading outside to see what she needed, then my eyes snapped right back to the phone.

It sat there, the screen dark, but tempting me.

A good wife would walk away from the phone because we all know that snooping in your significant other's messages is a great way to feel terrible about yourself or stir up problems, but the problems were already stirred up, weren't they?

How in the world could me looking at his phone cause any additional issues?

Even as these thoughts ran through my mind, I knew I was

going to check his phone. Try to get in, to read his messages, to look for pictures of some woman I don't know.

If I hadn't checked then I wouldn't know, but I did, and right now I wish I hadn't.

It was just too tempting, so I slipped the phone from the counter, sat down on the floor, nervously blew out a breath. I didn't want him to look in the window and see me with his phone, didn't want him to burst back through the front door and run to the kitchen, the memory of his phone left alone with me spurring him on.

So I hid. Like a little kid dipping into the cookie jar and then shoving their spoils in their mouth before anyone knows, I sat on the floor, the cold tiles making me shiver.

I tapped the screen. Turned it on. Swiped my thumb to bring up the keypad.

Tapped in our anniversary.

The screen vibrated.

Pin doesn't match.

My heart sank. I tried again. How many times can you type a PIN incorrectly before the phone shuts you out?

Pin doesn't match.

Do I try again and risk getting locked out? I pause, listening. He hasn't come in the house yet. He doesn't know I have the phone.

Not only do I have his phone, I also have my answer. If I had any doubt in my mind that he was hiding something from me, this gives me proof. He's hiding something, something big enough he's willing to change his PIN to keep me from finding out about it.

But it might not be an affair, right? It could be something else, couldn't it? I'm going to cling to that. This could still be a mistake.

I can still fix us. He'll come to his senses about whatever this is. He'll realize he's been stupid. This is a rough patch. That's all it is.

EIGHT

EVAN

"Chief Warner, this is Ariel Anders." Miriam announces the woman trailing into my office behind her like she's introducing someone at a ball, and I stand, my eyes flicking from my secretary to Ariel.

She's my age, maybe a bit younger, but dowdy. I take in her dark pants, black at one point in time, but faded now and pilled. Her sweater hangs over the waistband, tugged a bit to one side like it got caught around the agitator in the washing machine. When she looks up at me, I'm struck with the feeling that I know her, or I've seen her before, but she's completely unremarkable, so why would I have paid attention to her?

Even her hair, which is thick and red and would look stunning on someone half her age and with a better body, is tied in a fat braid down her back and looks more like a piece of rope than anything else. Her face is doughy, her hands clasped together in front of her body like she's not quite sure what do to do with them.

"Ms. Anders," I say, coming around my desk, my hand out

to shake hers. Miriam sees that she's not needed and disappears, nodding once as she exits my office, like she's pleased about how this interaction is going.

"Ariel, please." The woman shakes my hand. It's a bit sweaty, her palm, but I resist wiping my hand on my pants. "Thanks for calling and meeting with me this afternoon."

"I should be thanking you." She smiles at me now, looking relaxed. "Seriously, this is perfect timing for me."

"How so?"

"The family I was cleaning for has recently moved and so when Miriam told me she knew someone who might need my help, well... let's just say it was a blessing."

"Hopefully it will work out for all of us." I sit down and she lowers herself carefully into the same chair Miriam had been sitting in when she told me about her. "I don't know what Miriam's already said, but I have a daughter, Jessica, and she and I just lost her mother."

"Lola." Ariel nods. Her mouth frames my wife's name like a prayer. "She told me about that; it must be awful. I can only imagine what it would be like to lose a mother as a teenager. Simply terrible."

I nod. This woman might not be much to look at, but that doesn't really matter, does it? All that matters is if she can help me out, can take some of the pressure off of raising a teenager, can ensure that our house doesn't explode with dirty laundry and that we both get hot meals at least once a day.

"She's taken it hard, as you can imagine. Lola and Jessica were close and so of course she's struggling." I hesitate, then turn my family picture around so Ariel can get a look at my wife.

"She's beautiful." For a moment, the two of us stare in silence—Ariel, at the picture, me at her—then she gives her head a little shake like she's clearing away a thought and looks up at me. "Why don't you tell me everything you think you need done? What are you hoping to gain from employing me? How can I help?"

Without taking much of a breath, I launch into the role she would fulfill—not as a mother, of course, but as someone who does almost everything that a mother would do. Cooking, cleaning, laundry, grocery shopping. She wouldn't be expected to handle any of the finances. That's my job and it's one I've always handled on my own.

But hiring someone to do the lawn? That would be her purview. Making sure the mail got in on time before someone could dare snatch it from the mailbox in some kind of a prank? Ariel's job. Mostly, though...

"I need you to make our house run the way Lola had it running before she died." I finish and exhale hard like I just ran a marathon.

Ariel doesn't answer at first and I hesitate, unsure if I've somehow upset her or made her second-guess her agreeing to come here to talk to me. Finally, she shifts, then leans forward, putting her hand on the desk between the two of us.

"Miriam gave you my references, didn't she?"

I nod. I flipped through them, of course, but it's not like I had any time to sit down and call everyone. From what I saw, though, this woman is just what I'm looking for. I love that she's not much to look at because it means nobody in the neighborhood will be talking about me looking for a new wife.

If she were half my age and looked like she'd walked out of a magazine, then I might need to worry. As it is, though, I should be in the clear. I can't imagine anyone looking at Ariel and thinking that I was doing something inappropriate with her in my own home. She's perfect, obviously the answer to my prayers.

"Then you know that I'm your best option for the job."

I nod again. What is it about this woman that commands so much of my attention and makes it difficult for me to speak up?

I don't normally get like this with people, especially not with women, but she seems not only totally in control of our conversation but also very comfortable sitting here and talking to me.

"When would you like me to start?"

There it is again, how she just takes control without waiting to see if anyone is going to offer her any. Not only will she run the house the way I need it to, but I can easily see her dealing with Jessica's teenage drama.

"I'd like you to come by today so we can make sure we're on the same page. If you're interested once you've seen the house and the work I want done then we can go from there." Judging from the expression on her face, my answer surprises her as much as it does me. She blinks at me and then nods, a smile spreading across her face.

"That's fine. I'll have you know that I was living in the house with the last family I was taking care of. I'm going to be looking for a place to stay before I can help you and your daughter."

Even though she didn't directly say that she wanted to move into my house, the implication of what she's thinking is clear and it hangs in the air between the two of us. I reach out and take a sip of my coffee. It's lukewarm and tastes burned but drinking a little bit of it gives me time to try to gather my thoughts so she can't tell I look so scattered.

"Unfortunately, our home isn't large enough for you to move into."

She exhales, nods. "I totally understand. I just wanted to let you know that it might be a bit before I can find a place to live. As soon as I find somewhere to rest my head of course, I'm all yours."

She stands and I follow suit, my mind racing. "Hold on," I say, putting a finger up between the two of us to get her attention. "Just give me a moment to see if this will work."

Miriam answers as soon as I press the intercom button on

my phone and call her. "Do you know anywhere that might have a room where Ariel could stay while she works for my family?"

A slight pause, then she exhales hard.

"Give me a little while to think on it and see what I can come up with. Housing is a nightmare right now, but I bet I can find something."

It's not the answer I want, but I trust Miriam to find something for Ariel, and I don't have the time to look myself. I've no doubt she'll find somewhere Ariel can get moved into, get settled, then prepare herself to come work for me and for Jessica.

Miriam and I have worked together for a long time and she knows everything about me, from how I like my coffee, to what to say when I arrive in an obviously bad mood. There's only one thing she doesn't know about me and as long as that secret stays hidden, then everything's going to be just fine.

NINE

Jessica stares at me, looking more like a caged animal ready to gnaw off her arm to get away from me than my teenage daughter. I stare back, trying to figure out when my baby girl went from some loving little creature who wanted me to let her paint my nails to someone who would rather pull out her nails than spend time with me.

"I can't believe you hired someone." Jessica's voice is high and tight, a sure sign that she's not only shutting down mentally and about to refuse to hear anything I say to her, but that anything I do say will probably get twisted around and thrown right back in my face when this conversation is done.

"Jessica, you know as well as I do that we need help. She's going to be helping out around the house, making sure things get done, and making sure we have food in the fridge and on the table."

"So she's going to be my new mom." Jessica crosses her arms and leans back in her chair. She no longer looks like she's going to jump off the edge of her seat and rush at me, but now that she's going on the defensive, I know I have even less of a chance of getting her to really listen to and hear what I'm saying.

"No. Jessica, no." I shake my head and lean forward, lightly touching her knee. Her eyes flick to where my hand rests on her knee and she jerks her leg to the side to let my hand fall. "She's not a new mother, not by a long shot. I don't want someone like that in the house, and trust me, when you see her—"

"When I see her *what*?"

"She's nothing like your mother."

Jessica opens her mouth like she has something to say and then snaps it shut, shaking her head a little bit. Silence grows between the two of us, thick and uncomfortable. Every second one of us doesn't speak makes it seem that much harder to break the silence in the future.

"But what if she finds out—"

Whatever my daughter was going to ask me is drowned out in the sound of the doorbell. I stand, faster than I normally would, wiping my hands on my jeans. Relief floods through me that Jessica didn't get the chance to finish her question.

Even though I know full well what she was going to ask, the last thing I want is to have those words hanging in the air between the two of us.

"Jessica, I want you to be kind. Be the kid I know you can be."

Glancing back over my shoulder at my daughter, I'm not surprised to see that she hasn't moved from her chair. She's going to let Ariel come into the living room to greet her instead of being polite and coming to the door, and I feel a flash of anger rise in me.

"I want you to understand that Ariel is coming here to help us, not to hurt us, and the sooner you accept that she can make this house a better place to live, the better off we'll both be. She works for us, as an employee, and you need to be respectful."

I'd thought about picking up the house a bit before Ariel came over but just didn't have the energy. There are piles of junk mail on the coffee table, stacked so precariously that I keep thinking just walking past them will be enough to send them sliding to the floor. I can't remember the last time the baseboards were cleaned, but those are really the least of our worries.

The bathroom, the kitchen counters, the entryway floor, the rugs... The list goes on and on, and it's clear Jessica and I can't stay on top of everything.

We need Ariel.

Jessica still hasn't moved when I grab the door and swing it open. You'd think, after all we've been through together, that she would be a little bit kinder, a little bit more willing to do what I ask of her, but that's a problem for later.

Right now, the two of us really just need to make a good impression on Ariel. I hardly know the woman, but I already know she's going to change our lives.

TEN

ARIEL

It's strange to see Evan outside of his office, outside of the suit he was wearing when we met earlier, with his hair pushed up slightly in the front, almost like he's trying to look younger than he really is.

He's framed in the doorway, his broad shoulders tapering down to a smaller waist, his jeans hugging his hips perfectly, the T-shirt he has on screaming casual, but I know better. Evan isn't the type of man to do anything casually. Everything he picked out to wear when I came over this evening, everything he's going to say, even the way his hair is pushed up at his forehead, has all been purposefully chosen to reflect who he wants me to think he is.

And I refuse to fall for it. Why? Because I've been watching him. Because I know who he is without him trying to bamboozle me into thinking he's someone else. Evan may believe that he's slick enough to get away with anything he wants, but I'm already onto him, and working for him in his house is only going to make it easier for me to do what I really want.

"Ariel, you found the place okay, I'm so glad." He steps out of the way, still holding the door open for me like it might otherwise swing shut and lock me out of the house. "Why don't you come on in, meet Jessica, and see if you're still up to the task of making sure our house doesn't implode on us."

He throws me a cheeky grin, one that probably makes all the young women look twice at him, then I'm stepping through the door, into his house, breathing in the scent of a vanilla candle burning somewhere, heat burning the back of my neck as I try to appear like I've never been here before.

Like I've never sat across the street in my little rental car, watching him and Jessica leave the house in the morning. Like I haven't pretended to make a delivery, gone up and peered in the windows, looked around for any clues that would tell me more about the type of people who live here. Like I didn't look the house up on Zillow to try to see interior pictures.

"This home is gorgeous," I say, and it's not a lie. The hardwood floors are made up of wide wood planks, the throw rugs look casual but expensive. I check out the art and family pictures on the walls, my eyes flicking quickly over Lola's face peering out at me from a few photographs.

The last thing I want is for Evan to be watching me when I really look at her. I know he's not on the street any longer, not directly involved in hunting down criminals and looking for coincidences, but I doubt those instincts really leave you, no matter how long you've sat in your office high on the fourth floor.

No, if all goes well right now, I'll have plenty of time to look at the pictures of Lola later, when I'm alone, when he and his daughter don't get to watch me to see how my expression changes.

Walking past me, Evan gestures for me to follow him into the living room. I feel like my head is on a swivel as I try to look around me and take it all in, and I'm sure Evan and Jessica are both watching me, trying to figure out what I'm thinking, trying their best to read my mind.

I keep my face passive, manage to look interested but not too interested, focused on what's going on around me, but not judgmental, and then I see Jessica.

She's curled up in a chair, a blanket pulled up to her shoulders, the glare on her face laser-focused on me like she thinks she'll be able to force me to leave her house just by staring at me. Her long hair is pulled back into a ponytail and I can see that she's wearing a hoodie under the blanket.

On the coffee table in front of her is a thick book—fantasy, with an elf on the front cover—as well as a large coffee mug, still steaming. Her eyes lock on to my face and she doesn't look away.

I do. Dipping my head, I turn from her a little bit, not wanting to stare her down. It's one thing to see her in passing as she walks to school, another to be in her living room, looking her right in the face, waiting for her or her father to realize the truth.

"Hi, Jessica," I say, glancing back at her and then quickly looking away. "It's wonderful to meet you."

It's almost impossible for me to really look at the teenager curled up in the chair. I know I should. Making more of an effort to connect with her would probably help me out in the long run, but it's not the long run I'm really worried about right now.

It's the fact that right now it's difficult for me to breathe.

It's how hard it is to look at Jessica, let alone speak to her.

Evan clears his throat. I turn to look at him and notice that Jessica doesn't. Her eyes remain locked on me.

"Why don't you follow me to the kitchen? That will be your domain, and you can get your bearings a little while Jessica decides when she's going to come say hello." The implication in his voice is clear—Jessica better get up out of the chair and come speak to me before her dad gets really angry with her.

I wonder if Lola saw that anger on a regular basis.

The two of us reconvene in the kitchen, him leaning against the counter by the coffeepot, me standing a few feet away, trying to decide what I should do with my arms. What stance will make me seem most approachable and friendly?

"I'm sorry she's being rude," he begins, but I cut him off.

"She's hurting," I tell Evan, and even though I try to keep my voice even, I have a feeling there's a bit of pain in my words too. "She just lost her mother, the most important woman in her life, and then you bring someone into the house to help take care of the things her mom used to do. Not that I'm not grateful for this job," I say, speaking quickly, "but I understand where she's coming from. The pain. The pressure to let someone new in when you really don't want to."

"This is going to be fine. She'll be fine." Evan sounds more like he's trying to convince himself of the fact rather than me, but I keep my face still and neutral. "Now, why don't we discuss what exactly I need you to do and then we can talk about compensation, make sure the two of us are on the same page. I think you'll find that Jessica and I are both really easy to talk to and this should work out just the way we want it to."

He grins and, when I nod, continues talking, but I'm already tuning him out.

I'm willing to do whatever he needs doing around the house, no matter if that's deep cleaning the toilets or cooking healthy meals.

He pauses and I nod again, smiling at him. I have no idea what he's talking about right now, but he grins back and launches into another explanation of what I'll need to do at the house before producing a list from the counter outlining all of my new duties.

I take it, but all I can do is smile at him.

Evan has no idea, and he can't ever know why I'm really here.

Lola would want me to protect Jessica.
From him.

ELEVEN

LOLA'S DIARY

I found the letter.

Well, if I'm being fair, it's more a scrap of paper than anything else. Just a tiny ripped piece of paper so small that it shouldn't be anything. In fact, it's insane something like that could ruin everything.

How Evan thought I wouldn't find it, wouldn't see it tucked there in the pocket of his pants before I washed them, is beyond me. For a moment, I just stood there, my hand trembling, unsure if I should pluck it from where he'd tucked it or if I should ignore it, throw the entire thing in the wash, enjoy knowing that it was going to break up into a million little pieces before I pulled everything out to go in the dryer.

If I destroyed it then I wouldn't have to know for sure if my suspicions were correct, but even as I had that thought, I knew I had to pull it out.

I had to see what it said even though I was pretty sure I already knew exactly what would be written on it. The handwriting would be unfamiliar, like getting a letter in the mail from someone you've never met, but the words are old as time. Women all over the world have read them in romance novels and heard them in heartbreaking movies.

I just never thought I'd be one of those women.

My fingers trembled as I plucked the note out by the corner of the paper, being careful not to rip it. Intrusive thoughts filled my head, screaming at me to tear the note into confetti, to flush it down the toilet, to light it on fire. They were the same thoughts I'd get driving with Jessica in my car when she was a screaming infant, only those told me to drive the car into a tree or made me wonder how it would feel to drown in the car, Jessica strapped in the backseat, if I were to drive into a lake.

Intrusive thoughts. Nothing more.

Evan's work pants puddled to the floor at my feet, and I ignored them, finally unfolding the note in my fingers. It smelled, and I lifted it to my nose, taking a tiny sniff.

I don't wear floral perfume, but whoever wrote my husband this note and stuffed it in his pants pocket sure does. My stomach rolled and I closed my eyes, breathing deeply and slowly to try to keep from getting sick.

The wave of nausea passed, and I flattened the paper, using the top of the dryer to smooth it out the best I could. It was wrinkled, like Evan had had it in his pocket all day long, and when it was flat, I finally stepped back, my hands up in the air like I was afraid to touch it any longer, and looked down at the words scrawled there, a love letter to my husband.

> *Evan, you are perfect. You make me feel amazing, alive, incredible. I miss you already even though you were just with me. Come home to me soon. xoxo*

The words were childish, the letters looped and large, like a little girl writing to her first crush. I knew in an instant that whoever wrote this letter hadn't ever really been in love, not the type of love that will tear you open and destroy you if you aren't careful. She'd never had a child in her, never felt the real love that comes so fast after giving birth, how that wave of love becomes a tsunami dwarfing anything you've ever felt in the past.

There's nothing real here, no real passion, just the hot-blooded desire of a girl who's in love for the first time.

With my husband.

That's the rub... that's the thing that's going to push me over the edge. If this were a note I'd found in a parking lot then I wouldn't think twice about it. I might smile, wondering if it's for the high school quarterback or for the nerdy boy next door who's spent a long semester painstakingly tutoring calculus, this note his long-awaited reward.

But I didn't find it in the parking lot. It isn't from some high school girl mooning over a first crush. It's for my husband, and the thought that it might be from a young girl fills me with panic. Is he stupid enough to go down that path? I never would have thought so, but he's obviously stupid enough to have an affair, stupid enough to get between this woman's legs often enough for her to think that the two of them are in love.

But is he stupid enough for her to be as young as I fear she is?

No. He wouldn't.

Reading the note made my stomach twist but not just because of the words written on it. My stomach twisted because I knew what it meant for my family, how it would tear us apart, and I turned, grabbing the toilet and throwing up. My breakfast, my coffee, it all came up in a rush, and afterwards I wiped my mouth with toilet paper before flushing and brushing my teeth.

The entire time, the note was there. An accusation. Proof that our marriage wasn't nearly as strong as I'd thought it was. Proof that Evan wasn't happy at home, that he was willing to find his happiness somewhere else, proof that I needed to do something to stop this before it got out of hand.

And now I don't know what to do. I need to talk to him, need to tell him I know about the note, that I can't handle the thought of him tearing our family apart like this. I know how quickly young women fall in love, how just one kiss can balloon into something in their minds that change their lives and complete them, but I don't know how Evan feels about this.

It's obvious she's fallen hard and completely. The note on my dryer tells me this has probably been going on a while and that I need to be very, very careful.

But what it doesn't tell me is how serious it is, and that's what I need to find out from my husband. I need to know if we can get through this, not only for me but for Jessica. She needs both of us and I'm willing to try to work through this if he is.

I'll go to couples counseling. We can do it together, get through this rough patch. But first I need to know if there's even a chance of reconciliation.

That's the thing I need to ask him.

But only when he hasn't been drinking. Only when I'm sure I will be safe.

TWELVE

ARIEL

By the time I make it to the Warner house on my first day, it's
still so early in the morning that I hear mourning doves calling
from the trees while drops of rain drip from branches.

I let myself in through the front gate then pause at the base
of the stairs leading up to the deck. It was one thing to walk up
them yesterday with Evan and Jessica waiting for me. The sun
had still been warm and was beating down on my back, chasing
away any chill I felt about coming here.

Now, though, it's damp, it's dreary, and if I believed in
ghosts, I'd be looking over my shoulder for Lola. The stair
railing wobbles a little when I grab it for balance and I hesitate,
then quickly move up the stairs before turning on the deck and
looking back down them.

Right there, at the base of the stairs, on the damp sidewalk,
with slugs crawling across it, that's where she died. Lola fell
down the stairs, smashed her head on the ground, lay there until
she bled out, her body giving up well before an ambulance was
able to get to her.

That's what the news said anyway.

My hands clench into fists at my sides as I think about the terror Lola must have felt, how weightless she was until she hit the ground.

And the fact that it was the man who vowed to love her—to protect her, to keep her safe—who hurt her.

To protect and serve, indeed.

Exhaling hard, I force myself to relax my hands, then turn back to the front door, putting a huge smile on my face before I ring the doorbell. It sounds cheery, too out of place for somewhere this dark and dangerous. Luckily for me, I only have to wait a moment before the door swings open, Jessica on the other side, her eyes darting to my face and then away again.

She takes my breath away. She's just as beautiful as Lola was at this age, maybe even more so. Even if I just saw Jessica walking around downtown and didn't know who she was, I'm sure I'd be able to pick her out of a crowd. It's her long thin nose, the way her thick hair falls around her shoulders, how her right ear tips over just a little bit at the top.

She's already dressed for school, in tight jeans with strategically placed tears and a hoodie that's too large for her but somehow shows off just how slender she really is. Nothing in this house, including her clothes, is very fancy, but somehow Jessica comes across as more confident than most other teenagers I've ever met before.

"Good morning," I say cheerily, stepping into the house. She hasn't moved to let me enter but I'm going to force my way in with kindness. "I brought some groceries for breakfast and to pack you a lunch and thought I'd get started right away."

"I'll buy a lunch at school." Her voice is flat as she closes the front door behind me and throws the lock. A moment later she brushes past me, leading the way to the kitchen. A cloud of perfume envelops me as she passes me and I hold my breath for a moment, trying not to breathe it all in. It's overwhelming, fruity and bright at the same time. "I haven't taken my lunch since I was in elementary school."

"Of course you haven't." Following her into the kitchen, I smile at her. It isn't returned. "But I still wanted to be prepared, and now I know. Do you have anything in particular you want for breakfast?"

She grabs a mug of coffee from the table next to a plate covered with toast crusts and crumbs, staring at me as she does. If she feels guilty about already eating when I'm here to make her something for breakfast, she doesn't show it. The look on her face isn't apologetic: it's tight, her jaw twitching a little bit as she looks at me.

It's important I remind myself how much she's hurting. It would be easy to take her attitude personally, but she just lost her mother. She and Evan have found their new routine together since Lola died, and here I am, ready to change it up again.

"I'm not hungry. Maybe Dad will want you to cook for him though." Taking a long sip of her coffee, she walks to the coffeepot, tops up her mug, then turns to leave.

"Jessica." I keep my voice quiet and calm, hoping it will be enough to get her attention and make her turn around to look at me.

It works. I notice the tight grip she has on her mug, how her cheeks are bright with heat. She's angry at me for even existing in the same space as her mother, and I get it. I'm sure she's drawing comparisons.

She has to be. There's no way anyone will ever be able to take on some role of a mother for Jessica and have the girl not compare her to Lola. And, if they're anything like me, she's going to find them lacking.

But that doesn't mean I'm not going to do the best by my Lola that I can. She needed me; she reached out to me.

And now I'm here.

"I lost my mom when I was young too," I tell her. "And so I know you don't trust me, you don't know me, you don't want me in your house, and I don't blame you for any of that. I just want you to know I'm on your side, okay?" I pause, hoping that my words are going to get through to her and wondering if she's going to give me a chance this quickly. "I'm here to—"

"I know why you're here." Her voice is sharp, a knife cutting through the air and held up to my neck to make me stop talking. But then she exhales. She seems to fold in on herself, crumpling a bit, her shoulders drooping down. "You're here so Dad and I can have some sort of a normal life again without having to do the cleaning and the laundry and the cooking by ourselves. You're the mom without being Mom. *That's* why you're here. It's not to connect with me, not to offer me 'condolences.'" She makes angry air quotes around the last word, her coffee mug at a terrifying angle as she does. "You're working for us."

"I'm not trying to be your mom."

She pauses, her face still for a moment. The corners of her lips turn down and she closes her eyes. One tear runs down her cheek.

"I know." The admission is strangled. Her voice sounds tight. "I know that. I'm sorry. I'm so sorry. I just miss her so much."

"Of course you do. I'm here to talk if you ever want to." As I speak, I try to listen for any sounds Evan might be making. I have a very good feeling he wouldn't want me to add *counseling services* to my to-do list.

She stares at me. I'd give anything to be able to tell what she's thinking. The pause goes on so long I'm half-tempted to speak up just to fill the silence but then she finally breaks it for me.

"Thank you." She sets her coffee cup down on the counter with a *thunk*. That's it, just *thank you*, two words from a wounded girl, then the wall that was there between us a moment ago is back.

Still, I think it's weaker than it was before.

It feels like all the air in the room is sucked out when she turns and walks through the door. I hear her feet in the hall then the pounding of them on the stairs as she flees this conversation, but it isn't until her bedroom door slams shut that I exhale hard, blowing the air out in a loud whoosh, then grab the counter and lean against it.

Even from here I can hear the loud music coming from her bedroom.

That went better than I thought it would. From what Lola told me right before she died, she and Jessica didn't really talk about me. About any of her friends or family, to be honest. She was private and didn't talk about her past.

Even if they had, Ariel isn't my real name. Even though Evan and I only met once, at his wedding to Lola, when he was already drunk and falling over, pawing at her, I wasn't about to use my real name in this town in case he or Jessica put two and two together.

I need to make sure she understands that she can trust me. The truth is all going to come out in the end, and when it does, it could get ugly.

THIRTEEN

EVAN

I head home from work right on time, unwilling to spend any longer hanging around the office than I need to. In the past I used to stay late, hoping to see Dakota before she went in for the night shift. And in the past few weeks, since Lola died, I've been staying late to avoid clashing with Jessica.

Now, though, I have no reason to want to be here longer than necessary. Dakota is out of my life. We had to end our affair after Lola died. Nobody in town would feel bad for me if I hadn't, if instead I had just paraded Dakota around. I'm the grieving widower.

My wife is gone. And Dakota is out of reach.

Just thinking about her makes it hard for me to breathe. She's exciting. Refreshing. When I was stuck in the rut of working and parenting and trying to be a good husband even though Lola and Jessica were always fighting, Dakota was there for me.

A relief. A *release*.

I think about the stolen kisses in the break room and taking her to the hotel, how her eyes lit up when I'd take her out for dinner, because nobody had ever taken her to such nice places. She'd kiss me, leaning over the table, planting her hands between the plates to reach me, and I didn't care if everyone saw, because we weren't in our town.

I wasn't that stupid. It was easy to lie about going to work conferences and take Dakota out of town for a few days, to revel in how alive and fresh she was, to forget about the stale, dark, depressing state of my family life.

And now I have to live with seeing her at work but never touching her. The love I felt for her rivaled what I'd felt for Lola when we got married. Lola would have hated knowing that, but it's true.

Lola was safe. But Dakota was alive. Exciting. Vivacious.

I exhale hard and slam my fist into the steering wheel. As much as I'd like to daydream about Dakota and what we had when we were together, I have to get home to see how my new housekeeper did. It did make me nervous to hand over a house key this morning and tell her to make herself at home, but what choice did I really have? She was there, her hand outstretched, and it wasn't like Jessica or I could sit home and babysit her just to make sure nothing went wrong.

The house is still standing when I get home. The white picket fence is locked up tight and I unlatch it, my ears pricked as I hurry up the walkway to the front deck. Even though it's been almost a month since Lola died, and her blood washed away a long time ago, I still get chills as I walk over where my wife lay, bleeding out, her head twisted, her neck broken—

Enough.

Lola is dead, ghosts aren't real, and there isn't anything that can get me now.

I let myself into the house, surprised to find the front door locked. Jessica has a terrible habit of strolling into the house, leaving everything unlocked behind her, and then wondering why I'm upset with her. It must be Ariel who came behind her and locked up.

As soon as I step inside, I'm hit with the smell of dinner, meaty and rich, and I feel like I'm in a cartoon as I follow my nose through the living room to the kitchen. I'm so interested in what Ariel must be making for dinner that I barely notice how clean the living room is, that the stacks of books on the coffee table have been carefully shelved and that the rugs have been vacuumed.

One day. She's been here one day and already it feels like an entirely different house.

Pausing in the kitchen door, I watch as Ariel opens the oven, grabbing a huge pot and carefully lifting it out. She pushes the oven door shut with her hip before lifting the lid of the pot and inhaling deeply. I watch all of this, watch how fluidly she moves in my kitchen, how comfortable she seems to be here, and I'm struck by something.

When she pushed the oven door shut with her hip—that simple movement, like she's done it a thousand times before—that was familiar.

I'm still staring, my mouth open slightly as I try to figure out where I've seen someone do that before, when Ariel turns and gasps. Her hand flies up to her chest and she actually jumps before leaning back against the counter.

"Evan, you scared the daylights out of me! When did you get home?"

"Just now." A pang of regret shoots through me that I could scare her so easily. That wasn't my intention at all. "Whatever that is smells so amazing that I forgot how to speak for a moment."

This makes her laugh, a hearty sound. It fills the kitchen

and I'm grateful the windows are closed so the neighbors won't be able to hear her.

"This is just a pot roast and some vegetables," she explains, peeking back in the pot. "If I'd known you would be so easy to please then I wouldn't have been agonizing over what to make for dinner today."

"I'm a fairly simple man. Jessica, on the other hand..." Widening my eyes, I point up at the ceiling. "Is she home, by the way? The front door was locked, and she doesn't usually do that, so I wasn't sure if she'd made it back from school or if she had an activity this afternoon."

"She was home." Is that a bit of hesitation in her voice, like she knows I'm not going to be exactly happy with whatever she's going to say to me? "She was home but then told me she had to go study with Britt. I asked her if you knew, and she said yes. I figured, since she's a teenager and I'm not her mother..."

Her voice trails off, but she doesn't need to finish her thought for me to know exactly what she was thinking. I didn't hire her to be Jessica's nanny. On the flip side, she probably wants to know why my daughter would be so comfortable lying to her and to me, since it's probably obvious from the expression on my face that Jessica didn't have permission to go to Britt's this afternoon.

It's not that I'm going to make her and Ariel sit down and bond, but I wanted her to be around, get used to having someone else in the house. She'd been upset by the prospect yesterday, and I was hoping she'd see it different this morning when she'd had some good sleep and was looking forward to dinner.

"You did nothing wrong," I tell Ariel, giving her what I hope is a comforting smile. "I probably just forgot that Jessica and I had talked about her going over to Britt's. That's where she practically lives sometimes."

"Oh, good." A smile back, but I get the feeling it's a little fake. Ariel is obviously worried she upset me, but she has nothing to be concerned about. This is between me and my daughter.

We're silent, the two of us obviously trying to figure out how we're supposed to act around each other. She wipes her hands on the apron she has on, then clears her throat. "Should I set the table for the two of you then? Do you think she'll be home for dinner?"

"Set it for three." The words are out in the air between us before I really realize what I'm saying, but now it's too late to take them back.

"Three?"

I nod, trying to look more confident than I feel. "Three. Why don't you join us, Ariel? I'm sure getting to know you a little better could be really good for Jessica and will make her feel a lot more comfortable having you in the house."

This is stupid. My brain seems well aware that what I'm doing right now is not a good idea, but I can't seem to get my mouth on board with that. Why I'm inviting the help to dinner her first night here is beyond me, but it's done and all I can do is hope that she's going to turn me down.

"You know, that might be a good idea." Ariel throws me a huge smile and I'm surprised to see how nice it looks on her face. She's still not attractive, not by a long shot, and that's a good thing, but that smile is nice.

"Great. I'll get changed and call Jessica. I'll call Britt's mom and see if she can bring her home, so if you want—"

"I'll go ahead and set the table, get everything ready. I also made dessert, so I hope you're ready for a surprise."

Oh, I'm already surprised at what came out of my mouth just now—inviting her to stay for dinner—but there's no way I can tell her that. Instead, I give her the best smile I can manage, then hurry to the stairs. As I head up to my room, I pull my phone from my pocket, ready to dial my daughter.

Something at the top of the stairs gives me pause.

I wouldn't have thought, not with all the work Ariel clearly did downstairs today, that she would have had time to get upstairs to work. In fact, I meant to tell her that my bedroom was off limits. Did I remember to do that?

I must not have, because I always shut my bedroom door when I leave for work and right now it's cracked open.

FOURTEEN

LOLA'S DIARY

He denied it of course, like he could actually look me in the eyes and think that I'm so stupid as to believe that this note I found in his pocket was just something he picked up, something random, not a bomb disguised as a piece of ripped pink paper, not the one thing that can easily tear our family apart.

I watched him deny it, watched as he held his hands up between us like he was stopping traffic. I've always loved his hands, how big and strong they are, but now I don't want them on me. I think about them touching another person, touching someone else in the way he used to touch me, and just looking at them made me feel sick.

But I refuse to throw up anymore for this man. I refuse to let him do that to me, to let him have that power over me. He thinks he can get out of this by denying it over and over again like a broken record, but I'm not stupid, and I'm not going to just sit here and take it.

I have Jessica to think of, after all.

My sweet daughter—*our* sweet daughter—she's the child I

longed for and swore I'd do anything to protect, and now I have to make good on that promise and keep her safe, not only from her father's anger but from whatever anyone in town is going to say about him.

About us.

She was at a friend's house while we talked. Britt may not be the best influence on our daughter, but I needed Jessica out of the house so Evan and I could talk. I needed to make sure that she didn't hear anything I accused him of, that she wouldn't have to listen to her father lying through his teeth to me.

Because that's exactly what he did.

It was hard to listen to. I kept a running mental list of the lies as he spun them, him grasping for each one like he honestly thought *the next one* would be the one I'd be willing to believe.

I found it on the ground. Ha! Like he would stop to pick up litter.

Someone put it there as a prank. His staff is too afraid of him to prank him, and he and I both know it.

It was left on my desk by a co-worker. A co-worker named Evan? I'd love to meet them!

You don't understand. Oh, I think I do. But it was nice for him to finally start to show some real emotion.

"Where do we go from here?" I asked him, doing my best to keep my voice calm and level, looking him right in the eyes, my hands folded in my lap. He raged, stomping around the kitchen while I sat at the table, exuding calm. On the inside, of course, I felt like fireworks were going off, like I was about to explode and fly from the chair, but I wasn't about to let him know just how much he'd affected me.

He, on the other hand, couldn't have sat down and stayed still if his life depended on it. He was on the move, shifting position, walking this way and that, slapping his hand down on the counter from time to time like that sound was going to make me believe him.

In short, he was a child, caught with his hand in the cookie jar. Or, in his case, not his hand, his...

"I'll end it." He stopped, planting his hands on the table in front of me, staring at me, for once not breaking eye contact like that would prove to me just how serious he was. "Lola, I'll end it. You're right. It's wrong."

No apology. No admittance that he'd messed up, just that *it* was wrong. That *it* is going to hang over our heads for the rest of our lives, I'm sure of it. Two little letters, just one minuscule word, and it's going to change everything in the future.

"End it." I stood, making sure he couldn't reach out and touch me. The last thing I wanted was to feel his hands on me until I was sure it was over. It always burned when he touched me, like he was searing my flesh, marking me for his own, and I loved it. Now, though, the thought of him doing that again after touching someone else is too much for me to bear.

"I will. It's done."

He wanted me to stay and talk to him, I know he did, but there wasn't any way I could do that. I needed to get out of there, get some fresh air, stop this sick feeling in my stomach from making me feel like I was going to throw up. I knew he wouldn't follow me out to the front deck, and I was right.

So now I'm writing this while he's in the shower. I love Evan. I've loved him from the moment we met. He's been everything to me, and even though I know some people will judge me for forgiving him, I want this marriage to last.

I want him. Our family. Even though he was with someone else, I want to believe it was a mistake and that it's over, that he'll choose me in the end. He has to end it with her, get counseling with me.

And if he doesn't?

He has to end it. He ends the affair or I end the marriage.

I've never been more serious about anything in my life.

FIFTEEN

ARIEL

WEDNESDAY, AUGUST 30

I can hear Evan in his room changing from work clothes, but I still don't move from the kitchen until his shower turns on.

The pipes in this house rattle and sing a little bit but I still wait. Instead of rushing to the formal dining room to look through the buffet there for anything I might be able to use to prove he killed Lola, I make myself count to thirty.

It's better to wait a bit longer just to ensure he doesn't let the shower run to get hot.

I know he did it. I *know* he did, the way some old-timers know the rain is coming when their knees ache or how twins can tell when their sibling has been hurt. It wouldn't stand up in a court of law, the feeling I have, and that's why I need proof.

Proof, like letters. Any sort of pictures showing Evan doing... what I don't know. But I will when I see it. Maybe insurance papers. Computer searches related to killing your wife and collecting insurance. I'll have to use his computer to look for those search results though, so that will wait until later. Until I'm more comfortable trying to hack into his computer.

I'm looking for low-hanging fruit right now.

"Twenty-eight. Twenty-nine. Thirty." Exhaling hard, I leave the kitchen and beeline into the formal dining room. Other than running my duster across the furniture and vacuuming, I haven't spent much time in here. It's obvious Jessica and Evan don't use this room often, if at all.

The light turns on after I grope at it, and I don't wait. In front of me is a large dining table with six chairs around it. An arrangement of fake flowers sits in the middle of the table. Directly on the other side of the table is a huge window overlooking the backyard. I ignore the view and turn to the buffet, first opening the large double cabinet doors in the middle of it.

Stacks of china greet me, each plate and bowl carefully separated by others with small pieces of cloth.

"Not here," I mutter, closing the doors. On each side of the double cabinet doors are three drawers and I grab the top one on the right, yanking it open.

Silverware. Good stuff too, nestled in velvet.

The second drawer has linen napkins.

The bottom is stuffed with candles.

"There's no way it was going to be that easy," I mutter, duck-walking to the other side of the buffet. Before opening the top drawer, I pause, tilting my head to listen for Evan.

The shower's still running.

"Plenty of time," I murmur, grabbing the top drawer and pulling it open. Photos and pieces of paper are stuffed so tightly into the drawer that some pop out.

"Crap."

Grabbing the three photos from the floor, I glance at them, then put them on the top of the buffet. Part of me wants to stare at every photo of Lola and really drink her in, but I can do that later. It was silly to think I'd find what I was looking for so quickly.

But I still hoped.

The shower's still going, right?

It is.

I know I'm pushing my luck, that looking through these drawers right now is reckless, especially when I can take my time searching for proof later, but I just want to find it as quickly as possible. I want to end this, rescue Jessica. The faster I can do that, the better. Even though walking away from this right now is the best idea, I can't help myself.

I'm hyper-focused on it now. Digging deep into the photos, I lift a stack of them out and put them on the floor next to me. The colors are bright, the smiles on everyone's face so large, so real, that my stomach twists looking at them.

Did Lola know what was coming? Did he know from the time they got married that it would end up like this?

Sweat beads on my brow and I take a moment to wipe it off then lift out another stack. This time, instead of just being pictures, there's a manila folder on the bottom of the pile.

I pull it out, letting the photos fall to the floor. Sitting back on my heels, I take a deep breath to try to steel myself for whatever I find in the folder. A moment later, I sink all the way to the floor.

My heart pounds in my ears. I'm vaguely aware of a new sound in the house but I can't tear my eyes away from the paper on my lap. I'm too focused on what I just found. Even though I'm not sure what I'm going to find in the folder, I know for a fact that it's going to be big. It's a feeling I have, like I'm on the edge of a cliff and everything in my life is about to change.

All I have to do is open it.

Taking a deep breath, I do just that. My hands tremble and so I clench them into fists before relaxing them and laying the folder open on my lap.

When I open my eyes again, I make myself look at Lola's life insurance policy. Here it is, the papers I needed to find that prove to everyone that Evan was the sole beneficiary. Jessica contingent.

Not that I expected anything different, not really... but it feels like proof. Proof Evan stood to benefit when Lola died. Proof he had a lot on the line. Proof of... something.

But aren't most husbands the sole beneficiary?

It's probably nothing, and that's frustrating.

I wish I had known more about what was going on before she died. I wish we'd kept in contact, that I'd been a part of her life. But she'd called me, at the very least. She'd let me know how terrible things had gotten. And I might not have been able to save her, but I can still protect Jessica.

Guilt washes over me. Things fell apart between the two of us; I know they did.

But I was going to try to be better.

I'm making an effort with Jessica. She has to know the truth eventually, although right now is not the time. She's too busy mourning Lola to be able to understand what happened, but I'll explain it all in due time.

She deserves to know.

"Oh God." I exhale hard and close the manila folder. It takes all of my self-control to put it back in the drawer where I found it. I want to hold on to it, want to take the papers with me, but that wouldn't do any good and I don't really have anywhere to hide them.

After we get rid of Evan, I can come clean with Jessica about everything.

"It's in the past," I tell myself, giving the folder a little pat before piling on some pictures. They're scattered all over the floor and it's probably going to take me longer than I thought to put them back where they go.

And now I hear it. The sound I thought I heard a moment ago, right on the edge of my hearing. No, *the absence of sound.*

The shower stopped.

SIXTEEN

"Oh my God." The hair on the back of my neck stands up and I turn to the door, a flash of fear shooting through me. Evan's out of the shower and that means he'll head downstairs soon.

I move faster now, grabbing photos without worrying about bending their corners. The manila folder is now completely covered but I still have more photos to cram in the drawer.

Who puts this many photos loose in a drawer like this? I give my head a little shake, trying to hurry, trying to—

There's a picture of Jessica on top. She's a baby, with fat little cheeks and her fist clenched around a rattle. I pause, drinking her in. This is what I missed out on.

I missed out on—

"What are you doing?" Evan's voice, low with danger, cuts through my thoughts. I gasp, turning to look at him, my fingers tightening instinctively on the photo I'm holding.

"I dusted in here today and had noticed this drawer wasn't closed all the way. While you were showering, I thought I'd come in here and see if I could fix it."

Without looking, I set Jessica's baby picture in the drawer. I try to maintain eye contact with Evan while grabbing the last photos from the floor, but I have to break it to look down after a moment.

"You were dusting and didn't take care of the drawer then?"

He doesn't believe me. Of course he doesn't; it's a silly lie, one I wouldn't believe either. In two long strides he's next to me, and I hate looking up at him from the floor like this, but I do anyway, well aware of how strong he is, how easily he must have killed Lola.

As soon as I drop the last photos in the drawer, he reaches out. I gasp, jerking my fingers back so he doesn't catch them in the drawer as he slams it shut, then stand, wiping my hands on my apron. Can he see how flushed my skin is? That I'm having trouble catching my breath? That I'd do anything to be away from him right now?

"The drawers need to stay closed, Ariel. I highly doubt there's anything in them you need." His eyes are dark. His breathing shallow. I watch as his nostrils flare with every breath and I have the terrible feeling that he's smelling me, smelling for fear, for the lies I've told.

"Closed, got it."

I'm stepping around him when the front door swings open and then slams shut. Relief that Jessica is home safe washes over me, but at the same time I wince, wishing she didn't slam the door, hoping she won't draw her father's ire.

"Jessica." He bellows her name, pushing past me on his way out of the room.

I stagger and grab the doorframe, sucking in air like I just surfaced from a riptide.

"Hi, Dad." Her voice is quiet, and I freeze, fear dancing up my spine.

Is she okay?

All thoughts of self-preservation fly out the window and I hurry out to where the two of them are in a stand-off in the hall.

Jessica glances at me, gives me a smile, then looks back at her dad.

"You okay, Dad? You look annoyed."

He stiffens. I see the way his back tightens, how he draws himself up a few inches. It's clear he's trying to intimidate her, and I step forward, wanting to make myself known, wanting to try to keep her safe.

"You're home late. Care to tell me what you've been up to?"

"Britt and I were just hanging out. I lost track of time, so I'm glad you called her mom."

"Hanging out?" There's no inflection in his voice. "Hanging. Out. We've been waiting for you to get home for dinner."

That's not entirely true.

I risk a glance at Evan. His body is tight, and he leans forward a little now, like a starter at a race, waiting for the gun to go off, waiting for Jessica to do something that will give him reason enough to lunge at her.

"Really, Evan, she's okay." Without realizing what I'm doing, I reach over and lightly pluck at his sleeve, wanting to get his attention off his daughter and onto me. I can handle him being angry at me; I can handle the rage pouring off him. The last thing I want is that same rage directed at Jessica. It's bad enough that Lola had to face it.

"I'm talking to my daughter!" Evan explodes, turning to look at me.

I gasp, I know I do, the sound slipping from my open mouth. His face is dark, his eyes squinting as he stares at me. I feel a chill dance up my spine and there's a little voice in the back of my head screaming at me to go, to get out of here, to save myself.

But I can't do that to Jessica. Saving myself when I know she's in danger would be the cruelest thing I could do right now. No, even though it terrifies me to sit here while Evan is so angry, I can't abandon her. I'm not going to let her suffer the way Lola did.

"Dad." Jessica's voice is quiet, but it seems to be enough to get through to Evan. He blinks twice, still looking at me, and I have the uncanny feeling he wasn't really seeing me for a moment. It feels like he forgot I was here and now suddenly, with Jessica talking to him, he's back.

"Ariel, I'm sorry," he says, his voice full of contrition. "I'm sorry, I don't know what came over me right now, but it's not fair for you to have to feel the brunt of it. I apologize."

"It's fine," I lie. "It's fine. We've all had those days when it feels like everything is too much to bear." I look him straight in the eyes, wanting him to know that *I see him*. I know who he really is.

"We have. It's just been a long day and I was worried about Jessica not being safe." There's a current of danger running through his words. I pick up on it right away and wonder if Jessica hears it as well. "It won't happen again."

No, it won't. I'm going to make sure he never loses his temper again.

SEVENTEEN

EVAN

WEDNESDAY, AUGUST 30

I scared her, that much was obvious. After my showdown with Jessica in the hall, I thought for sure Ariel would turn tail and run, but she didn't. She's dogged, determined to do the best she can while working here.

But she didn't say much. In fact, she remained mostly silent the rest of dinner, watching as Jessica picked and poked at the food on her plate. If she was unhappy seeing my daughter refuse to eat the food she made, she never showed it.

Not like Lola. Lola would have fussed the entire time, doing and saying anything to try to get Jessica to actually take a bite of her dinner. The fact that Ariel never mentioned it, never even seemed to notice it, is inspiring.

I could be more like her, could try to do better holding my temper in check. It's a fairly new problem for me, not one I really know how to deal with. When Lola and I were first married and I was still on patrol, I did everything in my power to make sure I never came across angry or short-tempered.

When you wear a uniform and a badge, everyone wants you

to be the bad guy and so they're always looking out for you to make a mistake, to be too rough with someone, to take out your frustration on someone you're arresting. I perfected looking calm all the time and never letting anyone see me upset.

But as I moved up the ranks, that changed. I keep slipping, but only at home, never at work. Nobody at work would believe I could even snap at someone for anything trivial the way I just snapped at Ariel.

And now I need to make sure she's not going to quit and leave the two of us hanging.

Jessica excuses herself, and Ariel and I both watch in silence as she gets up, carries her full plate to the kitchen counter, then sets it down. She barely spoke during dinner, and I know it's because she's upset I lost my temper with her.

When Jessica is upstairs and has slammed her bedroom door like she does every evening after dinner, I turn to the woman I hired and clear my throat. "Ariel, I'm really sorry for how things went down earlier. I shouldn't have snapped at you. Jessica and I... well, the stress we're under is undeniable and sometimes it gets the best of me."

"It's fine." Ariel smiles at me. She takes a sip of water and carefully puts her glass down before speaking again. "I know you're stressed or you wouldn't have hired me to come help you two out. Don't worry, I don't hold it against you."

Is she serious? I search her face for any sign that she's joking. I can't find one.

"Please know it won't happen again. Especially now that you're here, I think the two of us will be much happier. I know dinner tonight was difficult, but I don't want you to think meals are always like this. I hope you'll join us again."

"If you'd like that. I don't want to impose."

I shake my head and smile at her. "No, no imposition. You're a lifesaver, Ariel. What you've already done cleaning up the house and making dinner? It's more than I was able to do in a week."

"It's just my job, no worries." She stands and starts clearing the table. "I'll get the pie out for the two of you, but then I must be going. Today had a few hiccups, Evan, but that's to be expected. I'm not worried, and I don't want you to worry either."

Relief washes over me. "And about Jessica, I know she was a little rough around the edges tonight—"

"Jessica is dealing with a lot, and I don't fault her one moment for how she acted today. I honestly hope you won't either." She throws me another huge smile. "She's a teenager and they all deal with grief differently."

I watch as she pulls the pie from the refrigerator, knocking the door with her hip to swing it shut. She carries it to the table and puts it down in front of me with a flourish. "Now, on that note, I'm out. I love pie but I don't think I could eat another bite."

After grabbing her purse from the counter, she stops and gives me a little wave. "Until tomorrow, Evan." A smile, like nothing bad just happened.

I swear I notice an expression there I've seen before. It's uncanny, how familiar she looks even though I only met her recently.

I blink and it's gone.

Ariel either doesn't notice that I seem shocked for a moment by her appearance or doesn't care. She's still smiling at me, her head tilted a little to the side.

"Thank you." I hesitate, then stand, wanting to say one more thing to her. "Ariel, I appreciate all you're doing, I want to make sure you know that."

"I do." Still smiling.

"But my bedroom is off limits. Don't go in there again."

EIGHTEEN

ARIEL

THURSDAY, AUGUST 31

I'd love nothing more than to return to the house after Evan and Jessica have already left for the day, but I need to be there to make breakfast for the two of them before they leave. Even though I have a key, I don't want to come across as making myself too much at home on my second morning. Steeling myself, I take a deep breath, then force myself to knock on the front door. It's a low, hollow sound, and it perfectly matches the pit in my stomach.

I'd love to walk away, maybe skip town completely and leave Jessica to figure this all out on her own, but I can't do that. No, I didn't make a promise to Lola to keep her daughter safe, but that's only because we didn't know how dangerous Evan really is before it was too late. Now that I know that, I have to be here, as much as I'd like to leave.

I hear footsteps from inside and I straighten up, putting a huge smile on my face so that whenever someone opens the door, I'll look like I want to be here. Part of me hopes it's Jessica, so I can try to show her some kindness and make her see that her life will get better when I get rid of her father, but it's Evan.

"Ariel." There's no hint of the anger I saw last night when Jessica came home. "So glad to see you. I'm running a bit late and would really appreciate an omelet with toast if you don't mind."

"I'll get right on it." Honestly, I'm relieved to be jumping right into my job for the day. It's a much better alternative than feeling like I have to tiptoe around him while I try to figure out how upset he still is with me. He might still be angry, and I'd wager he is, so I leave my purse on the coat tree in the living room and hurry into the kitchen.

At the same time, why does he want so badly to keep me out of his bedroom? Maybe Lola had a diary that outlined how afraid she was of her husband. Now *that* would be something I'd love to get my hands on. There are a thousand places in the house she could have hidden it. I mull that over as I survey the kitchen.

It's clear Jessica has already eaten. There's an empty plate on the kitchen table next to a mug of lukewarm coffee. Feeling efficient, I grab them both and dump the coffee, putting the empty dishes in the dishwasher before snatching an apron from the drawer and pulling it on. Evan didn't say what he wanted in his omelet, so I decide to get creative and pull a few things from the refrigerator.

Eggs obviously. Swiss cheese, some spinach I can wilt quickly, cubed ham, and a bit of cream to make the eggs as fluffy as possible. I should be able to have it all on the table in under ten minutes if I hurry, and then Evan can see that I'm not only good at my job but someone he wants to keep around.

I've already cracked the eggs and whisked them with the cream, salt, and pepper when Jessica meanders into the kitchen, heading straight to the table. I pour the eggs in carefully, enjoying the smell of the melted butter, but before I can grab a spatula to lift the edges and cook the still-runny egg, Jessica is right next to me at the stove.

She's standing too close, like we're friendlier than we really are, and I can smell her perfume on her.

"Good morning," I say, taking a step back to get some space between the two of us. "I'm making your dad an omelet, but I can easily make you something as well."

"Did you see my coffee?" She lowers her voice. "Dad doesn't like me drinking more than one cup, but I wasn't finished with that one."

"I'm so sorry," I say, grabbing a spatula and moving the eggs around a little bit to keep them from burning. "I thought you were done with it, so I put the mug in the dishwasher."

"I wasn't done with it." There's a note of hesitation in her voice. "Do you think he'd know if I got another one?"

Poor kid. First she loses her mom, then she has to walk on eggshells around her dad.

"It was cold. I can't imagine he'd be mad at you for replacing it, can you?"

She doesn't immediately answer, and I take a deep breath, holding it and counting to ten, then turn to look at her.

There are tears in her eyes.

"Jessica, what's wrong?" Absentmindedly, I reach over and poke at the eggs, but I don't take my eyes off her. She's so cute, so young. Jessica has an air of innocence around her, but how long that will last in this house, I'm not sure.

"It was my special coffee." Her voice breaks. Quickly, like she's angry, she scrubs her wrist across her eyes, wiping any tears there onto her pink hoodie.

I didn't know she had special coffee. She's fourteen, and why a teenager has *special coffee* I'll never know, but—

"My mom and I drank it together. I'm out. I need more."

Ahh, there it is. Now guilt sits heavy on my shoulders, and I give her a small smile. "I totally understand wanting that coffee back, Jessica. How about this: I'm sorry it's gone right now, but I'll get more for you today from the store if you just tell me what kind it is."

Without waiting for an answer, I sprinkle cheese in the omelet, pile it with fillings, then flip it closed before sliding it onto a plate.

Now it's ready and in just a minute more I'll have the toast on the plate, will get it on the table, can offer it to Evan—

Jessica reaches in front of me, her elbow knocking into my arm, and the plate tumbles from my hand. I stare in horror as it flips upside down, shattering on the tile floor, egg and cheese spattering out from the broken shards of the plate.

"Oh no." Jessica's voice catches in her throat as she steps away from me. She tucks her elbows in, then wraps her arms around herself. I look at her, my cheeks heating. "Oh, I'm so sorry, I was just grabbing the pepper."

"It was just an accident. Stuff like this happens all the time —don't worry about it." I feel stupid and want to match her tears, but more than that I want to set a good example for Jessica. "I bet I can get it cleaned up before your dad gets down-stairs, what do you think?"

"I don't know." She chews her thumbnail, then catches me looking at her. Shoves her hands in her pockets. "I know my dad was really hungry and now what are you going to give him for breakfast?"

"Hmm, good question. I'm not sure I have time to make it again." As if on cue, I hear Evan's footsteps above our heads. Both Jessica and I pause and look up.

I catch her eye. She forces a smile. "I didn't mean to bump you. It was an accident."

"Hey, I can handle it," I tell her, reaching out to touch her shoulder. It's the first time I've made physical contact with her, really touched her, and it feels good.

She shrugs away, a pained expression on her face.

"No, you better clean it up fast." Her voice comes out in a whisper. Her eyes dart past me to the door, then land back on my face. I'm suddenly intensely aware of the smells in the kitchen, the way the coffeepot clicks a little as it cools down, how I can still feel the residual heat from the stove.

"He's not going to get mad." I want her to listen to me and believe me. I want her to trust I'm going to protect her. "I've got this, okay? You run along."

She turns to do just that, poor thing, but before she can leave the kitchen, Evan's there.

"I came as soon as I heard a crash. Is everyone alright?" He hurries into the kitchen, stopping short right inside the door when he sees the two of us standing next to each other. I don't have to look at Jessica to know what her face looks like. I know it's bad.

Jessica is terrified of him, and I feel anger burn deep in my stomach. She's staring at Evan like she's afraid of what he'll do if he comes any closer to her.

"What happened here?" There's judgement in his voice, and he looks at each of us in turn.

"I dropped your breakfast. It was a total accident and I'm about to clean it up, but I told Jessica to finish getting ready for school. She doesn't need to be late because I'm clumsy."

"Is that what happened?" He turns his steely gaze on Jessica, and I swear—*I swear*—I see her wilt a little bit.

"She dropped it." Her voice is so quiet I'm not entirely sure I hear her correctly. "We were just talking, and I accidentally bumped her elbow, and she dropped it."

A heavy sigh. "You need to be more careful. Now you better go get changed."

He gestures to her pants and both Jessica and I stare down at them. Heat flushes up the back of my neck and my chest when I realize there's food on her clothing. It must have hit the floor and then splattered up, landing on her pants, but she can change; he can't be *that* upset about it.

"Jessica, go upstairs and get changed so Ariel and I can talk."

Evan still hasn't moved from his spot by the door, and I feel like I'm an animal on display in the zoo. He's staring at me, obviously trying to figure me out and see if I'm lying.

For her part, Jessica glances at me over her shoulder, concern etched deep in the furrow between her brows. She mouths something at me, something I don't catch, then she's gone, hurrying from the room, skirting Evan so she doesn't accidentally brush his shoulder with hers. He turns to stare at her then looks back at me, a frown on his face, his finger tapping against his leg, pounding out a rhythm only he can hear.

I'm left alone with a man I think killed his wife, and he's angry.

NINETEEN

LOLA'S DIARY

THURSDAY, JULY 20

For a while I honestly thought that things were better. Evan was around more after work, not going out at night with his friends or with the girl who wrote him the note. I never asked where he was going, never thought I needed to. My dad wouldn't have dreamed of doing this to his family, of finding someone else to warm his bed, so why would I ever think that I needed to look out for my husband doing that?

Especially not from someone in his position. Not someone who does what he does. It never crossed my mind to be worried, to think there might be a problem in the future, and that's on me.

I take full responsibly for not knowing what was going on, but I'm smarter now. I'm more aware of what's going on around me than I've ever been in my life and I'm not going to let anything like this surprise me ever again.

Still, as careful as I'm being keeping an eye on Evan, I feel like I need to be that careful making sure he's not keeping an eye on me. He's so aware of everything going on and it scares me a little when I wonder if he knows how upset I am, how cautious I am around him right now, how I'm watching him to see what he might do next.

The only time I have to write in my diary is when he's in the shower or still at work. I'm too terrified to do it any other time, too afraid that he'll catch me in the act, that he'll somehow know that I'm writing about him and force me to show him what I've been putting down. It terrifies me to think he'd see what I've written even though I'm not the one in the wrong here.

Even though it's been weeks since I found the note, I've been on high alert this entire time. It's difficult to live your life like that—constantly feeling like you need to be aware of what's going on just in case something bad happens. I'm tired. I feel the exhaustion deep in my bones. This entire time I've felt like I was at the end of my rope, and I was just about to let my guard down, believing that he was telling the truth, that it was over, when proof that it wasn't hit me right in the face.

And I never saw it coming. That's the part that hurts me the most.

He was in the shower. Although, at the time, he didn't know something terrible was happening. I was separating the laundry just like my mother had taught me, making sure nothing was going to bleed, or run, or get ruined by our old machine, when I heard ringing.

It wasn't the sound of his personal phone. I know that ringtone, have heard it go off time and time again in the evenings when his friends want to talk and they want him to know there's no emergency, there's nothing to worry about, because the call is coming in on his personal line, not his one for work.

But his work phone makes me tense up. It means something's going on, something's going *wrong*, and I ran from the small bathroom where I was piling clothes in front of the machine. It's off our bedroom, but so is the master bath where he was showering. I remember thinking we didn't need two bathrooms like that right off our bedroom, not even with one masquerading as a laundry room, but it's amazing.

I ran into the bedroom.

His shower clicked off.

Evan must have heard the ringtone too, but after years of being married to him, I know that moving quickly is important. You have to answer the call right away, get whatever information you can, take care of what's happening. You can't drag your feet, can't pretend you didn't hear it. You're not rinsed off in the shower? You can do that later. The pot is about to boil over on the stove? You let it.

I grabbed the phone first and answered it without thinking. That's what I do. That's how I make sure he doesn't miss a call, doesn't miss out on any information he needs to do his job.

For a moment, I thought the other person had hung up. There was nothing, no static, no sound, no breathing. Just... silence.

Then a voice, a bubblegum voice, the voice of a young woman who has never been told *no* in her life, the voice of someone who hasn't ever learned that her actions have real consequences and can hurt real people, filled my ear.

"Is Evan there?"

Young. She's so young. Just a few years older than Jessica.

Three words. Three simple words strung together into a question and even though they didn't mean anything, the words, not by themselves, they meant everything. It was the way she said it, the way her mouth moved to form his name, like it tasted good on her lips, like she could already taste *him* on her lips.

And I knew.

My husband was there, a towel wrapped around his waist, his hair still wet, beads of water clinging to his broad shoulders, his abs, his pecs. It used to be that I couldn't tear my eyes away from him when he was like this, but now he looked dull, like he'd been ripped from the pages of an old magazine.

I went from wanting to see him, wanting to have those arms around me, wanting to feel his mouth on mine, to wanting to get as far away from him as possible.

"It's your whore." Even now, the memory of how those words felt when I spoke them makes my face burn.

I held the phone out to him, still hoping a little that I was wrong, hoping that he was going to scoff and hang up, hoping that he wouldn't take the phone and cradle it to his face as gently as he might touch her, but that was exactly what he did.

"Are you okay?"

That's what he asked her. That's what my husband, Jessica's dad, the man I'd sworn to love for the rest of my life, asked another woman. He asked her that while he stood in front of me, while my arms hung uselessly at my sides, while my jaw dropped open and I wondered how he could ask someone else that when I was most certainly not okay.

And when I wasn't sure if I would ever be again.

TWENTY

EVAN

"Care to tell me what really happened?" I do my best to keep my voice even and unbothered as I cross the kitchen to where Ariel has already dropped to her knees and is starting to pick up the broken pieces of glass. There are a number of smaller shards she's going to struggle to pick up without getting them embedded in her fingers, and I detour, grabbing the broom and dustpan before handing them to her.

She's quiet at first, carefully picking up tiny pieces of glass and dropping them into the dustpan. They each land with a faint tinkling sound. Finally, she swallows, turning and looking me right in the eyes. "I dropped the plate. Jessica and I were talking, and I turned and it just... it got bumped from my hands."

I'm just on edge, trying to figure out how the three of us can operate together in the same space without getting in each other's way. I stare at her, trying to tell if she's lying to me. In the past, I could pick up on a lie faster than anything but I'm unfortunately out of practice now. Still, there's something in the way she's holding her jaw that makes me think she's not telling me the entire truth. My wife used to hold her jaw the exact same way when she was spinning some sort of a lie. Maybe it's something most women do.

"She bumped you and it just slipped from your hands?"

"Yes."

"Jessica didn't have anything to do with it *slipping,* did she?"

Jessica doesn't want Ariel here. It's entirely possible she knocked it out of the woman's hands to make her look bad. I steel myself for what Ariel is going to say.

"No. It was an accident, I promise you. I'm really sorry, and I'll make you something else as soon as I get this cleaned up."

"Ariel, listen to me." Without thinking, I reach out and grab her upper arm. She inhales sharply, her eyes flicking up to mine, and I let her go, jerking my hand back and dropping it by my side. "You don't have to tell me if you don't want to, but I want you to know that Jessica can be difficult. I know that."

Footsteps on the stairs.

"She takes after... well, I'd like to say her mother, but that's not entirely true. I don't blame you for the breakfast, okay? She's just figuring you out and trying to understand where you two fit in together here in the house. Don't think for a moment that I don't realize that. Combine losing her mom with teenage hormones and anyone her age would struggle."

Ariel's staring at me with a mingled expression of revulsion and concern. I take a step back as she stands. "What did you think, Evan? That she would be perfectly okay with her mother's death? If she weren't struggling with it, then I'd be worried. You need to give her some slack."

That's rich, coming from a woman who doesn't know my family, who's never even met my wife.

"You're right." I force myself to respond to her. Of course Ariel is going to want to protect Jessica. My daughter is grieving after all, and that's what any woman would do. Protect the child.

"Thank you." Ariel steps back from me, snapping me out of my thoughts.

At that same moment, Jessica walks into the kitchen. She's changed from her dirty jeans to a pair of skintight leggings. They're so tight they look painted on. Ariel's eyes widen at the sight of what my daughter is wearing, but she doesn't say anything.

"You two get everything worked out?" Jessica sounds nervous. She has her hands clasped together in front of her body. Her fingers are locked in a knot, all twisted together as she looks between the two of us.

"We're fine," I tell her, forcing my tone to be as happy and cheery as possible. "Everything here is good; I'm just going to grab some fast food on my way into the office. Do you want me to drop you off on my way in?"

"Britt's mom is coming to get me." Jessica grabs a pear from the bowl on the counter, weighs it in her hand. "I'll be late tonight. Don't hold dinner up for me."

"We talked about this." I don't like how my daughter has taken to walking all over me. She's fearless. Ever since her mother died, she's been acting out more and more. I guess that's to be expected. I remember how Miriam had suggested getting her a therapist, but I dismiss the thought just as quickly. Even if I had thought hiring a therapist for her to talk to was a good idea, I know my daughter.

She'd never talk to someone. Jessica is a lot like me in that regard.

"Dad, please. I know you wanted to keep me home with you after Mom died, but it's not fair to do that to me all the time." There are tears in her eyes, but she has a death grip on her pear, and I can only imagine how bruised it's going to be when she finally decides to eat it.

"You can't just stay out all hours of the night. I'll be home for dinner, and I expect you to be too." There. I'm taking a stand. It's harder than I thought it would be, especially with Ariel a silent observer and Jessica angrily looking between the two of us, but enough is enough. I need my daughter reined in.

We all do.

"Fine." She turns to look at Ariel, then back at me. Her shoulders seem to deflate a little bit, curving her body in on herself. "I'll be here for dinner."

Good enough. For now. What I want is for Jessica to apologize for her attitude. But there's no way I'm going to continue to push it with her. Not only do I not want to air our dirty laundry in front of Ariel, I also don't want anyone in our family to get pushed to the edge. The last time that happened it wasn't pretty.

TWENTY-ONE

ARIEL

THURSDAY, AUGUST 31

Cleaning a house has never been my favorite thing in the world, but when Jessica and Evan leave for school and work, and I'm left all alone, it's not so bad. Thanks to Spotify on my phone, I have music while I scrub floors, wipe baseboards, and clean out the refrigerator. I don't know how two people can possibly be so messy, but it almost feels like they intentionally live in a way that is as dirty as possible.

"Can't be true," I mutter to myself as I work on a particularly sticky and stubborn spot on the lower shelf in the refrigerator. "They're just busy and can't stand being in the same room as each other so they probably don't realize how dirty their house really is."

And it is dirty. Even my first pass yesterday vacuuming and cleaning the bathrooms didn't reveal to me the full extent of how much work I was going to need to put in to cleaning this place up. Not only does the house need all the regular cleaning that most people do on a weekly basis, but there are random things that are begging to be done.

Like beating the sofa cushions and pillows to get dust out of them.

Using wood oil on the wooden furniture to help it shine and keep it from cracking.

Cleaning off the top of the refrigerator. Most people don't do this, and it ends up covered with inches of dust, and this one is no exception.

Did Lola clean at all? It's possible she hated it, that she was one of those people who would willingly do anything other than wash baseboards. Or maybe, toward the end, she was just under too much stress to worry about vacuuming.

As I clean, I think. Even though I know it won't help anything, I can't stop replaying my interaction with Jessica this morning. She's terrified of Evan—I know she is. Now that I'm in the house though, I can find some proof that he killed Lola.

A shiver runs up my spine even though I broke a sweat a while ago scrubbing. Stopping for a moment, I pour a glass of cold water and sit down at the kitchen table.

A journal. Wouldn't that be rich? Evan isn't the type of man to tell his friends he murdered his wife. He wouldn't pop down to the bar to spill the secret over a pint. No, he's quiet. Taciturn. He's going to hold that secret close to his chest, but every person makes mistakes. There's no way he can completely hide what he did.

And maybe he wrote down his secrets. They'll eat you up from the inside out if you don't let them out somehow.

I take a deep breath and drain my glass of water before refilling it and sitting back down. No, he won't have told all his friends how he killed Lola.

But I'd bet anything there's *something* here. Something hidden in the house.

And I just have to find it.

As much as I'd like to sit and take a load off for a while, I stand back up. The kitchen is pretty clean, just some daily maintenance needs to be done every afternoon to keep it in good condition, but I can leave it for now.

The house is silent except for Dolly Parton singing from my phone as I walk into the living room. The wide floorboards under my feet probably cost an arm and a leg to have installed. Even though they look great, there are a few that squeak.

I freeze as I put weight on one and it moans under my foot.

I don't believe in ghosts, but I do believe in evil, and this house is full of it.

"If I had something that I didn't want anyone to know about, where would I put it?" I spin in a slow circle, taking in the fashionable sofa, the TV stand groaning with a collection of old DVDs, the bookcases along the far wall.

"In my bedroom."

Grabbing my duster, I hurry up the stairs before I can come to my senses. Evan made it quite clear already he doesn't want me in his room, but he must be hiding something. Where else would he keep something that would incriminate him? I'll just have to be very, very careful.

The door swings open under my touch. I'd thought for sure he would have locked it to keep me out, but he'd come flying down the stairs this morning when I dropped the plate. Maybe the ruined omelet was the best thing that could have happened to me this morning.

His room smells like expensive cologne. It's warm in here thanks to the sun shining right in the windows. The last time I was in here I was just looking around, but now I'm ready to do some digging.

Dropping my duster on the floor, I walk over to his dresser. It's carved cherry, the gorgeous top covered by stacks of papers and socks he hasn't put away. I'm itching to clean it off, but he told me to stay out of his room.

I have to make sure he believes I have.

Pausing once to listen for any sounds of someone in the

house, I grab the brass pulls on the top drawer and carefully slide it open. It sticks a little and I have to jerk it from side to side to get it all the way out.

Underwear. Socks. Everything is in a jumble, tossed in straight from the dryer, and I don't feel any guilt as I paw through them, digging deep for something hidden.

I just wish I knew what I was looking for.

My fingers brush metal and a shock of excitement rushes through me. I pause, tilting my head to listen once more. The front door is locked, so if anyone were to come home while I was up to my elbows in Evan's underwear, I'd hear it.

But I'm still scared. My breaths come in little gasps as I trace my fingers along the metal in the bottom of the drawer. What in the world could it be? I've never been married, but even so, I can't think of a single thing a man would have in his underwear drawer that felt like this.

My fingers slide across cool, smooth metal, and I'm about to unearth it from its grave of underthings when I reach bumpy, rough metal, and I gasp.

He has a gun hidden in his underwear.

Like I've been burned, I yank my hand out of the drawer. Without thinking about it, I lean against the drawer, my hands flat on the surface, and slam it shut. There's a buzzing in my head that sounds like a bee, and I shake my head to clear it.

For a minute, I just stare at the dresser.

He has a gun, he has a gun, he has a gun, he has a—

Of course he has a gun. Lola wasn't shot to death, and the man is a police officer.

The thrumming of my heartbeat in my ears slows.

She wasn't shot.

He's a cop.

Of course he has a gun.

Him having a gun doesn't prove anything. As much as I'd

like to end my search here and send him to jail for what he did, it's not enough. I need to find more.

I step back from the dresser, my heart pounding. If the other drawers are anything like the top one, then I highly doubt I'll be able to find anything useful in them. Still, I have to check.

The three of them stick just as badly as the first one did. I shimmy them open carefully, well aware of the sweat that's beaded along my hairline on my forehead. The second drawer from the top has shirts, the third one has pants, and the bottom one has hoodies.

Nothing in them but clothing.

"Okay," I say, working the last drawer into place and then stepping back from the dresser. "Okay, there wasn't anything in there, but I have to keep looking."

But before turning away from the dresser, I scrutinize it, looking for any sign I've been in here.

Nothing I can see. Hopefully Evan won't see anything either.

I'll find something in this house that will tie Evan to Lola's death. Right now though, I need to do some more cleaning.

Back downstairs, I end up in the living room again. My heart has slowed back down but my legs feel weak, like muscles always do when you've had a shot of adrenaline and are coming down from that high.

I'm more shaken up by finding the gun than I'd like to admit. Just touching the metal made my skin crawl and I want to get rid of that feeling.

I'll pop out to the garden and pick some flowers for the table. Then I'll swing by the grocery store and grab some fresh salad—there isn't enough in the fridge for dinner.

Walking into the kitchen, I grab some shears and a vase from the cupboard above the sink.

Everything in here gleams. It smells fresh and clean, and I feel a burst of pride at how hard I've worked. Evan and Jessica won't know whose home they walked into when they get home for dinner.

I have the vase in one hand and the kitchen shears in the other when it hits me. "You sneaky bastard," I mutter.

Of course Evan would pretend like Jessica has an attitude because of something else, something other than just losing her mom. He wants to make sure there's a wedge between the two of us so we don't get close. If Jessica learns that she can trust me then it's very possible that she'll tell me the truth of what happened the night Lola died.

She wouldn't feel so brazen in doing whatever she wanted in this house without any repercussions, if she didn't know the truth. Evan killed Lola and Jessica knows it.

Evan can't have that. He knows that anyone getting close to Jessica is a danger. That's why he doesn't want the two of us to be able to connect. That's why he doesn't want her staying late with her friends. Every single person she's close to is one more person who might learn the truth.

And the last thing Evan can handle is the truth coming out. It would destroy him. Not only would he lose his job, his house, his daughter, but he'd end up in jail.

He's not protective because he loves her. He's protective because he wants to control her to protect *himself*.

Excitement courses through me and I push away from the counter. When I get too much energy like this, I feel like I need to walk it off. Pacing helps, and I start walking around the perimeter of the kitchen, my mind going a million miles a minute.

He doesn't want people getting close to Jessica so I'm going to have to be careful. I need to get Jessica to trust me, to think of me as someone she can turn to. He wants to keep his secrets, so I need to make sure it never seems like I'm asking too many questions.

I honestly believe Jessica knows the truth. I just have to get her to trust me so she'll open up.

This is great because it means half of my work is already done for me. I don't have to worry about how I'm going to convince Jessica that her dad is dangerous. Of course, I'm not just going to bring it up over an afternoon snack before he gets home from work one day, but the fact that she already knows Evan is a loose cannon means she should be more amenable to my plan.

Of course, that's not all it means.

It also means that Jessica is in grave danger from her father.

TWENTY-TWO

EVAN

THURSDAY, AUGUST 31

I'm not confident that Jessica is going to show up for dinner until I hear the front door open and slam closed, and then the familiar thud of her dropping her backpack on the floor reaches my ears.

She picked that habit up from Lola. My wife slammed doors even when she wasn't upset. It's a terrible habit and one I'd like to break Jessica of, but at least I always know where she is in the house.

It's only now that I know she's home that I relax. Even though it's impossible to keep her on a leash all the time, I can't help but want to do just that.

Ariel's just plating dinner as Jessica walks into the kitchen. My daughter has a smile on her face that tells me she's in a much better mood than she was earlier this morning.

"Hey, Dad." She wraps her arms around herself, squeezing her stomach tight when I go to hug her. Putting my arms around her is like hugging a plank of wood. There's no give there.

"How was your day? And Britt?"

"School was good. Britt's fine." She takes a tiny step back from me and I let her go, watching as she walks over to Ariel. "That smells really good."

"You think so? Thanks." Ariel hands Jessica a pitcher of ice water with lemon slices, and my daughter brings it right to the table. I'm standing back from the scene, watching it play out, watching my daughter interact with Ariel. She's more relaxed than she was this morning and I feel my shoulders sag with relief.

This morning I was starting to get a little worried about having Ariel in the house and had even started to wonder if maybe Jessica and I didn't need a housekeeper coming into the house every single day to cook, clean, and do laundry. But then I came home from a long day at the office, and what did I have to do? Nothing. No cooking, because everything was almost ready. No cleaning, because the house is starting to sparkle.

Instead of lifting a finger to do any work around here, I cracked open a beer, took it with me to the shower, and now I'm in comfortable clothes, waiting on my meal to be served. I feel spoiled and I'm sure some people would say I am, but Lola had a huge life insurance policy that all went to me when she died, and I'm pretty sure she'd be okay with me spending it like this.

She loved me. And she loved Jessica. Me spending Lola's insurance money hiring Ariel so she'll pick up the house and make our life easier is, in turn, just me taking care of our daughter.

Without all the hard work.

Sure, I'm benefitting too, but it's creating a better home life for Jessica. That's what I'd tell anyone who questioned Ariel being here.

It's what Lola would have wanted.

"Can you believe how good this smells?" Jessica pulls the chair out next to me and sits. "I'm glad I didn't stay at Britt's, although her mom was going to order in pizza from Marco's."

Ariel puts our plates in front of us then grabs hers from the counter and joins us at the table. "So tonight we have grilled steak salads with goat cheese, arugula, candied walnuts, a bit of celery, and a vinaigrette I whipped up. I hope you both love it."

"It looks amazing," I say, spearing a bite. "I don't know how you have the energy to make a meal like this after working in the house all day long. I don't remember the last time this place was so clean."

"Probably while Mom was still alive," Jessica offers. She shoves a bite of salad in her mouth and speaks around it. "I'm not saying she was the best housekeeper, but she didn't just slack all the time."

"Jessica." I don't want to warn my daughter in front of other people, but I need to keep her under control. Ariel seemed like she understood why Jessica is acting out a bit when we spoke earlier, but it's still embarrassing.

Ariel blushes but doesn't say anything. An uncomfortable silence grows between the three of us until I clear my throat. "So tell me, Ariel, where did you find a place to live? I appreciate you understanding that living here wasn't an option, but I still want to make sure you're in a good part of town."

"Oh, Miriam helped me with that. She's wonderful and so efficient. She seems to know everyone."

"She is." I like that the conversation has turned to a subject I'm not only familiar with but comfortable talking about. Miriam is safe. She knew Lola, just a little, but she has no reason to think that anything bad actually happened to her. She's steadfast and loyal to me, and that's really hard to find nowadays. "You know what I love about her? She leaves her personal life at home, where it belongs."

Why did I say that? It adds literally nothing to the conversation, but Ariel seems interested and looks up at me from her place.

"She doesn't talk about her personal life at all?"

"No, it's just not appropriate. All I know about her is that she's great at her job, is efficient and willing to go the extra mile, and never slacks off on her duties."

"She sounds like a blast." A small smile plays on Jessica's lips before she takes another bite of her salad. "This is really good, Ariel." I've noticed she's pushing most of the meat to the side of her plate, but I don't think Ariel has.

"Oh, thank you, I—"

"If only there wasn't so much meat on it."

"Jessica. Manners." I reprimand my daughter without thinking.

Her face pales. "Sorry. Right, I forgot."

"You know better. Do better." I wipe my mouth with my napkin and then put it back on my lap. Any of the delight I had a moment ago while eating is gone. There's a gloom descended on the three of us, one that's been around more and more often and getting harder to shake.

"Well, we all forget our manners from time to time," Ariel says. She reaches out to pat Jessica's hand. I'm sure my daughter will yank her hand away, but she lets Ariel touch her. "You've been through a lot, Jessica, and I know you know manners are important. I also know sometimes we forget things."

"I just want to make sure you don't embarrass me." The words are out of my mouth before I can stop them. Jessica's mouth drops open in shock and Ariel gasps, her hand flying up to cover her mouth.

"I'll go to my room."

Jessica shoves back from the table and flees the kitchen. She pauses at the base of the stairs but then she's running up them, feet pounding on them like that will help her work out her anger. We hear her run down the hall.

Her bedroom door slams.

Ariel winces. I don't.

My heart beats out a staccato in my chest. Somehow, I need

to figure out how to get my daughter under control, but I have no idea how to do that. The most important thing is keeping what's left of my family together. It's the only way I can make sure this all works.

"Evan, listen to me." Ariel squeezes my arm before pulling her hand back. "Don't be so hard on her, okay? She lost her mother and now she's trying to find her way without her. Of course she's going to struggle."

As much as I should like that Ariel is defending my daughter, I don't. "Ariel, I appreciate your concern, I really do, but Jessica is my daughter, not yours. I know what's best for her and I'd really appreciate if you'd respect that."

I swear the temperature in the room drops ten degrees after what I just said. Ariel stares at me, her mouth dropping open just a little bit, like her brain is working overtime to catch up with what I just said.

"I'm sorry, I—"

"No apologies needed. Just know that I can handle my daughter. I hired you to keep the house in good shape, to make sure we have something to eat, and to ensure that nothing goes wrong when I'm not paying attention. I didn't hire you to keep an eye on Jessica. You're not her babysitter. Not her friend. You'd do best to remember that."

She nods and I feel a stab of triumph, but it's short-lived when I have my next thought.

How much longer will Jessica be able to keep everything secret?

TWENTY-THREE

LOLA'S DIARY

TUESDAY, JULY 25

Living in the same house as someone who doesn't love you any longer is a strange dance. It's like Evan and I have opposing magnetic fields in us, like we can't get too close without repelling each other. Evan floats into the kitchen to get something to drink and I float out the other door.

There's no contact between us. I turn my back on him at night, afraid to ask him to sleep on the sofa, afraid of Jessica finding out what's really going on. Neither one of us have told her, not yet. She's already such a teenager at fourteen; so wrapped up in her own life and the drama at school that she's clueless as to the fact that our marriage is over.

Just writing those words—our marriage is over—is enough to make me feel like I can't breathe. My chest goes tight when I think about Evan, but not the same tight it used to go when I first fell in love with him. I couldn't breathe around him then, couldn't seem to keep from going dizzy when he spoke my name.

Now, though, he doesn't call me by name. I told him not to

say it, not to say *Lola* ever again, not with the same mouth he used to kiss another woman.

And he hasn't. It hurts, all of it, but what might hurt the most is how quickly he was willing to give me up. I'm discarded, he's *upgraded*, even though I've always hated that term, the idea that women are appliances that so quickly go out of style that men need to constantly be on the lookout for the next best thing.

So I've decided to do the same thing. I don't want to upgrade to another man, don't want to put myself through marriage again, through the awkward stage that is dating. Evan has moved on to the next best thing and I'm going to do the same, only my upgrade isn't going to include washing someone's socks and underwear for them.

It's not going to include me putting someone else's needs before mine. Yes, I love Jessica, and yes, I'll still be her mother, but I'm not going to fall into the bed of another man thinking that, this time, things will be different.

I know they wouldn't.

I refuse to put myself through the possibility of this happening again and I'm not going to let Jessica think that this is what women have to deal with when they get married. It's not fair to her to see me struggle with Evan, to know that he's cheated on me like this, then see me immediately take my broken heart straight to another man for healing.

No, I refuse to do that.

Eventually, Evan needs to tell Jessica what he's done. He was convinced he was going to be able to turn things around, stop the affair, come back to me. He promised me he would do all of that, and he hasn't. I can forgive him for that, but that doesn't mean I'm going to stay.

It also doesn't mean I have to be the one to look our daughter in the eyes and explain why our family is broken. I'm going to leave that to Evan, and then I'm going to leave him.

Jessica needs to know that the reason our family is falling apart is because of what her dad did. I refuse to take any of the blame on this one. When I leave him, and I will, it will be to better my life, to take care of my daughter, to make sure nobody can ever hurt her or me again. When I leave him, he needs to have come clean to Jessica.

She needs to know that I'm doing this for her. I'm not running away from my problems; I'm not throwing in the towel just because marriage is hard. I'm leaving because it is, hands down, the right thing for me to do, not only for myself but for my daughter.

All I'm waiting on is Evan to come clean about what he's done, how he's ruined our family, how he broke the vows he made to me.

Then I'm out of here. My sister said I can come.

And I'm taking Jessica with me.

TWENTY-FOUR

ARIEL

The threat in Evan's voice was clear—*back off of my daughter and let me handle her.*

But what if he tries to handle her the same way he handled Lola?

He does a good job hiding the fact that he's a monster. I've seen his anger now and I can only imagine how terrifying it must be to have it turned fully on you without anything to temper it. It bubbles out of him, hot like lava, and he's barely able to contain it.

Lola had to deal with that.

The thought makes me feel ill. It's not fair for anyone to have to deal with that kind of anger, but she couldn't get away. After all the man did, she couldn't flee fast enough to save herself.

So it's up to me to make sure Jessica is safe.

Driving home to my little guesthouse, I keep running over the conversation in my mind. I'm picking apart every single detail I can, not only *what* he said but *how* he said it. It's obvious Evan wants to be in complete control.

But I can't give him that. What kind of a person would I be if I just turned and looked the other way when I honestly believe a child is in danger? As easy as that would make things, that's simply not the type of person I am.

Whenever I think about Lola, I feel a familiar stab of guilt. We were so close for the longest time, but it seems like everyone grows apart eventually. If she were here, I'm sure she'd thank me for keeping an eye on Jessica, no matter what Evan might want. That's the only thing keeping me going, and I have to remember that I'm doing this all for her.

It doesn't matter if I'm uncomfortable. It doesn't matter if Evan is mad at me for getting involved with Jessica and trying to keep her safe. All of her behavior makes sense. She's pushing me away, being rude to me, and not letting me get close to her because she's afraid of her dad. Even if she doesn't know the truth about Evan pushing Lola to her death, it makes sense that she'd be able to feel the tension in the house and want to get away from it.

The police think Lola fell, but I don't believe it for an instant. Evan is strong and he's used to getting his way at work. Lola's always been careful, and I really don't think she could have fallen. I don't care that he managed to convince his coworkers. He pushed her.

When I pull up to the guesthouse, I park under a large oak tree that hangs halfway over the driveway. In the fall the branches will be bare and skeletal, but right now the dark-green leaves cast much-needed shade and I exhale, leaning against my car for a moment after I get out.

I'm not afraid of hard work, but that doesn't mean I'm not tired. Spending so many hours at the Warner house working on my hands and knees is wearing me out. I'm grateful for the dinner the past few nights because otherwise I'm not sure I would have the energy to make myself something to eat. Still, with dinner as awkward and uncomfortable as it was last night, I might want to skip out for a few evenings.

And then it hits me. Evan scrawled a note on the calendar right before I left, and I peeked at it just long enough to tell what it said. He has a staff meeting tomorrow night, dinner served, and he gave me the night off. I know he doesn't want me to spend a lot of time with Jessica, but someone has to make her dinner.

And that someone is me. Staying for dinner with his daughter shouldn't be a big deal since he's already encouraged it the past few nights.

It's going to be my first time getting Jessica on her own without Evan there to interrupt or intimidate her, and I plan on taking full advantage of the situation.

TWENTY-FIVE

ARIEL

It's been a long day, but I'm not only prepared for dinner with Jessica, I'm actually excited about it. When Evan's home he moves through the house like a dark cloud, making it difficult for me to enjoy myself and to connect with his daughter. Now that he's not going to be here and it's going to be just the two of us, I feel like we'll finally be able to get somewhere and will hopefully be able to form a real relationship.

I pause, tilting my head to the side to listen. I hear Jessica's music, but it doesn't sound like she's come out of her room. Good. This is the last drawer in the living room TV stand to dig through and I'm hoping to find something here that will tie Evan to Lola's death.

I've already found her life insurance policy. Proof that he had an affair, that Lola wasn't just making it all up, would help my case. Anything written in his own hand would be even better.

I want to have something solid when I finally accuse Evan

of cheating on Lola. Irrefutable proof is going to be my best bet to get rid of him forever.

So far in the drawer I've found old batteries, dead remotes, magazines from three years ago, and three old cell phone chargers.

"Come on," I mutter, grabbing a pack of paper in the bottom of the drawer. I flip through it, so hungry it's difficult for me to focus on what I'm looking at, then it hits me what I'm holding.

I sink to the floor, bring my knees up to my chest, and drop my forehead to rest on them.

One big breath.

Another.

How many times did I write Lola, begging her to sit down and talk things through with me, or at least give me five minutes on the phone to explain my side? I can't remember all the letters I wrote, but they're here, all shoved in the back of a drawer.

All of them unopened.

She never opened a single letter I sent her, which means she never saw how I sobbed while writing them, never saw how my tears stained the paper. Anger rushes through me, cold and sharp, and I close my fist around the letters. They crumple.

As much as I want to rail at Lola for never opening my letters and never giving me a chance to patch things up between the two of us, she's no longer here.

"It won't do any good," I tell myself, tucking the letters back into the drawer where I found them. Lola hurt me, hurt me in the way only someone who knows your deepest fears can. But I'd still do anything to have her back, no matter how angry she was with me, no matter how much pain it might cause me.

I can't bring Lola back, but I can save Jessica. We need each other to heal.

It will take time, but I have that. If I can get her to open up to me, just a little, and can make her begin to see that I'm on her side and that I'm not interested in getting her in trouble with her dad, then the two of us should be able to get along just fine.

I put the letters back. My hands shake as I do and I'm half-tempted to take them with me, even to destroy them, but I can't do that. Jessica might want to read them when I tell her the truth.

I close the drawer. Lock those memories away.

I just have to make Jessica see that I'm on her team. That's my main goal here, and it's why I'm making something for dinner that I wouldn't traditionally make. When I first started work here and had to clean out the refrigerator and the freezer to make room for fresh food that wasn't spoiled takeout, I found a box of freezer-burned veggie burgers in the back of the freezer. Lola must have bought them for Jessica. After tossing them, I grabbed some of the same brand at the store so Jessica would have fresh ones.

I'm normally more inclined to eat a meat burger, but I've seen how Jessica picks at the meat on her plate when I serve her and her dad. I'm not saying she's a vegetarian, but she might be more interested in eating that way than I thought. If her dad had told me that, I would be catering to how she likes to eat, but of course he wouldn't.

Evan isn't going to do anything or allow anything in his house that might be at all inconvenient for him.

But he's not here, is he? And I've spent most of the day mixing up, proofing, and baking burger buns so that they're perfectly fluffy and browned. They each even have a sprinkle of sesame seeds on top and I grabbed some new condiments, a few types of pickles, and even a ripe tomato that I'm now slicing.

The veggie burgers are in the oven, which is the best way to cook them according to the box, and I'm just waiting on Jessica to come down from her room. When I told her earlier that I had a surprise planned for dinner I thought I caught a glimpse of interest on her face, but it was gone before I could decide if it was really there or not.

Moving quickly, I hurry into the kitchen and pull a pack of deli cheese out of the fridge before digging deep to find a veggie cheese I bought for her. In just a few minutes I have all of the burger toppings spread out on the counter, and I take my lightly toasted buns, open them on plates, then go to the bottom of the stairs to call Jessica.

She doesn't answer.

I'd have to be deaf to not be able to hear the loud thrum of music coming from her room. It sounds like someone is banging two pan lids together and screaming at the top of their lungs, and I hesitate at the bottom of the stairs for a moment before quickly walking up to the second floor.

Jessica's room is at the end of the hall. I have to walk past Evan's, and I pause as I do, glancing at the closed door. It's obvious he has secrets in there he doesn't want me to know about. Holding my breath, I reach out and turn the knob.

It turns but the door doesn't open. I stare at it for a moment before I realize what's stopping me: Evan's locked the door.

I hesitate, frustrated. I need to get Jessica so the two of us can have something to eat, but now I really want to get back into his room.

I searched his dresser. Found the gun. But what else did I miss?

Just in case I was imagining things, I twist the knob again, harder this time, saying a little prayer that it will turn, but the door doesn't open, and I swear. My hands are sweaty, and I wipe them on my apron before turning to look back down the hall to Jessica's room.

I'll have to get back into Evan's room but now I have to figure out how to be really sneaky about it. Pushing that thought from my mind so I can focus on his daughter, I walk down the hall to her door and raise my hand to knock.

Then I pause.

There's a strange smell coming from her room, and I know exactly what it is.

TWENTY-SIX

Where in the world did Jessica get her hands on some pot? That's the first question I have but it's quickly pushed out of my mind by the second one that runs through my brain. *How brazen is she to smoke it in the house with the chief of police living right down the hall?*

I realize with a start that my hand is still in the air in front of me, waiting on me to knock, and I finally do, lightly tapping the wood door. This close to her room, the sound of the music is almost overwhelming and I'm not sure if she's going to be able to hear me at all, but a moment later the music cuts off as abruptly as if someone pulled the cord from the wall, and she swings the door open to look at me.

Not all the way open of course. She barely opens it enough for her face to show and I glance down, not surprised to see one foot right behind the door, bracing it so that I can't push my way into her room.

Is that what she thinks of me? Or is that what it's like living with Evan? Is he so violent and disrespectful that Jessica thinks she has to actively take steps to protect herself and to keep him out of her room? The thought makes my heart break and I do my best to smile at her as I try to put her at ease.

"It's time for dinner," I say, ignoring her bloodshot eyes, the way the smell emanating from her room only intensified when she opened her door, how I can peek past her and see a joint on her desk. "I bet you're hungry."

Her eyes narrow and it's clear she's trying to decide how much I know and if I'm joking. I have no doubt she's trying to figure out how to get out of coming to dinner with me, but of course she's hungry: she's locked herself up here in her room all evening smoking pot. I'd wager she's about to come out of her skin with hunger unless she has some snacks stashed under her bed for when she gets the munchies.

She flushes. "I'm not hungry."

Liar. Her stomach rumbles and I'm sure she knows we both heard it, but we're both doing our best to ignore it.

"Shame, I made veggie burgers. And grabbed a few kinds of chips at the store because I wasn't sure what you liked." She blinks at me but doesn't move to follow me out of her room, so I continue, laying it on really thick. "And a brownie mix, if you want me to throw that together so they'll be baked right when we finish dinner."

Baked. Just like you are, Jessica.

"I'll be down in five minutes." The look on her face is pleading and I step back, letting her close the door. I hear the lock click and exhale hard, then turn and walk back down the hall. Evan's room is like a beacon, but I ignore it and make it to the kitchen before bursting out laughing.

The chief of police has a stoner daughter. How the hell he doesn't know it is beyond me. Maybe he does. Maybe he's well aware Jessica is hiding in her room, smoking in the evenings. Or maybe tonight was a special occasion because she knew her dad wasn't going to be around. Whatever it was, I need to be careful and help protect her from Evan.

We've all smoked a little pot in our teenage years, or least I did, and I turned out just fine. Jessica's self-medicating and I don't blame her for that. She just needs to be careful.

The last thing I want is for someone to catch on to his daughter's illegal activities. I can only imagine what would happen to her if the news caught wind of it. Everyone loves to see a powerful man brought to ruin, and while I would pay good money to see that happen to Evan, this isn't how I want it to go.

I want to make him suffer. I want him to look me in the eyes and know that the reason this is all happening to him is because of what he did to Lola. It's not enough for him to fall from grace because Jessica likes to smoke a little weed. I'll do whatever I have to do to keep him in the dark about that.

It'll be the first of our little secrets.

Five minutes on the nose, Jessica comes downstairs. She's chomping on gum, and I turn away from her, grinning. No doubt she also has some eye drops up there to counteract the red in her eyes and used them before coming down here, but no amount of eye drops and gum is going to be able to cover up what I know she was doing. She might think she's sneaky, but I remember being fourteen.

"Dinner looks good." She clears her throat and snaps her gum.

I wait to answer her until I have the veggie burgers out of the oven with the brownies in their place. This kitchen smells amazing and it's going to smell even better as soon as the chocolate in there starts to cook and melt. Poor Jessica is going to be gnawing at her arm in just a minute to get something to eat if she doesn't put something on her plate right away.

"Thanks. I have some veggie cheese for you as well as some toppings. I appreciate you coming right down, because it means we can both make our burgers however we want." *Treat the teenager with respect and they'll learn to respect you in turn.*

"Cool. This is way better than a frozen pizza."

"Glad you think so." I pause. "You know, you'll have to spit out your gum before we can sit down and eat. You don't want the peppermint ruining the flavor of the burger."

She freezes, her head down, her hand in mid-air as she reaches for some mustard. Slowly, like she's afraid of what she'll see, she lifts her head and looks at me. "You know?"

I want to laugh and tell her that I'd have to be blind and unable to smell anything to not know what she was doing in her room, but she's taking this seriously, so I will too. I nod.

"Are you going to tell Dad?"

There it is. Is that a bit of fear I hear in her voice? As brave and tough as Jessica tries to be, I have to remember she's still just a kid. Her being young and innocent is why I'm here in the first place—so I can protect her. I could tell Evan, could turn Jessica in and make her life a living hell, but that's not my end goal here. As soon as I told him what she'd been up to, any cracks in the walls surrounding her would close right back up.

It wouldn't matter how many veggie burgers I made the girl or what else I did to try to win her over, telling Evan would ruin any progress I'd made in the past and prevent me from connecting with her in the future.

"I'm not telling him." I stare right at her while I speak, wanting to see her face and make sure she understands just how serious I am about this. "But, Jessica, you need to be careful. What would he do to you if he were to find out you were smoking? In the house, no less. And where did you even get the drugs?"

She hesitates and I think for a moment she's going to come clean with me. Who cares that our dinner is getting cold? All that matters is that Jessica and I are about to turn a corner, about to finally connect. No, I don't love the idea of her sitting up in her room getting stoned, but if this little secret is what it takes for us to connect and for her to feel safe with me, then who am I to argue?

I won't tell Evan. I'll protect her. I need to make that clear to her.

"Dad can't ever know." Jessica presses her lips together as tight as they can possibly go and gives her head a little shake.

"He won't." Fine. She doesn't want to tell me where she gets the drugs? I guess it doesn't really matter in the long run, does it? What matters is that she's getting to see first-hand that I'm on her side, that she doesn't need to worry about me running and tattling to Evan.

"Thank you." Jessica breathes the words at me. They're so soft that I look up at her in surprise. It feels good to have her thank me for something, even if that something is helping her hide the fact that she smokes in her room.

Still, I'll take it. This may not be the bonding session I'd hoped it would be, but I feel like we've already made a lot of progress.

Besides, the night is still young. Evan isn't due home for another two hours or so. I'll hang out with Jessica until he gets here, make sure she sees that I'm really on her side. I'll make her comfortable.

She has more secrets, I'm sure of it. I'm going to learn them all.

TWENTY-SEVEN

EVAN

It's been a long day. Too long. The type of day that stretches out ahead of you, marked only by things that you don't want to do. Meetings. Reports. Complaints from officers on the road. Complaints from residents dealing with officers on the road. More meetings. Mediocre catering. Another meeting, just to cap off a long Friday, like it wasn't long enough already.

And now I'm finally almost home. Even though I'm glad to leave the office behind, there's a part of me that's a bit wary of pulling up in front of the house and seeing what's been going on since I was gone. This is the first time Jessica has been alone in the house for any length of time since we lost Lola. While I don't think anything bad will have happened...

Nobody said teenagers were easy, did they?

There's a familiar ache in my chest when I think about Jessica. How many pictures of her do we have from when she was a sweet little girl, dressed in fluffy dresses, playing with the neighbor's puppy, picking flowers? How many of her do I have smiling and laughing, her face bright with joy when I brought her ice cream, grinning as she showed off her new haircut?

Jessica is my little girl. She's the love of my life and the person I'd be willing to do anything for.

There's a car in the driveway. I recognize it immediately and stiffen, my thoughts immediately jumping from how sweet Jessica was as a little girl to wondering what the hell Ariel is doing here.

I gave her the night off.

Pulling into the garage, I try to calm myself down. What would she be doing here? I can think of a million things someone might want to do on their night off, and none of them involve spending unpaid time with a moody teenager.

Whatever's going on, I don't like it.

I take a few more deep breaths then get out of my car. When I slam the door closed behind me, the sound echoes in the garage as I walk to the door that leads into the laundry room. The house is silent, and I hate that my hand shakes as I turn the handle to let myself in.

How many quiet houses just like this one did I walk into while on the road, only to find—

Stop it.

The door opens silently, and I listen, my ears cocked, the silence so oppressive that it feels like all the air has been pulled from my lungs. Did something happen while I was at work? I didn't get a text from Jessica, but then why don't I hear anything in the house?

Even the music Jessica usually plays, loud and thumping, enough to make me want to pull my hair out when I hear it, isn't playing. The house seems empty without the sound of it thudding and I close the door carefully behind me, locking it by habit, then kick off my shoes and leave the laundry room.

The kitchen is empty, the light off. Something smells amazing in here. Chocolatey, rich and warm, and I wonder if the two of them did some baking. *Yeah, right. Jessica doesn't bake.*

And then I hear it. It's the TV, turned down so low that it sounds like two people whispering in the next room. Goosebumps break out on my arms, but I refuse to acknowledge them and instead I walk from the kitchen into the living room, being careful to keep my footsteps as quiet as possible.

What I see shocks me.

Ariel's sitting in the corner of the sofa, her socked feet propped up on the coffee table. Her eyes are closed, her head leaned back on the pillow propped up behind her, and my breath catches for a minute when I think that she might be dead.

Surely not.

I stare at her for far too long, looking for the rise and fall of her chest, and when I finally see it, I exhale, then look to her side. Jessica's there, a blanket wrapped around her, staring at me. There's an empty plate on the sofa next to her, a few dark crumbs on it. Cookies. Or brownies, I'd guess. That's what I smelled when I walked in.

Moving slowly, like she doesn't want to disturb Ariel, Jessica pulls one hand out from the blanket and wiggles her fingers at me. I wave back, then turn to look at the TV. It's some movie I don't know, with wizards and dragons, but the sound is turned low so it won't wake up Ariel and my daughter has the closed captions on.

What the hell is going on?

Tiptoeing across the room, I sit down on the other side of Jessica. Ariel wasn't supposed to be here but I'm not going to get mad at Jessica about that. I want to do better. "Did you two have a good night?" My voice is low, barely a whisper.

She nods. "Yeah, we had dinner and then hung out. We started the movie, but Ariel passed right out." A smile plays on her lips, and I feel myself relax.

When I saw Ariel, her head tilted back, her eyes closed... I can't help that the first thought I had was that she was dead.

I clear my throat. "Great. That sounds great. Dinner was good?"

"Yeah. Veggie burgers."

"Wonderful." I don't know what else to say. We need to wake Ariel up and get her on the road so she can get some good sleep, but she just looks so peaceful. I'm about to get up and wake her when there's a soft beep from a phone on the coffee table.

Ariel's phone. Jessica never puts hers down and so the only thing that makes sense is that the woman passed out on the sofa left her phone on the coffee table and didn't hear it beep. It doesn't matter who's texting her.

But I'm still curious. It's wrong to snoop, but without thinking about what I'm doing, I lean forward, grab the phone, and tap on the screen to make it light back up.

It was a text, but one of many. The screen is locked though, so while I can see who sent it, I can't see what the text says.

"I already tried to read them."

That makes me glance at my daughter. Of course she did. Jessica wouldn't be able to stand the thought that someone was getting texts and she didn't know what they said. The screen goes dark and I tap it again.

There's no reason for me to feel this pit in my stomach when I see who texted our housekeeper. In fact, it's the same person who introduced the two of us, so it would make sense that the two of them might text every once in a while.

Still, there's something about seeing Miriam's name coming up on Ariel's phone that doesn't sit right with me.

TWENTY-EIGHT

LOLA'S DIARY

FRIDAY, JULY 28

I shouldn't have started packing without Evan coming clean to Jessica, but I'm antsy. Now that I know I'm out of here, I want to put this entire nasty business behind me. I need to find a job, a place to live. I need a new normal—I crave a new normal—and packing is the best way for me to feel like it's actually going to happen sooner rather than later.

But Jessica saw me.

Or, rather, she saw the suitcase under my bed, saw it poking out a bit from where I'd pushed it there in a hurry last night, nudging it out of the way before Evan got out of the shower.

It's always the shower, isn't it?

I could blame her for wanting to grab some money from her dad's wallet, which he always tosses right in the middle of the bed like he doesn't care what happens to it. I could blame myself for taking time to clean up the dishes even though I'm the only one who really cares whether or not the kitchen is clean.

I could blame everyone for something, for some role they

played in Jessica coming up to my bedroom when she shouldn't have, for me not being there to stop her, for Evan putting his wallet too close to the edge of the bed so she had to come around to where I sleep to get some money to go out with Britt.

But none of that matters. The only thing that matters is that my suitcase was sticking out, just a bit, just the corner, but enough for her to stub her toe, enough for her to get curious and pull it out, enough for her to flip open the top, her mouth dropping when she saw what was inside.

She flew down the stairs. I always hated that term, like she was a bird flying free, but still tethered to the earth, her feet pounding hard on the stairs like she was beating them into submission.

I was still at the sink, trying to make myself work through the pile of dishes I needed to wash before I'd be finished in the kitchen, but I turned as soon as I heard her enter the room behind me, heard the rage in her voice.

"Where are you going?"

That was it. Four words, just four little words, and everything I'd been planning, all of the escape routes I'd been mapping out in my mind, disappeared.

I told her we needed to talk. That I needed her to be calm. She screamed at me that she was calm, that I needed to explain myself *right now*, like I was the child and she the exhausted mother with a husband who has a mistress just a bit older than her daughter.

When I told her we needed to wait on her father, she shook her head, closing the gap between us, planting her hands on either side of me, gripping the counter so hard that when I looked down, I wasn't surprised to see her knuckles turning white.

My poor baby. How in the world is she going to handle the unfair twist her life is about to take?

"Are you leaving Dad?"

There's no way to explain how badly it hurt to have my daughter look me in the eyes and demand an answer like this. To have her hurting like this and know that she blames me. This is why I wanted Evan to talk to her first. This is why I needed him to tell her what he'd done, what he was doing to our family, how he had ruined it all.

And he didn't do it.

He's a coward and I know that now, although it isn't something I ever knew before. Nobody who knows Evan Warner would think him a coward, would ever think that the man who has put himself in danger for other people time and time again wouldn't be able to talk to his teenage daughter and come clean about an affair, but that's exactly who he is, exactly what kind of a man I married.

I told her that her dad had something to tell her. I promised her he would talk to her, that he would explain everything, that it would all make sense. Then I reached for her. I wanted to hold my girl, to make my daughter feel better about what's going on, but she pulled away from me, her eyes dark and untrusting, her fingers twitching against the open air like she was reaching for some rope to hold on to, some rope that would keep her from falling when the ground tumbled out from beneath her feet.

Standing there, with her staring at me like that, I'm terrified of what the future will bring. Jessica loves her father, has always idolized him. That's the way a lot of little girls feel about their dads. They're the first men they love, and to suddenly learn her dad isn't a good man?

She didn't take it well. Her body was stiff and angular, her face contorted as she tried to hold back tears.

Her entire life, I'd thought of her as soft and gentle, as my sweet daughter, but there wasn't any laughter in her, none of the joy she's had since she was a little girl, and maybe there won't ever be again. There was fear in her eyes, fear and pain all twisted together like a vine choking out a tall flower in the garden and Evan planted the seeds, but she doesn't see that right now.

Even now, a full day after that interaction in the kitchen, she's avoiding me, walking around me, a shadow hanging over her that I can't seem to break through. Evan talked to her of course, after she ran to him in the bathroom, crying, him barely having time to pull on boxers before she burst through the door, tears streaming down her face.

And what did she say?

Mom's leaving.

Mom's leaving.

Mom's leaving.

He didn't correct her, not at first, and I saw the cloud of sadness darken around my daughter.

But he finally came clean with her, and I guess that's something. He told her there was someone else, that he'd found someone he loved more than me. I scoffed. There were certain things about her he loved more than me, sure, but—

But it doesn't matter because Jessica's life will never be the same. She needs someone to put the blame on and it's impossible for her to see her dad as the villain in this story. Some little girls never can, I guess.

To her, *right now*, I'm not enough. I don't do enough, love enough, care enough, listen enough. I told her it wasn't me, wasn't my fault, that it isn't something the woman can be blamed for, but it was like talking to a wall.

He's taking my marriage and I don't want him to take my daughter too.

I just hope it isn't too late.

TWENTY-NINE

ARIEL

Miriam waits as I down the glass of water she handed me after I got back to her house. My mouth is dry, stuffed full of cotton, thanks to passing out on the sofa next to Jessica. I knew I was tired working all day long in their house, but I had no idea I was so exhausted.

That or I'm just not the target age for the type of movie we were watching.

Finally, I put the glass down on the counter. As quickly as I do that, Miriam grabs it and puts it in the dishwasher. She turns, leaning against it and crosses her arms on her chest. There's a moment of silence as we both do our best to gather our thoughts.

She breaks the silence first. I'm not surprised, because right now I have all the information and she's dying to know what happened. "Well?"

"I don't know. We made some real connections today, I think. Delicious dinner, a movie..." I don't tell her that Jessica was smoking pot in her room. The last thing I need is for

Miriam to get angry at Evan at the office and let it slip. Jessica trusted me but only because she had to.

I figured out she was smoking on my own, so it's not like she came to me to confess and share that secret. But maybe she'll share a secret with me in the future. *Baby steps.*

"What's the plan?" Miriam chews on a hangnail and I stare at her for a moment. Honestly, I don't really think she knows that she's doing it. Even though she's already dressed in her plaid pajamas and seems ready for bed, it's clear she has too much energy to fall asleep right now.

I feel the same. After my little nap on the sofa, I could stay up all night long.

"The plan hasn't really changed. Just the end of it has. I need to make sure Jessica really trusts me, that she likes me. She has no idea that when something happens to her dad, I'll become her guardian. That's not exactly something you can drop on someone, especially not when you're plotting to kill their father."

"I just—" Miriam begins, but I cut her off.

"Dakota will get justice, okay? I know you feel like he took advantage of her, but he didn't *kill* her. I promise you: Evan Warner is not going to walk out of this alive." I exhale hard. "I thought I could just prove he killed Lola and have him locked up forever. Honestly, at the beginning of all of this, I thought that would be enough, but he's so angry. He's terrifying, Miriam. It's not just me; it's also Jessica. I have to keep her safe."

No response.

"Jail is too good for a man like him." I don't admit that I haven't found irrefutable proof yet, nothing that will ensure he's locked up for the rest of his life, which is what he deserves. Miriam doesn't need to know I'm coming up short on that. "Jail wouldn't be easy for him, not as a cop, but he'd be fine. He'd survive if they kept him out of general population to protect him. *Thrive.* That's not fair to anyone. He deserves to die. It's the only option."

I don't mention that if they didn't protect him, he'd die. The other inmates would love to kill a police officer. I'm counting on it if my plan fails.

Miriam sighs and gestures at the kitchen table. Even though I don't want to continue this conversation with her, I sit, wanting to make her feel like I'm really interested in what she has to say.

"Dakota is heartbroken." Miriam's voice is low. Maybe it's just the dark pressing in on the windows making her feel like she needs to do her best to keep anyone from eavesdropping. "I think she'd go back to Evan in a heartbeat if she thought he would take her. If he's in jail, he can't do that. Jail is enough."

I scoff. "There's always a chance she'd try to go back to him if he were in jail. Him being dead removes any possibility of that happening."

Miriam doesn't respond, so I continue. "She's what, eighteen? Nineteen? Come on, you and I know that first heartbreak is really painful. She'll find someone else."

That's part of the deal. Miriam offers me a place to stay, and then I deal with Evan. It's not just for Lola, not for that revenge, but also for Miriam's granddaughter, Dakota.

The poor girl was just out of high school when she met Evan. She skipped out on college, telling Miriam that she wanted to get some life experience and some money saved up before she tried to go back to school. I have no idea why dispatchers only need a high school diploma to get hired, but that's what Dakota had, and it was enough to get her in the door.

It only took running into Evan a few times in the morning when they were both coming in for work or Dakota was getting off her shift for the friendly acquaintance they'd created to morph into something more.

I don't know all the details of how that happened, and I don't care to know them. It's a pretty classic tale, and one most women know by heart. Man meets girl, man sleeps with girl. Wife finds out, threatens to take daughter and leave man. Man becomes enraged and kills wife.

Here lies a *beloved wife*, indeed.

That's where I come in. Even though Lola and I weren't close, I wasn't about to let her suffer in a marriage where she was being cheated on, especially when she told me how afraid she was of her husband. When she didn't come to my house with Jessica, I knew her worst fear had come true and that I'd have to do something to get her revenge.

Miriam and I met when I came down for Lola's funeral. She caught me in the hall of the church, crying my eyes out, and hugged me without knowing who I really was. Miriam's bitter and wants revenge for Dakota, but she's still a loving person. I know more about her now, know that she bakes casseroles for anyone who loses a family member, that she serves on the hospitality committee at her church.

I know that she saw me crying and knew she had to reach out to me to see what was going on. As dangerous as it was, the words spilled out of me, and it felt good to tell her everything. That I knew Lola from the past. That I was here even though we weren't close. That I didn't know Evan and Jessica because we had been estranged.

God, I hate how everything fell apart between the two of us. I thought, when Lola called, that I was going to be able to help her, that I'd swoop in and pick her and Jessica up from the airport like a knight in shining armor.

But I'm no knight. I was too late.

Evan caught on to what was happening. He moved faster than I could, and he took my sister from me, right when we were finally reconnecting. Right when we were both willing to put everything behind us and move ahead together, he took her, he killed her, and now I'll never get to hug my sister again.

I'll never get to tell her how much I really love her. I'll never get to tell her how, even after everything, I would still lie in bed and think about her. I'd wonder how she was doing. I'd look her up online to try to catch a glimpse of her, of Jessica, just to make sure they were both happy.

Even though I wasn't ever going to be included.

And then, when I was finally going to be included, when Lola and I were going to put it all behind us, he took her.

Not just from Jessica. Also from me.

That's why, when Miriam approached me at the funeral and wrapped her arms around me like she really cared, I let myself sob onto her shoulder. Why I trusted her enough to tell her the truth of how Lola was trying to get away from Evan and how it ended up being too late.

And why, even though it could have backfired spectacularly, I told her the one secret I had that I knew more than anything to be true.

That I believed Evan killed Lola.

On hearing that, Miriam stiffened, her arms around me suddenly feeling more like a cage than a support, and I pulled back, needing air, needing to get some space between the two of us. I knew I'd messed up, that my confession was sure to get me in trouble, was sure to get right back to Evan.

But it didn't. Miriam pulled me into a small room and closed the door. There were two overstuffed chairs and a sofa in the room. Wedding pictures filled the walls, and the small side table held a Bible.

It was in that room she grabbed my hands, squeezing them hard while we sat across from each other, so close our knees were brushing. It was in that tiny room, used for brides to prepare before a wedding, that she told me who she was.

She told me she worked for him, that she had his ear, that he trusted her. She confessed this all to me in a rush and I sat there stunned, the hatred I felt for the man growing inside of me. He hadn't just ruined Lola's life. He'd ruined his daughter's, he'd ruined Dakota's, he'd ruined Miriam's.

How many lives should he be allowed to ruin?

Miriam shared with me how young Dakota was, how innocent. That she thought Evan loved her and would want to be with her for the rest of her life. Miriam told me how terrified she was for her, especially now that Lola was dead under such mysterious circumstances.

My sister's death was ruled an accident, but I found out that afternoon that I wasn't the only person who was suspicious of that ruling and of what role Evan may have played in making sure that's what people thought.

Right there under a cross, with the Bible on the table next to us, Miriam and I talked, our heads together, excitement coursing through our bodies. She wanted to make sure Dakota was protected and get revenge for the heartbreak Evan put her through. I needed to make sure Lola got the revenge she deserved, even dead and cold in the ground, while at the same time protecting my family.

There wasn't any reason the two of us couldn't work together and get what we both wanted. Protecting another person is the most noble thing you can do, especially if it means you're putting yourself at risk at the same time. Miriam and I are exactly the same in that way. No, we don't look alike, we don't have similar past experiences, and our personalities are incredibly different.

But we're both willing to kill to protect the people we love.

THIRTY

EVAN

It's been a week since I had to stay late at work for a meeting and Ariel and Jessica spent the evening by themselves. I remember how shocked I was to see the two of them on the sofa together, Jessica watching a movie turned way down low so she didn't wake Ariel up, our housekeeper passed out like she didn't have a care in the world.

I should have been happy. Really, anyone in my position should have been happy to see his daughter so comforted, so protected, so safe with someone with whom they were willing to sit quietly while the other person slept. But I'm not happy. I may have been for a moment after I got over the shock of Ariel being there in the first place, but the fact that Miriam texted her still worries me.

It just doesn't feel right.

If someone asked me why, I don't know that I'd be able to come up with an answer. But in law enforcement, we're taught to listen to our gut. We're taught to pay attention to the little voices in the back of our heads telling us that something is wrong.

Ever since Lola died, I feel like I've been on high alert, doing my best to pay attention to everything going on around me. I've been keeping an eye out for any threat.

And while, logically, I know I shouldn't worry about Ariel and Miriam texting, I didn't get the impression they were that close.

I'm going to ask my assistant why in the world she and Ariel are still in contact. It was one thing for Miriam to help her out and make sure she had a job and a place to live, but for some reason... I don't know. I don't like my personal and my work life overlapping, that's all. Ever since my affair with Dakota and how I broke it off with her when Lola died, I've wanted to keep everything separate.

I loved Dakota. Still do, if I'm being honest. She was fun and exciting, and she made me feel alive for the first time in... well, years. She made me laugh, and when we were together it felt like all the adult concerns I had—of bills and Jessica acting out, of Lola nagging me about date night, and problems at work—all seemed to disappear.

Being with her made me feel alive again.

Would we have ever gone the distance? I ask myself that sometimes, wondering if I would have been willing to take the step of leaving my wife for someone so much younger. Dakota was thrilling. Lola was comfortable.

I wanted them both.

And then Lola died, and I had to end it.

It seems like the best way to keep things from getting too messy.

The best way to ensure other people didn't know the truth. A fling is one thing. Committing to that person when someone as loved as Lola died would be another. Career suicide.

But none of that matters now, does it? Lola and Dakota are

both gone, and I have to pretend like I didn't lose everything the night my wife died.

Miriam's right on time this morning, just like always. The door to my office is open and I watch as she unloads her arms at her desk, dropping off her purse, her lunchbox, and her cell phone. The last one lands with a heavy *thunk* on her desk, and she lightly taps it like she's afraid she might have broken it.

I'm antsy. I want to go talk to her right now and figure out what she was doing texting Ariel last week, but I wait until she has her computer turned on and has the coffee running. Before she can pour me a cup and bring it to me, I leave my office and lean casually against her desk.

Miriam turns, her lips pursed, two cups of steaming coffee held out from her body a little bit, then jumps when she sees me. "Oh, Evan! You moved like a ghost and I didn't hear you. How are you this morning?"

"I'm fine." She hands me my coffee and I put it down on the desk next to me. "How're you? Everything good?"

"I'm great."

If Miriam can feel the tension in the room, she's not letting on and I realize how stupid this probably is. I should have talked to her immediately after she texted Ariel to find out what was going on. Waiting a week makes me sound insane and she'll probably wonder what in the world has gotten into me when I bring it up.

But I honestly feel like I've come too far to not push the issue now, even though it might be crazy of me.

"Hey, quick question. Do you keep in touch with Ariel?"

"Ariel?" Miriam settles herself behind her desk and pushes her purse out of the way before answering. "Not really, why?"

"Just wondering." I take a sip of my coffee. It's still too hot but I choke it down. "I know she really appreciated your help getting her the job at my house."

"I'm always happy to help anyone who needs it." There's a

pause, then she looks up at me, right between my eyes like she can't quite meet them. "Did something happen? Are you not happy with her?"

"What? No. She's great. Why? Do you know if she's not happy?"

This is ridiculous. I feel like I'm back in middle school trying to find out if the girl who sits across from me in US History thinks I'm cute. I'm the chief of police, for God's sake, and there's no reason for me to be dancing around what I really want to know when I could just ask Miriam and find out the truth without any other trouble.

"I haven't really heard," Miriam says at the same time I speak up.

"I saw you'd been texting her and didn't know if you two were friends."

Her mouth snaps shut, and she stares at me. I have the distinct feeling her mind is going a mile a minute as she tries to figure out exactly what to say to me about that. It's uncomfortable, trying to get an answer from someone like this, but I hold her gaze.

"You know, I think I did reach out to her recently to make sure everything was okay. She'd been so excited about the job, but you know how it can be to start somewhere new. Why, is it a problem if I text her?"

"No, not at all." I shake my head, suddenly feeling silly. "I don't know why I wanted to know, just that... I don't know. I didn't realize the two of you were friends."

"I got her the job," Miriam corrects. "That doesn't necessarily mean we're friends; it means I wanted to touch base with her and make sure she's settling in okay." She doesn't say anything else, but I can almost hear the accusation hanging in the air between the two of us. *Is that a crime?*

"Yeah, you're right..." Running my hand through my hair to push it back from my face, I let my voice trail off. What am I going to say—*I just don't like it?* "That was nice of you to check in on her."

I'm paranoid. I feel like one of the junkies I used to arrest when I still worked the streets, always afraid that someone was out to get them, always looking at other people like they were actively plotting to hurt them. Why do I feel like that? I don't want to admit it to myself, but it's got to be because of the guilt I feel over... well, everything.

I just don't like that there's some sort of connection between Miriam and Ariel.

But it really shouldn't be a problem. Even though it makes me nervous that Miriam and Ariel are suddenly being friendly, that's not the connection I need to worry about.

I want Jessica to be polite to Ariel, but that's as close as I want the two of them to get. Jessica is the one other person who knows the truth and she's the wild card out of the two of us. I thought I had everything under control at home, but it hits me as I lean against Miriam's desk, trying to do my best to appear as calm and collected as possible, that any danger I'm going to face regarding the truth coming out isn't going to come from outside my family.

It isn't going to be because my assistant is still close with my housekeeper.

It's going to be because of my daughter.

THIRTY-ONE

ARIEL

Everything is working out just the way I want it to. Not only am I getting paid more than I thought I would to cook, clean, and run errands, but I feel like I'm finally making some progress with Jessica. It's not that the two of us are suddenly bosom buddies by a long shot, but I get the distinct feeling she doesn't actively hate me any longer and I'm going to count that as a win.

While Evan bustled off to work this morning, Jessica stayed in her room. It's a teacher workday and while I would have thought she'd want to be up and out with her friends, she's still sleeping. Evan asked me to let her sleep and to give her plenty of space today. He even offered for me to have the day off so I could get some rest, but there's no way I'm going to pass up on an opportunity to connect with her without him around to babysit.

I feel like he's always hovering when I spend time with Jessica, and it's not like I'm doing anything crazy with her. Just last week she helped me out in the kitchen, making onigiri with me, the two of us laughing as we wet our hands to keep the rice from sticking. She kept having to push her hoodie sleeves up from her wrists to keep the fabric from getting wet, but that didn't matter. We just had fun. It felt good, like maybe I can do this parenting thing.

But Evan was there. He *hovers*, watching and listening, and I feel like I'm on a chaperoned date. So while he told me over and over again not to come in this morning, there wasn't any way I was missing out on solo time with Jessica, even if Evan does get angry with me. It's a risk, showing up like this when I'm not supposed to, but I want to get Jessica on her own. I'm willing to take that risk if it means the truth about what happened to Lola will come out sooner. I waited in the parking lot down the road until I saw him drive by on his way to work, then I pulled into the driveway and let myself into the house to check on her.

That's how I know she's still in bed, but I have a feeling she won't be for long. The smell of coffee and the delicious breakfast I'm going to whip up will have her following her nose right down the stairs in a minute.

While I wait for her to wake up, I dust the living room, taking the pillows off the sofa and plumping them, then putting them back so they look inviting. There's a picture of Lola, Evan, and Jessica on the coffee table, and I pick it up, lightly tracing my finger over Lola's face.

She was always the pretty one. I remember everyone whispering about how cute she was when she was younger.

And she was. I fought our mom anytime she wanted to put curlers in our hair, but Lola loved it. She loved the way her hair framed her face, and she'd dance around the kitchen, pretending to be a ballerina.

Until the one time Mom forgot to take the curlers out. Lola had slept on them all night like she was supposed to and come downstairs to have our mom unclip them and unroll them. This would free her curls to float around her head like a halo.

But I was the only one at home. Mom and Dad were both at work and Lola had slumped in her chair, her lower lip jutting out, ready to cry about the dang curlers.

I offered to take them out, but she was stubborn, always so stubborn. Three years younger than me and thought she ran the family.

She refused until it was almost time to get on the bus, then she panicked, begging me to help her. But I don't know how Mom did it. Lola's hair was wrapped tightly around the foam curlers, snagging in some places. I unclipped and tugged and tried to pull them free, but they only got more and more tangled.

So I got the scissors.

Lola's gorgeous locks floated like milkweed seeds down around my bare feet. She was almost bald by the time I was finished, with hair sticking up here and there, and bare patches of skin almost visible around her neck.

I remember the horror on her face when she looked in the bathroom mirror and how I handed the scissors to her to make things even. My hair wasn't as long as hers to begin with, so she made short work of chopping it all off.

We were almost bald getting on the bus, but we were bald together, and that was really the only thing that mattered. As long as we were together, we could face anything. It didn't matter what life threw at us, because I had her back and she had mine. We were as close as sisters could be, even though I knew the truth.

That Lola was always a bit better than me.

Even mostly bald, she was gorgeous. Being Lola's sister growing up was hard but now...

My stomach clenches and I put the picture back. It rattles against the coffee table like it's going to fall over.

I miss her. What I wouldn't give to go back and not lose our relationship. We hadn't been as close as other sisters, that much is true, but it didn't have to end the way it did.

I could have tried harder.

"What are you doing?" Jessica stands in the doorway, one hand on her hip, the other twirling some hair by her face. "You looked like you were going to cry."

"Oh, no," I say, standing and brushing off my apron. "No, just looking at this picture of you, your mom, and your dad. I can only imagine how much you miss her."

She tilts her head to the side and walks over to me. Grabbing the picture, she stares at it, then puts it back down. "I miss her. But you were crying."

Dammit. "It's just sad, that's all. To lose your mom when you're so young. And she was young too."

"Right." Jessica stares at me. She chews on her lower lip and then slowly smiles. "As long as everything is okay. That was just weird."

"I know. I was just thinking about my mom and how much I miss her." I pause, looking for some way to salvage this interaction. It's not at all how I wanted it to go.

What I really want to do is take her shopping. I want to get her out of the house so she and I can spend some time alone together, away from this place and its secrets, without Evan hovering and making her too nervous to really open up to me. I don't know for sure, but I have a feeling Jessica will feel more comfortable talking to me if she's doing something she wants. Sitting around the house, staring at each other, won't be comfortable.

But shopping? That might be just what we need to bond. What teenager doesn't love to shop?

"I'm not sure if you have plans today but I thought we could go to the mall. It seems like a lot more fun than just working around the house." I'm casual, keeping my voice even like it doesn't matter to me what her response is even though I'm really hopeful that she'll want to spend time with me.

"Shopping?" I don't have to look at her to hear the surprise in her voice.

"Yeah, you don't have school, your dad told me to relax today, and I thought we could hit the mall."

She doesn't answer and I shift in my seat, watching as she takes a bite of her omelet. I don't know why I'm so nervous, but it's probably because I just want her to like me. She's the last remaining bit of Lola I have left and while I wasn't a great sister before, I'm determined to be there for Jessica now.

"You want to take me shopping?" The surprise in her voice is evident and I nod before she even finishes speaking. "I don't have any money."

"I can buy a few things." The words spill out of me before I realize what I'm saying, but rather than looking surprised, Jessica looks impressed.

"I mean, not a lot. Your dad is very generous with his pay, but I still don't have a ton just to throw around. What do you say?"

She pokes her fork at me. "I'd say that it sounds great but I'm not sure Dad would really like it. He wants you here, cleaning and cooking."

But you're my family. You're all I have left.

"That's true." I pause, thinking. "I'll get the cleaning done; you don't have to worry about that, but I really do need to go shopping. Maybe you can help me find something that will make me look younger. More hip, I don't know."

Now she's smiling. I feel a warm glow rush through me at the sight.

"I could do that."

Putting down her fork, she wipes her mouth with her napkin. She pushes her sleeves up and leans on the table. "Stay here, let me get changed."

I barely hear what she's saying because I'm too busy staring at how she pushed up her sleeves.

There's a huge bruise on her arm.

"Hey, are you okay?" Before I can stop myself, I lean forward to get a better look. "That's a nasty bruise."

"It's nothing." She jerks back from me, yanking her sleeves back down. "I fell."

Alarms go off in my head, but I plaster a smile on my face. "Alright, as long as you're okay."

"I'm fine." The words come out in a mumble. She pushes her chair back and hurries from the kitchen. I hear her feet pounding on the stairs then the sound of her bedroom door slamming shut. While she changes, I clear the table, replaying what just happened over and over in my head.

Just because she has a nasty bruise on her arm doesn't mean Evan hurt her. Everyone trips and falls from time to time. I can't jump to conclusions. Still, I need to move faster.

I'm just wiping down the kitchen counter when Jessica reappears in the door. She's wearing too much eyeliner and a red hoodie that looks two sizes too big. I watch as she adjusts it, lifting the hem up far enough for me to see the glint of metal against skin.

"Your dad let you pierce your belly button?" I try to sound casual. Cool. It's the most skin I've seen her show since I started working here.

She freezes. Yanks the hem back down. "No, of course not. He doesn't know, and please don't tell him. You know how he can be."

Yes, I do. I cross my heart. "Never. Your secret is safe with me."

"Huh." For a moment the two of us just stand and look at each other. "You know, Ariel, I was really worried about Dad hiring you to come here and help us out, to be honest. But I like having you here."

"Thanks." It's not a compliment, not really, but then Jessica loops her arm through mine and starts pulling me to the door.

It's one of the first times she's been so raw and honest with me, and I feel my heart lurch in my chest. Jessica has no idea how much what she just said means to me. She can't know, not for a while.

She laughs again, throwing her head back. It's intoxicating, the sound so familiar.

There's no doubt in my mind I'm doing the right thing.

THIRTY-TWO

LOLA'S DIARY

THURSDAY, AUGUST 3

I have to get out of here.

Of course, I don't want to leave Jessica behind. I *can't* leave her behind, that's the thing Evan has to know even though he doesn't want to see it. He refuses to get therapy, refuses to go with me to couples counseling, even though that's the thing that will save our marriage.

Instead, he drinks.

Just because he can drink to forget everything going on doesn't mean it never happened. He's the embodiment of every country song, losing himself in whiskey and leaving his family behind.

I'm tired of cleaning up the empty bottles, tired of seeing the liquor store charges on the credit-card statement. I just can't do this any longer.

Especially when I know where he was last night. I found the hotel receipt in his pocket after he stripped for bed and passed out. I'd told him if he ended things, if he was willing to get counseling, then we could work it out.

And he told me he would do it, but he lied, and now it's time for me to go.

And I'm taking Jessica with me. I need to know that my daughter is safe, that I won't have to worry about some other woman coming into my home and raising her. I have to be there for her, to hold her hand when her heart breaks, to whisper to her that everything will be okay. I'm her mother, for God's sake, and the thought of Evan moving anyone else into my house to raise my daughter makes the hair on the back of my neck stick straight up.

I'm moving in with my sister. Tonight. I'm going to leave tonight, and I hope to God that we're gone before Evan knows something's up. My sister and I might not be close, we might not talk as often as we should, and yes, there's a good reason for all of that, but I'm willing to put the past in the past if she is.

I need my family right now and my sister is all I've got.

Evan thinks I'm leaving this weekend. He thinks I'm going to be able to stay under this roof with him for a few more days, but he's wrong. While he's at work tonight for a department meeting, I'm going to disappear with Jessica.

I know she's hurt, that she'll miss her dad, but I love my girl and she loves me. We'll be fine. We'll make it.

We have to move quickly though. Evan's department meetings usually last a few hours, so that should give us time to pack and leave.

I don't like driving in the dark, or in the rain, but I don't have a choice. Jessica and I will be fine. We'll get out of here, start a new life. I won't have to worry about Evan drinking or having an affair. We won't have to worry about him being angry.

As long as we get out of here before he gets home then everything will be fine.

THIRTY-THREE

ARIEL

MONDAY, SEPTEMBER 11

I'm exhausted and the shopping bags cutting into my arms are so heavy I'm half-confident they're going to leave permanent grooves in my skin. Jessica opens the front door and walks in before me, stepping off to the side to watch as I carefully lower everything we just bought down to the floor.

Sweat beads on my brow and I wipe it away, feeling a bit self-conscious in front of Jessica, who still looks perfectly put together. Then again, she only carried two of the bags, so of course she doesn't have a river flowing down her back. I'm hot and sticky and walk over to turn the AC on as she starts rummaging through everything we bought.

True, a lot of the items we bought are ones she green-lit for me to wear to help me look a bit younger, more hip, and attractive. It was strange feeling like a doll as she dressed me then turned me this way and that to look at my outfit. No matter what I had on, she had something to say about it. I wanted her to feel invested in me.

And I got it.

Better yet, I loved every moment of it. This is what my future is going to be like—me hanging out with Jessica, spending time with her, listening to her problems. I want to get to know her before this all comes to an end with Evan. I want her to feel comfortable around me.

Bonding. It was bonding and I've missed so many years of Jessica's life. Right now, I want to bond with her however she'll let me. I just want to spend time with her. Getting ice cream, going for a walk in the park, talking about boys.

I want it all.

And that's why we went to the mall. That's why I did my best to spoil her even though I did have to stick to a budget.

She's been a little short with me around the house. I've seen her talk back to her dad, but that has to be because it's stressful here. One-on-one, out in the mall, things were perfect.

I can do this. I know it'll be hard, especially when Evan is out of the picture, but I'm tough. And Jessica's worth it. Today was a good moment with her, one both of us really needed to show us how well we could bond.

And I think I did an incredible job showing Jessica how much fun we can have together. How the two of us can get along.

I picked her up a new hoodie—not a crop-top hoodie, which I think defeats the purpose of trying to get warm—as well as a new necklace. She yanks them both from the bag and rips off the necklace tag, slipping it on over her head before turning to me to model it.

"Looks lovely," I say, holding my finger in the air and rotating it in a circle to get her to turn around. That's what she's done to me all day to get a good look at my outfits and she laughs, slowly rotating in a circle for me to see how she looks. To *check her fit* as the kids say.

And then I see it. Sticking out of her back pocket, the tags still on, is a wallet she'd asked me to get and I'd told her to put back. She keeps spinning, the wallet now out of sight and I close my eyes, trying to picture paying for everything.

Did she sneak it onto the counter for me to buy without me knowing?

"How do I look?" She's grinning at me, but I grab a bag and dig out the receipt, my fingers shaking as I pull it tight to straighten it out. "Ariel?"

"Fine," I mutter. "Let me look at this."

Shirts for me, the hoodie for her. She lives in long sleeves and jeans, never showing off more skin than necessary. We picked up a necklace for her, a pair of earrings for me. Even a pair of heels and a dress she told me made me look irresistible and would turn heads. There are some books she really wanted and a notebook she swore she would use for math class.

Some pens. Sunglasses for me.

No wallet.

I know I told her to put it back. She'd been unhappy with me, but I'd been so busy paying for everything else that I hadn't paid attention to watch to see if she'd really done it. Why should I? She should be responsible enough to put something back when I tell her to.

"Jessica, what's in your back pocket?" I'm angry, hot rage making it difficult for me to think straight, but there's no way I'm going to blow up at her right now, not when we've had such a great day and I feel like we've really connected.

She pales, the smile sliding off her face. "My back pocket?" I watch as she reaches behind her and pats it like she has to convince herself what may or may not be in there.

"Jessica. I saw the wallet in your pocket. The one I asked you to put back."

"Oh my gosh, did I forget?" Jessica yanks the wallet from her pocket. I notice how she has to really tug it out of there. She pushed it down far enough into her pocket to keep it lodged tight when we walked out of the store and made our way home, and now she has to work it out. "How in the world did I do that? I feel like such an idiot!"

I'm listening to her, but I'm much more interested in the expression on her face. Her eyes are shifty as she looks at the wallet then back up at me.

No, not back up at me. Up over my head, like she doesn't really want to make eye contact with me. One finger taps the wallet, and she undoes the clasp, shutting it again with a loud click.

Her movements are frantic, and she closes it as quickly as possible.

But not before I see what's in there.

"Did you stuff it full of jewelry?" She doesn't expect me to lunge at her and grab it from her, which is probably the only reason I'm able to pull the wallet from her hands. I notice how she tries to grab it back, but I take a step away from her, holding the wallet so tightly I don't think she could get it from me if she tried.

"Ariel, wait!"

"No, Jessica."

Taking a deep breath, I push the latch. The wallet falls open easily, practically pops open, it's so stuffed with jewelry that it probably was difficult to latch. Holding it in my left hand, I poke through it with my finger. There's so much here and I almost don't want to touch it, don't want to get my fingerprints on it.

"I didn't mean to."

There's a quaver in her voice and I look up in surprise.

"I promise, Ariel, I didn't mean to. I was just goofing off and then I forgot I'd put jewelry in there and then I didn't put it back, but I wouldn't steal it on purpose—it was an accident." She reaches out but when I pull the wallet closer to my body, she lets her hand drop between us.

It clenches into a fist at her side.

"Jessica." I take a deep breath. Somehow I have to figure out how I'm going to deal with this. "Jessica, you and I both know you don't stuff a wallet full of jewelry and then forget it's in your pocket."

She's crying now, tears dripping down her cheeks. Her shoulders round forward and she buries her face in her hands. I hear her inhale and then exhale before she looks back up at me. "I'm just under so much stress, Ariel. You have to see that." Her voice breaks.

Dammit. Compassion grows in me, and I remember how much fun we had today, and just how hard her life has been. Parenting is, at its best, almost impossible. When things go wrong, it's a nightmare, and even though I know I'm going to have to be firm with her eventually, right now I just want to take care of her.

I can do this.

She's all alone.

"I won't do it again. We can take it back to the store; we can tell my dad—"

"No." My voice is sharp. She looks up, surprised.

Was that a smile on her lips? There and gone before I could recognize it?

"No," I say, calmer now, "we're not going to tell your dad, Jessica. You just need to promise me that you won't ever do this again, that it really was an accident. I need to know that you're not going to make a habit of this or I can't help you out."

"I won't." She grabs my hands, squeezing them tight. "I promise you: this is not a habit. I just... I messed up. I know that. I just miss my mom." Again, her voice breaks and now I turn, putting the wallet and jewelry down on the small entrance table.

I miss her too.

"Come here, darling," I say, holding out my arms. Jessica hesitates, but only a moment, then she steps forward, letting me wrap my arms around her. "It's okay. I know you miss your mom. Just... this can't keep happening, okay? You're better than this, Jessica. I know you are."

"Thank you." She's so thin that I want to not only wrap her in my arms but also in a blanket. I want to put her on the sofa, make her soup, and tell her things will be okay. I want to do everything in my power to protect her.

Even if that means letting her get away with stealing the jewelry.

I think about other kids—troubled kids—you sometimes read about in the news. It could always be worse.

Jessica is smart, she's in pain, but she's not troubled. She's acting out, sure, but I understand it. I'm not going to blame her for that.

I will admit, though, she's not what I thought when I first met her. There's more to her than meets the eye, a hidden side of her that she's only just now letting me see. If she really took the jewelry by accident then I'd honestly be surprised, but I'm not going to go there with her right now.

She stole it. And I'm going to help her cover it up.

I can't let myself think the thought growing in the back of my mind. She drinks a little, she smokes pot... maybe I don't know her nearly as well as I want to think I do. Has she always been this difficult to parent or is this new?

I'd thought we'd had such a perfect time at the mall together. Which version of Jessica is the real one?

And what does it mean for me if this is who she is at the core?

What if she's more troubled than I thought?

"I just want to keep you safe," I whisper into her hair. My eyes are closed but I don't need to be looking at her to know that she's just stiffened up in my arms.

"Safe from what?" Her voice is tight. The question hangs in the air between us, and I know I shouldn't answer but I can't help myself. I feel like she and I have made a huge break-through, that maybe we can come out of this on the other side closer than I ever imagined.

I shouldn't tell her. The words form on my lips. *Your dad.*

But how would a teenager take it? Jessica is such a wild card with more emotions packed into her little body than I thought possible that I fear she might overreact, might tell her dad what I said, might even try to run away. No, telling her the truth about her father right now is not a good idea, not until I know for sure that I can keep her safe.

"Just the world." It's a lie.

Can she tell?

More importantly, does it matter?

THIRTY-FOUR

EVAN

MONDAY, SEPTEMBER 11

I feel a ball of anxiety drop straight into my stomach when I pull up into my driveway and see Ariel's car.

What the hell is she doing here? I gave her the day off on purpose, hoping that Jessica would have some time to herself to just be quiet, and yet here she is. This is the second time I've told her not to come to the house and she's done the opposite.

How dare she think she can just stop by?

Anger rushes through me and I grip the steering wheel hard, the leather squeaking under the pressure. I take a deep breath and release it, then unclench my jaw, trying to calm back down.

I'm not going to go in there yelling and raging. I'm going to keep my cool, try to figure out what's really going on. It's clear Ariel is up to something, but without knowing what it is, I need to be careful.

Letting myself into the house, I move quietly and quickly, not really wanting to alert Jessica or Ariel to the fact that I'm home. Sure, if they were paying attention to the driveway then they might have heard me pull up, but the fact that nobody has greeted me yet makes me think they must be involved in something else.

And I'm right.

I'm so quiet when I walk into the living room that the two of them don't hear me and I get an eyeful of what's going on. There's a pile of shopping bags on the floor, clothes spilling out of one of them. Standing right by the door, like they could barely make it into the house before they had to hug, Jessica and Ariel are embracing.

My daughter looks so small wrapped in the housekeeper's arms, and I stop in the doorway. Grabbing it for support, I stare at the two of them, trying to figure out what's going on.

"It's okay. You just have to trust me. I'll keep you safe."

Even from across the room I can hear what Ariel's murmuring to Jessica. She keeps running her hand down my daughter's back like she's trying to comfort her. I know I shouldn't be bothered by this scene, but there's something about my daughter finding comfort from someone else that upsets me.

No, that's not it. It *terrifies* me. It wasn't too long ago that she was in my arms just like this, sobbing over her mother. I have no reason to think she might be telling Ariel the truth about what happened to Lola, but I still stop short. My heart races in my chest and it's difficult for me to breathe.

I have to do something. I have to—*stop her, get her out of here*—stay calm, I have to stay calm.

I clear my throat.

Jessica and Ariel jump back from each other. They look guilty, like I just caught them doing something they weren't supposed to. But they were just hugging, right? Still, there's something eating at the back of my mind that makes me think there's more to this scene than meets the eye.

"What's going on here?" I do my best to keep my voice light so they won't be able to tell just how angry I am right now.

"We were just saying goodnight." Ariel's face flames. Lola's used to do the same when she was lying to me.

I shake my head to clear it. My wife is dead and thinking about her right now won't do anything but make me feel guilty about that night.

"I told you you didn't need to come today." I'm seething. Keeping my cool is getting harder and harder. My stomach twists and I feel my hands clench into fists. When I take another deep breath, I try to relax my face.

Jessica's staring at me. She sees my anger. I know she does.

Then she takes a small step back.

She lifts one shoulder. Drops it. Tries to look unconcerned. Even with a calm expression on her face, however, I get the feeling she's worried about what I'm going to say.

Or what I'm going to do.

I know I heard what she said.

She told Jessica she's going to keep her safe.

What the hell does that mean? Why does she think she needs to protect my daughter? That's my job.

"I was bored and I thought I'd come by and check on Jessica. When she told me she didn't have any plans for the day either, I thought it would be fun for the two of us to go shopping."

I eyeball the bags on the floor. They didn't just go shopping. They went on a shopping spree. Jessica doesn't have access to that kind of money to buy everything she would want, and it surprises me to think Ariel would want to pay for my daughter to get new clothes.

"That was unnecessary."

Ariel smiles and, for just a moment, I wonder if I'm overreacting. She's just being nice. Just taking care of my daughter. That's all a father wants, isn't it? For people to be willing to do whatever they have to in order to keep their kids safe?

No, I'm not. I heard what she said. And I told her to stay away today.

There's no reason she would just *check on Jessica*. Unless she thought there was a reason Jessica might need her help.

"I'll get out of your hair." Ariel smiles at me, her mouth tight, then reaches out and lightly squeezes Jessica's arm.

My daughter doesn't look at her.

"Goodnight, Ariel." My voice is stiff, my words clipped. I want to scream at her. I want to grab her by the shoulders and shake her. Instead, I gesture to the door. Ariel nods, grabbing her purse and a bag from the floor. As she walks out the front door and closes it behind her, Jessica and I are silent.

Neither one of us move as we listen to her walk across the deck and down the stairs to the sidewalk. Her car rumbles on and we still stand still, the two of us looking at each other. My daughter's eyes are wide.

Ariel's car motors out of the driveway and my daughter gives her head a little shake like she's trying to clear it. Moving quickly, she leaves the pile of bags on the floor and walks across the room. Her head is bent, turned a little bit away from me.

"Where do you think you're going?" I stop her, moving to the side so she has to stand still and talk to me.

"My room." Her voice is flat. There's a note of something there. Fear?

I'm doing my best to stay calm.

"Am I in trouble?" She takes a small step toward the stairs. When she speaks again, her voice is softer. "Dad, she thinks you hurt Mom."

What?

I eyeball Jessica, debating what to say. "You're not in trouble, Jessica, but we need to talk. I'm getting rid of Ariel."

That's the only option I have.

THIRTY-FIVE

I pace. It's the one habit Lola always made fun of me for, but I can't help it. My feet eat up the path down the hall to the bathroom then I loop back around, making a circuit through the living room into the kitchen. The entire time I'm moving, Jessica is still, perched on the sofa, her hands clasped tightly in front of her, her eyes locked on me.

She's like one of those waving cat clocks, only her eyes don't flick back and forth. They move slowly, tracking me, catching up with me when I appear again from the hall, never letting me out of her sight.

"Dad?" Her voice trembles a bit and I turn on my heel, stopping in front of her. It's the first time either of us have spoken after Jessica told me what Ariel thought. Her voice cracks and she swallows, trying again. "Dad, what are we going to do?"

"I'll take care of it." It's my answer for everything.

Problem at home? I'll take care of it.

Problem at work? Leave it to me to handle.

Problem with my wife wanting to divorce me and take my daughter?

I can handle anything.

"How? She thinks you hurt Mom!" Jessica stands and I motion for her to keep her voice down. "She thinks you hurt Mom," she repeats, quieter, moving closer to me so I'll be able to hear her. "What do you think she's going to do? What is she even doing here?"

Who is she really?

"She's not going to do anything," I tell Jessica, "because I'm not going to give her the chance. I'm going to fire her, okay? She'll be gone and out of our lives. Then if she continues to come around and she's not wanted, we can press charges."

My daughter chews her lower lip. "Do you think that will be enough?"

"It will be fine," I say slowly, picking my words so I don't accidentally upset her. "I don't think we need to do anything drastic. I'll fire her."

She doesn't respond.

"She probably just meant that she wanted to keep you safe... like in general. From whatever might hurt you."

Jessica falls silent.

"This will be fine. Do you understand?"

Jessica chews her lower lip for a moment. "I don't know, Dad. I want it to be fine, but how can you be sure? She was really intense."

I'm not sure what to say. Jessica isn't usually dramatic, and she seems to have a pretty good grasp on when people are telling the truth or lying or when they might want to hurt her, but this seems extreme.

"I'm going to fire her," I say again, firmer this time. "I know having her around has made things a lot easier on the two of us, but there's no reason to keep her if she's stressing us out."

Ariel was the perfect fit for our family, but sometimes perfect fits change.

"That will take care of it?" There's relief in Jessica's voice, but it's mixed with something.

Fear. Hope. I'm not sure what, but I want to keep my daughter as happy as possible. Happy. And safe.

Most parents wonder what kind of a person their child will be when they grow up. We all worry and hope that our kids will be awesome, that they'll change the world and be kind and loving. We all hope for the best.

I have to stop this.

"Jessica." I make my voice as firm as possible to try to get her to listen to me. "It's really important that you understand this, okay? You have to let me handle Ariel. I'll get her to leave, to leave our family alone. If you get involved then I don't know what will happen." I pause, not wanting to continue but also knowing I need to make this as clear as possible if I'm going to be able to avoid any problems in the future. "I know you liked spending time with her and she bought you things, but I don't like her not listening to what I tell her. I'm ending this."

Her eyes narrow. Her cheeks, pale just a moment ago, flush. I feel like she's staring straight through me, and I'm not surprised when she clenches her hands into fists and exhales hard. "Fine, Dad. As long as you think it will all be okay."

"It will," I say, but Jessica has already turned around, her hair whipping out behind her like a kite. "It will," I call after my daughter, but Jessica doesn't look back. She runs out of the room and flies up the stairs.

Probably to smoke some pot. I should stop her, but at least it will mellow her out a little bit.

The chief's daughter smoking pot. I looked the other way right after Lola's funeral and now it's become Jessica's way to calm down. I need to put a stop to it, I know that, but right now is not the time.

"God, that's a terrible thing to think," I mutter to myself.

The pile of bags is still on the floor but I barely glance at them as I wander back into the kitchen to pour myself a drink. Jessica has her way of dealing with stress and I have mine. Just one drink will take the edge off and help me come up with a plan of what to say to Ariel.

I'll get her to leave. It was nice having her around, but if she's hanging around Jessica trying to—*to what?* Get information from her? Do some amateur sleuthing? Try to pin a murder on me?

That thought gives me chills.

I won't let any of that happen.

It's time for her to go.

THIRTY-SIX

JESSICA'S DIARY

THURSDAY, AUGUST 10

Mom's been gone a week and only now do I feel like I can sit down and write about what happened.

Looking back in my diary, it's silly the things I used to write about. I was always so worried with what my friends thought at school and getting good grades that I thought that was the worst I'd have to deal with. When I got a C on my math test two weeks ago, I thought it was the end of the world.

Now though...

Now I don't really know how to put my thoughts to paper. My mom is gone, and I miss her so much I can't think about her without crying. I don't know what to do without her, how to survive without her in the house, but I have to do that.

She died and everyone in town thinks it was an accident, but they weren't here.

They didn't see their father push her down the stairs. Dad was so angry because Mom and I were going to leave. We were going to live with her sister since Dad can't stop cheating on her, but before we could go, he killed her.

I was inside packing. Well, that was what I was supposed to be doing. He was supposed to still be at a meeting, but it ended early and they were yelling at each other, which is all they seemed to do anymore, like they just couldn't stand being near each other, and I'd looked out the window. I'd seen my mom standing there at the edge of the deck, her hands clenched into fists at her sides.

I saw Dad's back. He walked right up to her like he wanted to scare her, but Mom didn't flinch. She never once flinched, never once backed down, and that was because she loved me.

And then he pushed her. He put his hands right on her shoulders and shoved her back. I saw it all and I screamed, but there wasn't anything I could do to stop it. I screamed and screamed and it was only when Mom was on her back on the sidewalk that Dad turned and saw me in the window.

He ran up the stairs then. I wanted to hide, but where was I going to go? I'm too big now to hide under my bed and, besides, I didn't have enough time to try to hide. I was frozen in place, just terrified, and then he was in my room yelling and carrying on, telling me that she deserved it.

My mom may have deserved a lot of things, but she didn't deserve to die.

I was sobbing. The tears streaming down my cheeks made it difficult for me to think straight. He grabbed me by the shoulders and forced me to sit on the bed. For a moment, I thought it was all over for me. I thought he was going to hurt me.

Why would he hurt Mom? What does he think is going to happen?

"Jessica." He wasn't crying. I hated him more for that. "Jessica, I need you to calm down. Your mother fell."

"You pushed her!" The words exploded out of me, and I tried to get him to let me go. "You pushed her and now you want to act like nothing happened!"

"No." It was his story and he was sticking to it, and I hated him even more for that. "No, she fell. But the police are going to come and you're going to go into a foster home if you don't help me. You want that? You want to live in a home where nobody really loves you? Where you aren't sure if you're going to get any food? Where you might have to protect yourself against whoever lives there when you're supposed to be sleeping?"

No. Of course I didn't want that. Why would I want that? I shook my head, but I couldn't look him in the eyes. That is, until he grabbed my chin and forced me to. My skin crawled with the feeling of him touching me, but I couldn't pull away from him.

"She fell. You need to say it."

I couldn't. Saying that would mean I was turning my back on my mom and what really happened to her. I tried to pull away from him, but he wouldn't let me go.

"Say it, Jessica. Say that your mother fell."

He was squeezing my chin harder. It hurt. I wanted to jerk away from him, but every time I tried to move, he pulled my chin right back to center so I was looking at him. When I closed my eyes, he squeezed harder. What choice did I have?

"She fell."

God, I wish I could take those words back. Just thinking about saying them now makes me cry. I can't believe I turned on my mom like that, but what choice did I have? I've never been afraid of him before, but I was right then and I still am now.

"She fell. Good girl."

When he let me go, I swore I could still feel his fingers pressing hard into my skin.

"She fell. I'm going to go make sure it looks like she did. You need to do something for me, okay?"

"Okay." Inside, there was a voice screaming at me. I didn't want to do whatever my dad was going to ask me to do, but I didn't have a choice. He was going to make me help him.

If the police ever find out what really happened, I'm going to be just as guilty.

"She packed some suitcases. They're by the front door. Empty them. Put everything back where it goes. The police are going to come, and we can't have them thinking for one moment that anything was wrong here or they might not believe that she just fell and that it was an accident."

I was too numb to respond.

"Jessica, do you understand? What do you need to do right now?"

My mouth was dry. I cleared my throat. Next to my bed was a glass of water but I couldn't get my body to move so that I could pick it up. What I wouldn't do for a long drink of water right now, but even though it was so close, it was incredibly far away.

"What do you need to do?"

"Clean out her suitcases. Make it look like everything here was fine."

"Good girl." He leaned forward and kissed me on the forehead. I wanted to pull back in revulsion, but I didn't. I couldn't move.

But he could move. He got right up from my bed and hurried out of the bedroom and down the hall. I heard him on the stairs then heard the front door open.

And then, and this is the worst part of it, I stood up and did what he asked me to do. Now, I wish more than anything that I hadn't. I wish I'd called the police before he did and told them what really happened. I wish I'd done everything in my power to make him suffer and pay for what he did to my mom, but I couldn't.

I was scared. I was in shock. None of how I was feeling is an excuse, but what else was I supposed to do?

My dad wanted me to cover up my mom's murder, and I did it. And now I have to find a way to live with it.

THIRTY-SEVEN

ARIEL

Last night was not my finest night.

I know that.

As great as the day with Jessica was, I shouldn't have gone over there. Or, if I really felt like I needed to, I should have left well before Evan got home. But I didn't. He caught me hugging his daughter and whispering to her that I was going to protect her.

From him.

Evan is dangerous. I knew that coming into this, knew I was putting myself in a situation where I needed to be careful, and what did I do? I let my guard down as soon as I was connecting with Jessica. I trusted that we would have a moment alone and Evan showed up.

And now he knows I'm onto him.

That changes the entire game.

"Oh God." Groaning, I put my car in park in the Warners' driveway and sit there for a moment. I need to get out, get up to the front door and start my day, but just pretending that yesterday didn't happen is really nice right now.

How would I be acting if I hadn't let it slip to Jessica that I'm worried her dad might hurt her? How would this day go if I didn't know how out of control Jessica really is? The pot doesn't bother me. It's almost a rite of passage. But I know that jewelry and wallet didn't end up in her back pocket by accident.

She's mourning, sure, but mourning isn't an excuse for all of her behavior.

Jessica can lie to me all she wants, but it's clear there's more to her than meets the eye. I've seen little flashes of the real her, the Jessica I think she is when she's done pretending for the sake of everyone around her.

At first, I thought it was just normal teenager stuff. To be completely fair to her, I haven't spent a lot of time around teenagers. I know they're moody from all the movies I've seen.

Hormones.

But now, for the first time since meeting her, I question if her behavior is all due to Lola's death. I've never seen her be violent, have I?

Tapping my fingers on the steering wheel, I think. Jessica has gotten angry at me before. She's stomped from room to room when she's upset, she's pushed her chair back from the table so hard it's almost tipped over, but...

Wait.

She bumped me so I'd drop the eggs in the kitchen. And then she smiled, but it wasn't a real smile, was it? It wasn't all friendly and sunshine, a Colgate smile fit for a commercial.

There were too many teeth. It never reached her eyes.

She stole the wallet. And I *know* she was lying to me about forgetting it.

Isn't that all normal teenager stuff? Sure, that's not *nice* behavior, but is it *bad*? I don't know, but just thinking about it gives me chills.

Although I might not like her behavior right now, I have no reason to think it won't improve once I get her out of this house and moved into mine. For a short period of time, I'd thought that keeping her here in this house where she grew up would be a good idea.

She could finish out her high school years at the same school. She'd be able to keep her same friends. Having some sense of normalcy would probably be good for her, but maybe not. Not if she's smoking pot and shoplifting and dealing with Lola's ghost around every corner.

No, once I get rid of Evan and step forward as Jessica's guardian, I'm getting her out of here. New school, new friends, new start.

I just have to get rid of her father first, and from the suspicious expression on his face yesterday, that might be a little bit more difficult than I'd originally thought. The life insurance policy is good but not surprising. I need more. I need something that will not only point the blame at Evan, which is where I think it should have been pointed in the first place, but shine a beacon on him.

I don't want him to be able to slither out of it this time.

Finally, I take a deep breath to fortify myself and get out of the car. I'm going to put yesterday out of my mind. As much as I want to talk to Jessica about her behavior and how she can change it for the better, I don't think that's going to do any good.

No, I'm just going to go into the day treating it as a fresh start. Whatever happened yesterday is in the past and today is going to be great.

That's what I keep telling myself as I hurry up the stairs to the front door. Yes, I have a house key and I even made myself a copy of it just in case, but I always like to knock in the morning before going in. It seems polite and will keep me from catching Evan and Jessica before they're ready to have another person in the house.

My hand is raised to knock when the door swings open.

I have to stop myself from stumbling back when I see the expression on Evan's face. His brow is furrowed, his eyebrows angled down over his dark eyes. I can see twitching in his jaw and his lips are held together in a firm line. Even his body, which is normally relaxed, is tight, like he's an explosive just waiting to go off. He looks furious.

"Evan, good morning." I plaster a smile on my face, doing my best to look like I'm not scared by his appearance. "How are you doing?"

He doesn't smile in response. I guess that's not totally abnormal for someone in a position like him. Maybe he knows he has a terrible meeting coming up this morning. Maybe he just slept wrong.

Maybe he found out about his daughter shoplifting.

I shift my weight from one foot to the other.

"Ariel, I have to say that having you work for us made our lives a lot easier. Until just recently." Evan tilts his head a little bit to the side like he's trying to gauge my reaction.

"I'm sorry? What happened?"

He definitely knows about the shoplifting.

"Some of Lola's jewelry went missing and I'm afraid I'm going to have to let you go. I'm not going to press charges, but you're no longer welcome on our property. If you return here, I'm afraid I will have you arrested, make sure you're charged, and then see you thrown in jail."

His face is stony. There isn't a hint of a smile.

A chill races up my spine and I reach out to grab something for support, but there's nothing there. Evan doesn't move to help me, and I stare up at him, trying to understand what just happened.

"I didn't take—"

"I don't want to hear it. You need to leave now, Ariel. This is your only chance to walk off my property without being in handcuffs, and I suggest you take it before I change my mind. Give me your house key."

My mouth hangs open like a dead fish's and I have to force myself to close it. The key dangles from my hand and I hold it out, watching in horror as he snatches it from me. Nodding once, I turn on my heel and stumble down the stairs.

Once in my car I sit, panting, my heart pounding, trying to figure out what just happened.

But it's not like I really have to guess.

He overheard me telling her I was going to keep her safe.

I knew it. Last night I could tell he was upset when he got home. He told me to stay away and I didn't, and now I have to deal with the consequences. But that's not all I'm worried about.

What if he knows who I really am?

What if he's been one step ahead of me this entire time?

I thought I could come here and get justice for Lola but what if the only thing I've done is put myself and Jessica in danger?

Fear chills my body. My hands feel so cold that they're cramping while my heart ticks faster and faster, racing toward tachycardia. I'm sitting still in my car but still feel like I just ran a sprint.

And then I glance up at the house. Immediately, I wish I hadn't. Evan stands on the front deck, his arms crossed, his eyes locked on me. He looks like a statue, and I fumble the key, finally turning it, making the engine of my car roar to life. Before I throw it into reverse though, I stare up at the house, my eyes searching the second-floor windows for Jessica's.

There it is.

And there she is. She's standing in the window, the curtain pulled back so she can see out. I can see her outline, but I can't make out her face.

Is she smiling? Is she angry? There's no way to tell, but it's not like I can stick around much longer. Even if I could form any words right now to try to ask the two of them what really happened, there's just no way I can walk back up to the house.

I didn't take the jewelry. It's a threat based on a lie, but a good one, and Evan knows he has the upper hand. I finally back down the driveway and shoot through the neighborhood. Ignoring the *slow: children at play* signs, I press down harder on my gas, glancing into my rearview as I do.

I keep expecting to see Evan behind me. I can just picture his car eating up the space between ours. He might tap my back bumper; he might call in a chase. He might refuse to let me go.

But he's not there.

Blowing through the stop sign at the end of the street, I turn onto the main road toward town. It doesn't matter how much distance I put between Evan and me, but it feels better to know he's not right there behind me. I have to get away from him and then I have to figure out what I'm going to do.

My heart slams in my chest as I park my car in the back of the house out of view of the street and let myself into the little guest cottage. It's only after I have the door locked and bolted that I make myself a cup of tea to try to calm down. Once I'm no longer crying, I call her.

She'll know what to do. She's my partner in crime and she has to help me.

"Ariel? Is everything okay?" Miriam's voice sounds muffled when she answers the phone and all I can do is hope Evan isn't close enough to hear her side of our conversation.

"Miriam." A flood of tears springs to my eyes and I angrily wipe them away. "Miriam, I don't know what to do. I think I really messed up." I take a shaky breath and make a fist with one hand, squeezing hard so that my fingers cramp.

The pain is sharp. Bright. It helps me focus.

"What do you mean? What did you do? Does he know?" She's hissing the questions at me, and I wish she would just shut up and take a breath so I could answer.

"He doesn't know," I say, although I'm not entirely sure if that's true. He knows *something*, that's for sure, although I don't know what it is. Evan isn't stupid. Even though he doesn't know the whole truth of what I'm doing—I hope—it's obvious he suspects something.

"Then what happened?"

"He fired me." My stomach sinks at the words. I've worked so hard for this. Coming here, leaving my house to do this, trying to make a home here... It's too much for me to fail now. "He told me he knew that I'd stolen some of Lola's jewelry, and he told me to leave or he'd have me prosecuted."

She's silent. I don't have to see her to know her mind is working overtime as she tries to figure out what to do next.

"Did you?"

"Did I? What—no! Of course I didn't. But that's crazy, right? I didn't steal the jewelry—he has to know I didn't, and for him to tell me he won't press charges if I don't show back up? He just wanted to get rid of me. He wanted to scare me off."

"You must have done something to upset him. Evan isn't erratic like that, not really. Obviously you said or did something that spooked him and now he feels like he has to be on the defensive. Think, Ariel. What did you do?"

I wasn't careful and I got caught.

"I don't know." I hesitate, thinking of what else to say.

"You know. What did you do?"

Crap. "I told Jessica that I would keep her safe. I didn't think Evan was right there or that he could hear me, but I must have been wrong. He must have heard everything and figured it out himself. That or she came clean with him about what I said."

"Jesus, Ariel." Miriam exhales and sighs. "Okay, you sit tight. Are you at my guesthouse?"

"Yes." *Where else would I be?*

"Let me talk to Evan, see what's going on. I'll just touch base with him, make sure he's happy with you working for him, that kind of thing. Don't worry," she says, speaking louder and faster when I start to interrupt, "I know how to handle him. He won't suspect a thing."

She hangs up and I stare at the phone in my hand before dropping it down to her kitchen counter.

No, she's wrong. Miriam thinks she can handle Evan and that he won't catch on to her, but if there's anything I've learned about the man, it's that he's always one step ahead of you.

I don't care how careful Miriam is, I honestly don't see how this won't blow up in my face.

THIRTY-EIGHT

EVAN

Every little thing that could go wrong has.

It started with firing Ariel, not that I really had a choice in the matter. I needed the woman gone, needed her out of my house, had to get her away from my daughter. I don't know who the hell she is or what she wants, but something is wrong with her.

It was the right call—it was my only call—but my day has just gone downhill since then. I can't seem to focus. My coffee was terrible. The internet is shit today and keeps dropping out. I jump every time my cell phone vibrates.

Sighing, I close my eyes and rub my temples. Maybe massaging away some of the tension I feel right now will help me get over the stress of what's going on, but I doubt anything short of never having met Ariel will do the trick. She's onto me, I know she is.

How? I have no freaking clue.

What does she want? No idea.

Most importantly: how dangerous is this woman? That's the

question I need to answer and the one I can't. Every interaction I had with her was fine. *It was normal.* She was a good cook, always kept the house tidy for me, never caused any problems.

Until she did.

My eyes fly open, and I yank my desk drawer open, pawing through the contents to look for the references Miriam had given me to call. I never did, not when I had my assistant vouching for the woman. Why the hell would I? I needed someone ASAP, someone good, and Miriam promised me Ariel was the best.

And she was.

Until she wasn't.

I grab my phone and angrily punch in the first number on the list. Curiosity drives me to do the one thing I should have done before ever offering Ariel the job. I want to find out who this woman is and what she really wants. I need to know what kind of a person I'm up against, because it's obvious there's more to her than I thought at first.

The phone rings. At the same time, I hear Miriam's phone start ringing. It's been blowing up all morning, calls and texts coming in right and left. I keep meaning to tell her to turn it off so she can get some work done, but that would involve leaving my office and talking to her, and I don't want to see a single person right now.

Nobody answers the phone. There's no voicemail and I hang up.

Frustration makes me want to flip my desk. People would pay attention then, wouldn't they? They'd pay attention to the fact that I was losing it.

That's the last thing I need. I'm just angry, and angry people do stupid things.

Like push someone down the stairs.

"Dammit." Standing up, I stomp to the water cooler in the corner of my office, fill a cup, then drain it. The cool water tastes good and I do it again, only stopping at the sound of a knock on my door.

"Yes." I may not be in the mood to see or talk to anyone, but that doesn't mean I can totally shirk my duties today. Crimes are still being committed; people still need my help.

Miriam leans in the door and I have to stifle a groan. Normally her happy attitude makes my day better, but I'm not interested in it today. I need a real release, like Dakota, but that would be a stupid idea. I would love to be with her, have her in my arms, but nothing would make people more suspicious than to see her walking into my office right now.

Dispatchers don't come talk to the chief. We're our own separate entities and that's one of the reasons nobody at work suspected anything. When we're in this building, we're on two separate planets.

I can go see her. But her coming up here to see me?

It would raise eyebrows on a good day.

And especially today I don't need her coming to my office, not when I know I wouldn't be able to control myself around her.

Ending it with her when Lola died was my only option. I didn't need the extra scrutiny. We'd already been caught once by Lola. I don't need the entire department looking closer at what really happened.

"I just wanted to check on you." Miriam throws me a megawatt smile and I push all thoughts of Dakota out of my mind. "You don't seem like you're having the best day."

"It's fine." I try to look like I'm telling her the truth, but honestly I'm upset she could see through my charade. "Just another day."

"We all have days like that. Need me to order in something special for you for lunch? Or did Ariel pack you some leftovers?"

I pause, looking at her. "No, she didn't." No reason to get

into the real meat of why I'm having such a terrible day. I can only imagine the horror on Miriam's face if I told her my housekeeper thinks I killed my wife. That I'd fired her. That I think she's poking around my house, trying to butter my daughter up.

But it's not just her being nosy, is it? There's something more to her, I'm sure of it.

I'm terrified I made a huge mistake letting Ariel into my home in the first place. She's up to something—she has to be. The only question I have is whether or not Miriam knew what Ariel wanted before she introduced us.

"Oh, is she not working out okay for you? I thought she was going to be the perfect fit and that you were happy with her."

"Who says I'm not?"

She flushes. "Your tone, you just—"

I cut her off. "She's your friend, right? You could always ask her how things are going."

"I wouldn't say we're friends. I know her from church." She hasn't walked all the way into my office and almost looks like she's using my door as a shield. "I just thought that you and I have known each other so long and always been there for each other that it wouldn't be a big deal for me to ask you."

She's rubbing me the wrong way. I'm not entirely sure what it is, but there's something about the way Miriam is talking to me and peering at me like she's afraid she's going to set me off that is doing just that.

"If you really want to know, Miriam, I fired her. She was stealing from me."

Miriam's eyes fly open. She flutters her hand up to her chest like she's going to grab a pearl necklace even though she's not wearing any jewelry. "What?" The word comes out in a breath, like she honestly can't understand what I'm saying. "She was *stealing* from you? No, not Ariel." Before she finishes speaking, she starts shaking her head.

"You seem really sure about that." I stand up, walking across my office to join her by the door. For a moment I think she shrinks away from me.

"I'm just surprised, that's all. Ariel seems so on top of it, and she doesn't seem like the type of person who would ever steal. To think that she would... Well, you know best. You just don't always know people the way you want to, do you?"

"No." My eyes don't leave her face. I'm trying to remain as calm as possible but inside I'm seething. "No, Miriam, you really don't. You could know someone your entire life and they could still surprise you when you least expect it."

"Exactly." She bobs her head. "Well, I'm really sorry she didn't work out. I'll get back to my desk and let you get back to whatever it is you're working on."

She scoots away from the door, walking backwards a few feet before she turns and flees to her desk. It's only when she's tucked in safely behind it, her chair pulled close so she can work on her computer, that she risks a glance up at me.

I'm still watching.

And thinking.

I don't like what I'm thinking about, but some things are starting to become clear.

THIRTY-NINE

I was in a play once in college. Something by Shakespeare, and the only reason I agreed to do it in the first place was because it gave me an excuse to hang out with the girl I liked. Not Lola; I didn't meet her until years later. Of course, I had no idea that acting in a Shakespeare play would mean wearing tights and jumping around on stage for half an hour every night, but I was willing to do it to win the girl.

And it worked. It was good practice for me keeping my emotions in check when I really want to blow up at someone. I'm not saying that I'm the world's best actor by a long shot, but I did a pretty spectacular job keeping my face calm today and not letting the rage bubbling up in me out at work. Miriam knows something about Ariel, I just know she does.

It's too much of a coincidence for her to poke her head into my office to ask about Ariel on the very same day I fired her. There are a lot of people who believe in coincidences, but I'm not one of them. Nothing on this planet happens without reason, without purpose, and most of the time the reason something happens is because someone somewhere is being an idiot.

I was that idiot. I shouldn't have trusted Ariel. Even though

I still don't know who she really is, I'm not going to let this go. She came into my house, tried to get close to my daughter, and was lying to me. There's more to Ariel than meets the eye—I'm sure of it.

Those aren't things that I can just forgive or overlook, not when she could ruin everything.

It would be nice to ignore her, to pretend she never stepped foot in my house, but that's just not a good idea. If Ariel knows something about what really happened to Lola—or what she *thinks* happened to Lola—then I have to stop her from spilling her guts to someone.

To Miriam, quite possibly.

I press down harder on the gas and before I know it, I'm in the garage. My body feels like it's on autopilot as I walk into the house, throwing my keys on the counter. When I left work, I fully expected to have to order in a pizza tonight for dinner, but Jessica has two plates on the kitchen table already, the smell of macaroni and cheese actually making my mouth water.

"Hey, Dad." She sounds shy as she stands behind one chair, holding on to it like she needs the support. "I know today was kinda a crappy day and I wanted to help out."

"You are incredible." A wave of gratitude washes over me and I walk over to her, pulling her into a hug. "Look at you, ketchup on your mac and cheese, pepper on mine. It's like you're my own personal chef."

She laughs and the sound is magical. It's been a while since she's felt comfortable really laughing like that, or maybe it's just been a while since the two of us had something to laugh about. Either way, I'm happy to have this moment of peace with my daughter, even though I know it won't last long.

I have things to do.

"I thought we could watch a movie after dinner," she begins, but I stop her, holding up my fork.

"That sounds amazing, but I have a bit more work to do at

the office." Her face falls and I ignore it, continuing. "I'm sorry to dine and dash, but that's exactly what I'm going to have to do if I'm going to get everything done."

"Okay. That's fine." A long exhale and then she takes a few bites of her dinner before speaking again. "Do you really think Ariel stole Mom's jewelry? Or did you just tell her that because of what she said to me?"

"You're a smart girl, Jessica. What do you think?" Checking my watch, I try to gauge what time to leave. It's already getting dark outside, which will ensure nobody sees me.

"Do you think she's dangerous?" Her fork is down now, her hands steepled in front of her face like she's a therapist.

"You need to let me worry about that, okay?" The macaroni I already ate suddenly sits heavy in my stomach and I push back from the table. "Let me worry about Ariel."

"Dad, I'll—"

"You'll stay in this house while I'm gone. You'll put these thoughts out of your head. You'll eat some ice cream from the carton and then put it back, thinking I won't notice. You'll forget to load the dishwasher and I'll fuss at you later for it. This is not a discussion we're having, Jessica. I know you want to help, but right now the only thing you can really do is sit tight."

Shock flickers across her face. Even I'm surprised that I spoke to her like that—it's not something I've done before. Maybe I should have. Maybe we wouldn't be in this position if I'd put my foot down with her before. Maybe Lola would still be alive and I'd be with Dakota.

But that line of thinking isn't going to get me anywhere and it sure as hell isn't going to help out with what I have to do now. It's strange to leave Jessica here when I'm not sure what she's going to do, but I have something I have to check.

"Clean this up. Stay home. Don't do anything dumb." Leaving it at that, I grab my keys and head back out to my car. It only takes me a moment to pull up The Last One, a database that allows law enforcement to see personal information on anyone they want to look up.

A lot of people don't know that officers can find out all kinds of information thanks to this national database. Addresses, driver's license information, phone numbers, known associates, and vehicle information all pop up with the touch of a button.

I type in Ariel's name. The wheel spins for a moment, letting me know the app is thinking, but it shows up with no results.

"What the hell?" I feel a prickle of sweat on the back of my neck and I wipe it away. How could I be so stupid to not look her up already? Ariel has to be a fake name; it's the only thing that makes sense.

Knowing that, I play the only other card I have and type in Miriam's name. Her driver's license picture pops right up on the screen. So does her address. Two more taps on my screen and I have it entered in my GPS and I'm on my way.

The drive to Miriam's takes almost no time at all. I'm not sure what I'm expecting to find there. All I know is that I need to go to her house, need to see what she's up to. She's involved in this thing with Ariel, I'm sure of it. As much as I'd like to think I'm wrong, I know I'm not. Miriam gave me her information. She acted like Ariel was the best thing in the world. Then this morning she seemed to know something had happened. And let's not forget the fact that they were texting.

Much like me, Miriam lives in a small neighborhood with cute little houses flanked by large trees. Unlike my neighborhood though, the cars parked in the driveways here aren't as nice. There are some kid's toys strewn in front yards, which is something that never would be allowed thanks to my HOA.

I have to fight the urge to pull up to the house and bang on the door. Instead, I park on the street across from her house and kill the engine, sinking down a little in my seat so I can keep an eye on what's going on at her place without her seeing me.

At first, nothing happens. There are lights on in the house, making it possible for me to see Miriam walking around from room to room, but besides that I don't see anything.

I just feel like a creeper. "Come on," I mutter, rubbing my eyes and then looking back at the house. "There has to be something here that will prove to me I'm not insane. That Miriam knows something. *Something.*"

Then I see it. I thought she was alone in the house. She's been walking in front of the windows, the lights in her house so bright I can see the look of frustration on her face. While I'm watching though, she turns around as someone else enters the room behind her. Sitting up, I grab the steering wheel, my fingers clenching it so hard they begin to cramp.

Who is in there with her?

I ask the question even though the answer is obvious. *Ariel.* She walks right up to my assistant, giving her a hug before they separate. The urge to march up to the house and hammer on the door burns in my chest. Something is going on in there and I don't have to know what it is to know I don't like it.

Gritting my teeth, I run through my options. Yes, I could go up to the house and demand to know what's going on, but I'm sure the two of them would pretend like it's some innocent get-together. They'd act like nothing out of the ordinary was going on. *Girls' night.*

Just getting together to drink wine coolers and complain about me, about the fact that I fired Ariel and was rude to Miriam today. It's what women do when something bad happens to them, isn't it?

I can imagine the way they'd both stare at me, how'd they'd laugh at me after I left. A united front.

I could drive away and deal with this in the morning. Doing that would give me enough time to dig harder into who Ariel might really be, since it's obvious now that Ariel isn't her real name.

But it doesn't matter what they say about me after I leave. I have to know what's going on.

I'm just not the type of person to leave when I know I'm close to the truth.

Grabbing the door handle, I prepare myself to walk up to the house and demand answers when another car pulls into Miriam's driveway. I shrink away from the window although I don't think it's really possible the driver saw me.

Maybe if I'd opened the door already and the overhead light had clicked on, I'd be in trouble. But I was moving slower than normal, and I'm still shrouded in dark. From here I have the perfect vantage point to see who else is visiting Miriam.

I don't know what Miriam and Ariel really want with Jessica and me, and the thought of someone else involved makes my head spin. This is all getting out of control. There are too many players involved and I feel like I'm just catching up on what's happening. Someone else has come to join their little girls' night, but who is it?

They take their time getting out of the car. It's an old Mini Cooper, the back bumper dented. I let my eyes flick over that detail before I realize what I just saw.

A Mini Cooper. Back dented bumper. It's tricky to see just what color the car is but I can tell it's dark. Like green. Or black.

I want to throw up. None of this makes any sense and I press my hands against my window to get closer to whoever is going to get out of the car. My entire body feels like it's shaking, but there's only one black Mini Cooper with a beat-up bumper I've ever seen driving around town.

The driver gets out, all long legs and blonde hair that seems to glow in the overhead light of her car.

"Dakota." I don't even realize I'm whispering her name until it's out of my mouth.

I'm frozen in place, watching as the girl I had an affair with walks up to the front door. She's going to pause, realize she's at the wrong house, and then leave. She's going to knock and tell Miriam she left her purse at work.

Something. There has to be some way I can make this all make sense.

What I see happen next is so far out of my comprehension that I just sit in my car, my jaw hanging open.

Dakota walks purposefully up to the front door. She's not acting like she's lost or like she made a mistake coming here. I expect her to ring the bell, to step back from the door, to give Miriam plenty of time to come let her in, but instead she rummages in her purse. Thanks to the porch light shining down on her, I can see everything she's doing.

She's gorgeous and this should be exciting, to be watching her without her knowing, but I feel like I'm watching a horror movie. A moment later she finds what she wants in her purse.

A key.

There was no hesitation in how she moved, no pausing as she unlocked the door and stepped inside. She did it like I open my front door—as if I've done it a million times.

I don't know what the hell Dakota is doing, but it's clear she and Miriam have more than just a work relationship.

My head pounds and I start the car, pulling away from the curb with a screech.

Any confidence I had that I could figure all this out has flown out the window. I have to get out of here, have to try to figure out what's going on. Why would Miriam, Ariel, and Dakota all get together tonight?

And what the hell does that mean for me?

FORTY

JESSICA'S DIARY

MONDAY, AUGUST 21

I don't want to live in this house any longer. Mom is gone and whenever I think about bringing her up to my dad, I don't. I'm honestly afraid of what he might do to me if I talk about her.

She's a ghost in the house and I feel like I'm one too. I want to lock myself in my room and never come out, but I have school and there's just no way to avoid that. Dad hardly mentions Mom. He's just living his best life, happy, like nothing ever happened.

And the entire time I feel like I'm drowning.

I know he was having an affair and I honestly thought he'd start it right back up after he killed Mom. Of course there's no way I'm going to ask him about that. The girl hasn't been around, but that doesn't mean he's not meeting up with her at work or in a gross hotel room.

All I know is she isn't here, and that's what really matters to me. I don't think I could handle having her in our house, knowing this was where my mom was so happy. And maybe he knows that. Or maybe he's just waiting.

Every morning, like a mantra, he reminds me of the part I played in what happened to Mom. This morning I was getting ready for school and he stopped me, putting his hand on my arm to prevent me from leaving the kitchen.

I thought I was going to avoid the little reminder, but I was wrong.

"Jessica. Don't talk about your mother at school."

I nodded. It was the only way to get this over with.

"You're just as guilty as I am. If the police ever find out that her death wasn't an accident, you'll go to jail just like I will. You'll be locked up forever. I promise you—you'll never see the light of day again."

I nodded again. This little morning routine made me feel sick but there wasn't any way out of it.

His tone changed, his fingers pressing harder into the flesh of my arm. "I promise you, Jessica, if you turn me in, you might not even make it to jail. I'll take you out with me."

Then he pushed me away. It was rough and I lost my balance, but I caught myself on the counter. There's a bruise on my hip now. It's pretty deep and some of the girls noticed it when I was changing for PE. I told them I tripped running in socks in the kitchen and they believed me. Thank God.

There's no way I can tell them what really happened: that my dad threatened to kill me if I tell anyone the truth.

And worse, that I believe him.

FORTY-ONE

ARIEL

This is going to be the first time I actually meet Dakota face-to-face. Part of the agreement Miriam and I had to help each other was that I wouldn't have to deal with the girl who ruined my sister's marriage. That's what she is—a girl. She's barely out of high school, so young and wet behind the ears that when a man paid attention to her for the first time, she was more than willing to fall into bed with him.

I'm protecting her just as much as I'm getting revenge for my sister, but that doesn't mean I want to meet her.

Dakota played a key role in my sister's murder. I know I shouldn't hate her, that most people would say she's a victim herself at the hands of an older man, but it's really hard. When Miriam told me she'd be coming over tonight, I'd balked.

But what choice do I have? Dakota is her family, her blood, and just like I have a responsibility to take care of Jessica, she feels that same responsibility to Dakota.

The girl walks into the kitchen where Miriam and I are talking. Her long blonde hair floats around her shoulders like a halo.

I saw her at the funeral, in the back row with the other dispatchers, her black dress a little too tight, her heels a little too high. She looked like she was trying to be supportive for her chief, but I knew better.

She wasn't mourning Lola. She was mourning the fact that Evan had broken things off with her.

"Grandma," Dakota says, walking over to Miriam. I watch as the woman hugs her, pulling her close and patting her on the back. "I don't know if I can go through with this."

"What?" My voice is sharp and, just like a knife, cleaves them from each other. "Can't go through with what?"

They turn to look at me, Dakota sniffling a little bit like this is too much to bear.

"You can't hurt Evan." She's gripping Miriam, holding on to her for support, but the expression on her face tells me she's stronger than she's letting on. "I love him, I do. He just—"

"He killed my sister." I cut her off and cast a quick glance at Miriam. *Why would she tell Dakota about the change in the plan?* "He killed Lola and you don't think he'd do the same thing to you? Think about it, Dakota. I know you're not really using your brain right now, but this is not a good man. What happens the next time he wants the newest model? He's going to get it and it doesn't matter what he has to do to make that happen."

Dakota wipes her eyes, smearing a bit of her mascara. She's really not that much older than Jessica and the realization makes me sick.

"Dakota, darling, let me talk to Ariel. I know you're upset, and the three of us are going to do everything we can to help you and Evan."

I feel shock rush through me at what Miriam says but she and Dakota are too busy looking at each other to see the expression on my face.

"I love him."

"I know you do. We both know you do." Miriam swings her arm out to the side a little bit like she's trying to include me in that statement. "We just want to keep you safe."

No, I want to see Evan in the ground.

I have half a mind to ask Miriam what kind of game she thinks she's playing, but I don't have to to understand. She hates Evan, but not the way I do. I hate him because of what he did to my family; she hates him because of what he might do to hers.

Me wanting to kill him is about revenge. Her wanting to kill him is insurance. We're both trying to protect someone we love, and that's the only reason I think we can still make this work.

Besides, she and I have spent too long working on this plan for her to throw it away right now. She's comforting her granddaughter, lying to her about not killing Evan, saying whatever she has to in order to keep Dakota calm. I know what she's doing. The question is, does Dakota?

"I just want what's best for Jessica. I want her out of that house," I say, reaching out to touch Dakota on the arm. I want to try to make a connection with the girl, or at least make her think I am, but at the last minute my hand falls back to my side. It's too much to touch her knowing that she's the reason this is all happening.

"You'll hurt Evan."

I shake my head. I've lied a lot to get here so far, so what's one more lie to a stupid girl who doesn't know any better? "No, I just want to keep Jessica safe. You have to understand that we're all on the same page here."

She looks at Miriam then back at me. "You have no idea what it's like to love someone so much," she says, tears squeezing from her eyes. I have to try to keep my face neutral, to smile at her, but all I want to do is scream.

Why are we all taught we need a man to take care of us? Dakota would be better off without Evan.

"You can trust us," Miriam says, and I'm grateful she's

speaking up because I don't know what to say to her grand-daughter right now. "Ariel and I just want to make all this ugliness go away, okay? Now, darling, why don't you go into the living room and let the two of us talk?"

Dakota shakes her head. "No, I'm fine." She takes a shuddering breath and rubs her cheeks like that's going to get rid of the flush that's grown there. "I just wanted to come by and make sure everything was okay. I saw him in the parking lot going to his car and he seemed so sad. I could help him."

"You can. You just have to wait a little bit longer." Miriam hugs her, pulling her close and looking at me over Dakota's shoulder. "We're going to make sure everything is taken care of, okay? You have to trust me. Do you?"

"Of course." There's no hesitation when Dakota responds, and I see relief flit across Miriam's face. It's gone by the time she pulls back from the hug and lightly pats Dakota's cheek. "Thank you for taking care of me, Grandma."

"I'll do anything for you. Now, get home, get to bed. I know you have an early shift again in the morning."

Dakota nods and leaves the room, not even looking at me. Turning, I watch out the window. She hurries to her car, her head down, her hair a curtain over her face, making it impossible for me to even guess what she might be thinking. Neither Miriam nor I move or speak until she's backed out of the driveway and driven away.

She's the first to break the silence. She turns to me, and I look at her, wary. I believe that what she just told her grand-daughter was a lie, but I still want to hear it from her. I'm still going to get revenge for Lola; I just need to know if she's still in this with me or not.

"I told her that I'd do anything for her, and I meant it." Miriam nods like she's giving herself permission to keep talking. "My daughter was a single mom and raised Dakota all on her own. We lost her to drugs shortly before Dakota started seeing

Evan. That's the reason she was so taken in by him, I'm sure of it. She was vulnerable and Evan preyed on her. If she hadn't just lost her mom, then I don't think she would have been so dumb as to fall into bed with him."

"I'm sorry."

If Miriam hears me, she doesn't acknowledge that I've spoken. "I'll do anything to protect that girl. *Anything*. Dakota thinks that means I'll do whatever it takes to make her happy, but there are some times in life when you don't actually need the thing you think you do. She thinks having Evan will make her happy. She's wrong."

I wait. This isn't so much a conversation we're having as a chance for Miriam to get everything off her chest.

She takes a deep breath then looks me dead in the eyes. "We need to keep the plan in motion."

I nod. She doesn't know the truth about who I really am. I almost slipped up the first time we met, at Lola's funeral, and told her everything about me. It would have been so easy but it's best if people don't know. I've been thinking about it, thinking about what Miriam needs to know, and decided that less is more. Keeping Lola a secret means Miriam can't use our relationship against me if she has a change of heart around the plan.

She doesn't need to know the truth. She just has to trust me that I hate Evan as much as she does.

"But how in the world are we going to manage this now that he's fired you? You can't exactly waltz back into the house and poison him or bludgeon him or shoot him."

I don't tell her that I wasn't planning on doing any of that. Those would all kill him, sure, but I have a better idea.

Evan is going to kill himself.

FORTY-TWO

ARIEL

There's just one big complication, one hitch in my plan, one thing that might stop me from getting to do exactly what I want.

Jessica.

Obviously I don't know her as well as I hoped I did. I thought it would be easy to sweep in here, get rid of Evan, make sure Jessica trusted me and wanted to live with me. I thought I'd be able to protect her and bond with her and there wouldn't be any problems. Now though, I'm nervous. When a person shows you who they really are, you should pay attention.

Drumming my hands on my steering wheel, I make my way slowly across town. It's after lunch, well past the time I'd normally go to Evan's for work, but since I'm fired, it doesn't matter. He doesn't think I'm coming today and that should give me the chance I need to find something that will drive him over the edge.

I could have come here this morning right when he and Jessica left the house, but Miriam made me promise to stay in the guesthouse. She told me she'd be back at lunch to join me, so

I'd put off coming to Evan's house until I saw her for lunch. We ate sandwiches on dry bread and tried to avoid the elephant in the room.

Having Evan arrested for Lola's murder was the original plan but now I'm not sure how to do that. It was supposed to be easy to find the proof I needed about what he did to Lola and then turn it all over to the police. But I can't find what I need. It's just not there, no matter where I look or how much I dig. I thought it would be easy.

I was wrong.

I'm going to look once more, just in case I missed anything, just in case something pops up. And if I can't find something that ties him to Lola's death? Something so airtight there's no way in hell he'd be able to talk his way out of it? Then I'll kill him and make it look like suicide.

That should be easier, right? It's not the path I wanted to take, but maybe it's the one I have to. Still, killing Evan would be ideal but learning more about Jessica makes me nervous. What if she's not as kind and innocent as I thought she was?

The thought terrifies me, but I keep turning it over and over in my head. I may not want to think it, but it makes sense.

The drugs. The stealing. The anger.

I feel completely out of place when I pull into Evan's neighborhood and drive slowly by his house. Clouds cover the sky, casting a gloom on the home. The house is still, the inside lights off. It looks like nobody's home but there's no way for me to know for sure if Jessica is still at school. I parked outside her school early this morning to see if she got off the bus, and she did, but what if she came home early? What if she pretended to get sick so Evan would bring her home and head back to work?

Even though I know they're both probably gone, I still take my time, looping around the neighborhood two more times before parking down the street. When Evan and Jessica come home, they'll enter the neighborhood from the other direction. Hopefully that will be enough to keep them from seeing my car.

My palms are sweating, and I wipe them on my jeans before getting out of my car. Keeping my head down, I hurry down the sidewalk then hustle up the stairs to Evan's front door. No neighbors are out, but even if there were, I have to hope they wouldn't question what I'm doing. They've seen me here for a couple of weeks now and hopefully they'd just assume I got a late start on the day.

And what would I tell them if they wanted to know why I didn't park in the driveway like usual? I'm not entirely sure about that, but I have faith it's not going to come to that. This is going to work out.

Nobody will see me, nobody will question me, nobody even cares what I'm doing. That's the thing about humans that a lot of people don't realize—so many people are worried about what others think of them when in reality it doesn't matter. Nobody cares. People are all too busy worrying about themselves to think about another person, let alone judge them. Besides, it would surprise me if Evan went around the neighborhood telling everyone he'd fired me.

He wouldn't want everyone to know what happened. Sure, he might feel comfortable lying to me and telling me he fired me because I stole Lola's jewelry, but there's no way he's going to tell everyone in his neighborhood that, especially when he knows it's a lie.

Still, I'm nervous. I won't be able to fully relax until I'm in the house.

To my relief, nobody calls out to me as I fit my copied key in the front lock. I hold my breath and turn.

It sticks.

"Shit."

I wiggle the key, then yank it out and try again, turning it as gently as I possibly can this time while whispering a prayer I haven't said since I was a little girl. Whether it's because of me taking my time with the key or my cry for help, I don't know, but the key turns and the door swings open.

Now I move quickly, stepping inside and locking the door behind me. It's darker in the house than I expected, even with the curtains open. For a moment I consider leaving the lights off so nobody will know I'm here, but then I realize how ridiculous that is. My car is parked right down the street, a beacon for anyone who wants to pay any attention. Besides, people leave their house lights on when they're gone all the time.

So I flick on the switch, holding my breath as the bulb on the ceiling fan turns on and the blades being to lazily spin. It isn't until I wait long enough to rest assured that nobody is going to leap out at me that I exhale hard and look around the room.

It's filthy. I swear, I don't know how two people can make a house this dirty, but it feels like all of my hard work has been undone. I know I shouldn't spend time ogling the dirty plates left on the table, the empty microwavable packages of macaroni cheese that one of them had the forethought to make into a pile but not the ability to throw away apparently, but I can't help it.

It's all just too much.

"Bunch of slobs," I mutter, shaking my head. The only good thing is that I won't ever have to clean for this family again. One day soon, Jessica will live with me, and I'll make sure she helps me keep the house picked up and neat, and Evan will be rotting in his casket.

I just have to find something to put him there, some way to pin it on him killing himself. Whether people think it's out of guilt or grief, I don't care.

Up the stairs I go, my hand lightly tracing the handrail. Ever since learning how Lola died, I feel like I take my time more on flights of stairs. I test them when they're wet, eyeball how much room my foot has. I go slower, not wanting to do anything stupid that will send me falling downwards.

First, I walk to Jessica's room and push the door open. My heart slams in my chest as I look inside, hoping she's not going to be in there for some reason I hadn't already considered. I can't imagine Evan would have gone to work and let her stay home but there's always a chance.

But even though I'm scared she's going to be sitting at her desk or lying on her bed, she's not here. There's evidence of her of course. Piles of dirty laundry on the floor, rolling papers on her desk. I even see some jewelry under her bed and know exactly where it came from.

Stolen. Not the stuff she stole when the two of us were shopping, but still stolen. I can see the tags even without dropping down to my knees to look under the bed. She's been a busy girl and Evan doesn't seem to know, to care, or to want to stop her.

"Things are going to change, Jessica," I mutter, walking back out of her room. At the same time though, I wonder how much I can really change her.

"Focus on Evan," I mutter to myself, walking down the hall to his room. I haven't been in here to search his bathroom and closet since the first time. Now I grab the door handle, rattling it and giving it a yank to see if I can get it to come free.

Nope. It's on there securely.

Luckily for me, he's an idiot. The screws around the doorknob are easily accessible and all I have to do is grab a screwdriver from the garage to take care of this.

Carefully, so I don't fall, I head back down the stairs.

FORTY-THREE

The final screw slips from in between my fingers and falls to the floor. Immediately I bend down, grab it, and slide it into my pocket. When I leave here, I need to be able to lock this door back up the exact same way it was or risk Evan figuring out that someone was in his room.

One last chance. Even though I'd love to see Evan dead, the thought of killing him myself makes me feel sick. I'm going to have one more look for something that will point to his guilt in Lola's death.

And if I don't find it? Then Evan really has to die. I have to put aside how squeamish the thought makes me and remember how I would have happily killed him at Lola's funeral. That rage is still there; I just have to grab it, use it. I have to harness it.

But only if I can't find something to throw him in jail forever. A cop in jail.

We all know how that story would end.

Either I find something that, in combination with the life insurance policy, will get him thrown in jail where an inmate will take care of the problem for me, or I'll kill him myself. I don't see any other way this ends for Evan.

Of course, then I'll be left alone with Jessica. While that thought thrilled me just a short while ago, I have to admit that now it gives me pause. She's a handful. She needs therapy. I need to get her away from some of the friends here, the friends who are definitely not helping her make the best decisions. She'll have to learn to listen to me and respect me. There's no way she respects Evan. Not after what he did.

No child is completely free from the sins of their father, but I can save her. I can get her away from here and get her help, and Jessica will be okay.

I owe it to Lola.

I slip the screwdriver into my back pocket and walk into Evan's room, flicking on the light as I go. It's impossibly neat and I pause in the doorway, looking around.

The first day I'd worked here I'd come right on in and cleaned up this room for him. It hadn't been filthy then, but the baseboards had needed a good scrub, the coverlet on the bed needed to be washed, the windows were streaky.

Now, besides the junk on top of his dresser, there isn't anything out of place and that makes me nervous. I'd hoped to be able to move quickly in here, get in and get out, but I'm going to have to go slower and make sure everything ends up back where it belongs.

As it stands, if I were to move anything out of its spot, I have a very good feeling Evan would be able to tell. My palms are sweaty again and I rub them on my jeans.

"Okay, you've got this. Get in and find what you need, make sure you're not messy in here, then lock up the bedroom door and get the hell out of here. This ends today with either a trip to the police station or you getting your hands dirty." I glance down at my watch. "You have three hours. And go."

Even after my little pep talk though, I'm not entirely sure where to start. I spin in a slow circle, taking in the closet, the bed, the dresser. There's a small side table next to the bed with two books and a half-full glass of water on it. The closet doors are closed, but I have a pretty good feeling everything in there will be just as neat as the rest of the room.

Across the room from me is a window that looks out over the side yard. The curtains are pressed and hang straight down to the floor. If I didn't know any better and hadn't heard Evan thunking around in here in the morning getting ready for work, I'd think nobody lived in this room.

Next to the bed is a door that leads into the bathroom. I'm itching to get started but can't imagine he'd hide some proof of his wrongdoings in the bathroom, but to be thorough, I'm going to have to look. But only when I'm desperate. When I've looked everywhere else.

But first, the bed. Under the mattress was my favorite place to hide contraband when I was younger. Love notes from the boy who sat across the classroom? Under the mattress. A broken necklace I found on the walk home from school that Lola convinced me held a real diamond? Under the mattress.

Anything important that I didn't want my parents to find went right under the mattress. It was a real princess and the pea situation, but instead of keeping me from getting the sleep I needed, I swear that knowing my prized possessions were so close helped me pass right out and sleep through the night.

Of course, that was all until my parents found them one day, but that's beside the point. What matters is that Evan needed a good hiding spot for his stuff, and I can imagine him putting things under his mattress. Nobody would think to look there when dealing with a grown man. Nobody would think a grown man could be that careless—to hide things in plain sight like that.

But I do.

I'm energized now. Excitement and a bit of fear work together to propel me over to the bed. Before lifting the edge of the mattress though, I carefully study how the bed is made. If

I'm going to do this, I need to do this right. I need to make sure he'll never know I was here.

More confident now, I lift the edge of the mattress, shoving my hand in between it and the box spring and working my way around it. It's heavy, probably the type of mattress with a special sleeping foam that will allow murderers to sleep better but makes it more difficult to lift the dang thing, and by the time I'm done, I'm sweating.

And I don't have anything to show for my work. It takes a few minutes to get the bed made back up the way it was when I walked into the room, then I drop to my knees and look under it.

Nothing. When's the last time I ever met anyone who didn't store *something* under their bed? I honestly can't remember a time when I didn't have some box of junk shoved there, but the space under Evan's bed is perfectly empty. There's a dust bunny, but that's hardly a crime.

So it's got to be in the closet.

I stand back up, breathing heavier now. This takes much more exertion than I would have thought but I'm not nearly done. Rather than taking a break, I stalk to the double doors and throw them open. There's a little cord hanging in front of my face, and I yank it, filling the closet with light.

This, too, is all perfectly organized. I groan. "Why can't you be messier like your daughter?" Even though it *looks* nice, the thought of keeping everything in order while I search is daunting.

It's just so *pristine*. No way would I ever think any room in the house would be this picked up. I guess Evan likes control and wants his room looking a certain way. The rest of the house was in such disarray, but this place is tidy, just like his office was.

It's overwhelming, and honestly, I'm not entirely sure what I'm looking for. A box of letters perhaps? Notes between him and Dakota? Coupled with the life insurance policy, that's motive right there. Throwing Dakota under the bus would piss Miriam off, but I don't care. Letters could be stashed in a box, tucked in a boot, layered between sweaters. I'm already pulling some clothes off a shelf when I realize what about the closet is so odd.

All of Lola's clothes are gone. The entire closet is full of men's clothes. From the hanger in front of me to the shelves on both sides of the closet, it's all filled with Evan's stuff. There are sweaters, work uniforms, pants, and buckets of socks. Shoes and boots line the floor under the hanging clothes, perfectly in order like a row of soldiers.

On one wall there's a break in the shelving and that's where he's hung his ties. Above them is a mirror so he can check himself out and make sure he looks good before going downstairs. If there was any sign of Lola in the closet before, it's now gone.

Confused, I walk back out into his bedroom and spin in a slow circle. I've been in here before but hadn't noticed it at the time.

There isn't any sign of Lola anywhere. It's like she never existed.

"What did you do with Lola?" I ask as tears spring to my eyes. It's one thing to know she's dead, another entirely to have her erased from this house. Her home.

Like I'm being pulled by an invisible string, I walk back into the closet.

FORTY-FOUR

JESSICA'S DIARY

WEDNESDAY, AUGUST 30

I think my dad has finally gotten it through his head that we need help. I just don't have any energy to do anything around the house. Going to school and keeping this big secret inside is so difficult that when I get back to the house in the afternoon, I just want to pass out in bed and not move ever again.

And the house shows it. It's dirty and the laundry is out of control. I know I should throw a load in from time to time to help out, but why would I want to help out the man who killed my mom? Why would I want to make his life easier when he took my mom's life and turned mine into such a living hell?

I don't want to help him. I want him to suffer just the same way I'm suffering. I can't tell anyone what he did because he'll kill me, but that doesn't mean I have to enjoy living with him.

Today, though, was different. He brought someone into the house, this woman named Ariel. He promised me she isn't going to try to take Mom's place.

I don't point out to him that it would be impossible for her to do that since Mom is dead and Ariel is alive.

I can't imagine he'd like that very much if I were to say it. I can't imagine he wouldn't hurt me. But you know what, this could be a good thing. Having someone else in the house to take the pressure off him might make things better. I don't think Ariel is going to be a miracle worker, but I'm excited to have her around.

I know she's not my mom, but she's also not my dad, and that's a good thing.

He scares me. I'm so tired of the daily reminders that I'm just as involved in my mom's murder as he was. Even though I know it's not true, I can't help but believe it sometimes. There's just something about the way he gets into my head that makes it really difficult for me to remember the truth.

And that's this: my dad killed my mom. He made me help him cover it up. When he thinks I'm not listening or that I might not cover for him, he pushes me around. I have bruises from him. I'm terrified of what else he might make me do.

He scares me. I just hope Ariel can help make things better in the house. I hope she doesn't end up upsetting him. I need her to keep me safe.

FORTY-FIVE

EVAN

There's a stack of files sitting on my desk that I know I need to sort through, but I can't bring myself to lift the first one and flip it open. I already know what's going to be in there—any reports my captains wanted me to check out to ensure they were done correctly, requests for information releases from the news, and reports on daily stats for my street officers.

This is part of my job. Going through them and making sure everything has been done correctly is something I do all the time but right now I can't bring myself to even open the first folder.

I just can't stop thinking about Ariel. She's in my head and has settled down like she's going to live there. She's living rent free in my mind.

I trusted her.

But not anymore.

My desk is messy, and I tap the stack of files into order then push them to the side. Next, I drop my pens into the cup where they live when not in use. Finally, I pick up my coffee cup, fully intending to drain it, only to see that I've already done that.

Sighing, I push back from my desk and wander out to refill it. Miriam's at her desk and she glances up at me, her eyebrow raised, her mouth quirked into a question, but she doesn't say anything.

And neither do I. Instead, I focus on the way the coffee fills my mug, swirling and brown, then carry it back to my office. "I'm not to be disturbed," I tell Miriam, then I close my door behind me.

Lock it.

My body feels stiff and awkward as I walk back to my desk. I think I look calm—I hope I look calm—but on the inside I'm coming apart at the seams. Stress turns my stomach, and even though the coffee probably isn't going to help with that, I don't know what to do with myself right now.

Something isn't right.

Ariel isn't right.

I didn't find anything on The Last One, which tells me one thing: she's using a fake name. I, the idiot, didn't look into who she really was when she came to work for me. Frustration makes my stomach turn.

I did call her reference that one time, but did I push it when I couldn't get in touch with anyone?

No. I just wanted it to work out, so I ignored the bad feeling I had.

That's my mistake and one I'm going to have to handle myself. Now. By finding out who she really is so I can try to figure out what she wants.

It may be a little late to undo whatever trouble she's already caused, but I can stop her from causing more. And that's my plan for this morning. I have one more play to make and I have to hope it gives me enough ammunition to deal with Ariel.

To protect myself.

What I'm about to do could cause a hubbub if I'm not careful. Using police resources for personal reasons is frowned upon, but I don't have much of a choice at this point.

Everyone in the department was sympathetic when Lola died, but if I'm caught running someone's fingerprints without a report on file and a darn good reason, it could really rile people up downstairs.

And I definitely don't want Miriam to find out.

That's why I have to do all this on my own.

Luckily for me, I still know how to lift fingerprints. And, also luckily for me, our department received a huge grant last year to replace our outdated fingerprint equipment.

I glance over at my office door even though I know it's locked. My heart pounding, I reach into the box I brought with me and pull out a drinking glass sealed in a ziplock bag. In the bottom drawer of my desk I have my old fingerprint kit from when I was on the road. It isn't something most chiefs have in their office, I can pretty much guarantee that, but I held on to mine.

Why? Maybe I'm more sentimental than I ever thought.

Whatever the reason, I'm grateful I did.

Moving faster now, I snap on rubber gloves and carefully lift the glass Ariel used out of the plastic bag. I put it on my desk, pushing the file folders out of the way to make room for it. At first I'd been irritated when I found this glass sitting out of place in my living room and I'd blown up at Jessica, wanting to know why she'd left it there.

Instead of answering, she'd just gotten up and left the room. Gone upstairs. Slammed her bedroom door. Turned on her loud music. Like I don't know what she's doing up there. Smoking pot and talking to Britt about what a terrible father I am.

The thought makes me chuckle. If Britt only knew how far I'd go for my daughter.

Jessica didn't drink from the glass.

I didn't use it.

It has to be Ariel's. I need it to be hers so I can lift this print and figure out who the hell I let into my home. It's the only way I'm ever going to be able to relax. I may have gotten rid of her for the moment, but I've dealt with enough cockroaches in my life to know that you can't just scare them off.

Sometimes you have to make sure there's no way they'll ever come back.

It's been years since I've used my fingerprint kit, but I took hundreds of prints when I was on the road. My brush still has enough powder in it to take prints without adding more, and I take a deep breath, lightly buffing the bristles across the glass.

The fingerprint shows right up. It's perfect. No smearing. A full print, not a partial.

Beautiful.

It was always a joke when I was on the road, how the worse the crime is, the worse the condition of the fingerprint. Hunting a murderer or rapist? You're only going to find a terrible partial print. Someone jaywalked and lightly touched the hood of a car on their way across the road? That print will be perfect and will stand out like a damn Christmas light.

This one is textbook.

"I've got you," I whisper, breathing the words out as I dig back in my fingerprint kit.

I peel open a print lifter and lightly press the sticky tape against the fingerprint, then peel it carefully up from the glass, holding my breath until I'm sure I didn't screw it up. I'll be pissed if I ruin it now because there isn't any other way to get a fingerprint from Ariel. This is my last chance at finding out who the hell I let into my house.

It's only when I press the print lifter in place to the white card to seal it that I relax. Now I move quickly, carefully putting the lifted fingerprint on my desk so I can take it down to the lab while I clean everything up. In just a moment my desk is clean, my kit stowed back in the drawer, and I grab the card, slipping it into my pocket before leaving my office.

"I'm going out." I only want to say the bare minimum to Miriam today, but I have to keep speaking to her. Hopefully she'll just think I'm in a bad mood. The last thing I need is for her to figure out that I'm onto Ariel. Let her put the pieces of the puzzle together when I know what I'm dealing with.

Just a little bit longer and the playing field will be even again. I'll hopefully know who Ariel really is and she won't even see me coming.

I hurry down the stairs, not wanting to wait for the elevator. When I get to the second floor, I'm sweating a little, but more from excitement than from exertion.

I'm filled with relief when I see nobody is in the lab. Without knowing how long my luck will last though, I need to hurry.

My first step is to scan this fingerprint into the machine and look for points of minutiae. These will make it easy for AFIS to find any other fingerprints that might match. A strange bifurcation in the print? Point of minutiae. An unusual ridge ending? Point of minutiae.

All fingerprints are different, but I'm looking for anything that will really set this print apart. Then I'll run it through AFIS, be given a few prints to compare, and should hone right in on who Ariel really is. The Automated Fingerprint Identification System is set up to quickly scan for a fingerprint that matches the one we're trying to identify. With more than 162 million people's fingerprints uploaded, I'll have a pretty good shot at matching this print.

But it's not one hundred percent guaranteed.

I'll only have her prints if there was reason to upload them to the FBI. Like if Ariel was in the military. Or was fingerprinted because she's a criminal.

That's a lot of *ifs*. But I have faith.

The great thing about AFIS is that it works quickly. The most time-consuming part is looking for points of minutiae, but once I have those marked, the computer does all the work. If Ariel's prints are on file, I'll know in a few minutes.

But if not, I have a few more tricks up my sleeve. She may have had the upper hand until now, but that's changing.

I'm coming for her, and she has no idea.

FORTY-SIX

ARIEL

I found it.

The thing I've been looking for—and more.

My fingers tremble as I pull the blue notebook from behind a stack of jeans. If I hadn't been taking everything off each shelf to look behind it, I never would have found what I was searching for.

An envelope is rubber-banded to the top of the notebook and I pluck it free first, my heart beating in my chest.

My fingers tremble as I pull the papers from the envelope then carefully unfold them. I came to this house looking for a number of things, and this is one of them. Without these papers I won't be able to convince Jessica of anything.

They're not proof of Evan killing Lola, but something else. Something I haven't seen in sixteen years. Something maybe even more important.

"Oh, Jessica." My fingers brush the paper before I stop myself, clenching my hand back into a fist. The words on the page blur as tears fill my eyes. I sink to my knees, unable to stand any longer.

Adoption papers. I didn't mean to get pregnant, didn't mean to bring a baby into the world when I couldn't take care of her, and Lola stepped right up. She promised me that she and Evan would take care of Jessica. My beautiful baby girl. My only act as her mother was naming her, and then letting her go so she could have the loving, stable home she deserved. It almost killed me, to give birth to her and then give her away, but I didn't have a choice.

Not if I wanted to give her the life she deserved. If she'd stayed with me, I would have loved her. I would have given her all the love she needed, but that's not enough to take care of a baby, and I knew that. I didn't want to give her up. But I had to. For her sake.

I desperately wanted to be a part of my daughter's life. Lola told me no. She said it would be too confusing for Jessica, would make it too difficult, that we had to wait until she got older.

I disagreed, but she was Jessica's mother now. Once I signed the papers, my daughter was gone. Whatever I wanted didn't matter. Jessica belonged to Lola, and I was the aunt who never came to visit.

Because Lola wouldn't let me.

Lola wanted a baby. I needed a home for mine. If we hadn't fallen out, maybe if I hadn't pushed so hard to get to spend time with Jessica, then we might have already known each other before now. I've thought about her so much over the years. I've wondered what she looked like. Did she have my eyes? How did she wear her hair? What was her favorite subject in school? I hoped she was kind, that she had a lot of friends.

And then Jessica got old enough to have social media. It was all locked down of course, Evan and Lola making sure Jessica would be safe from predators. That meant I couldn't see her posts and what she was up to, but I got to see her little profile pictures.

I stared at them, screenshotted them, tried to memorize what my daughter looked like even though the shots were tiny and pixelated. Even when I thought about adding her as a friend, I knew the trouble that would cause with Lola.

So I didn't.

Wallowing in my guilt isn't going to do any good but I can't help it. I've been doing my best to think of Jessica as Lola's, not as mine, just to keep some distance between the two of us, but I can't do that any longer.

I tuck the papers back in the envelope and set them on the floor next to me. After I take the rubber band off the notebook, I put it on my wrist for safekeeping.

Now. This is it—it has to be.

My breath catches in my throat.

Is it possible he wrote in a diary?

Running my hands across the cover, I exhale hard, fighting back tears. I still need to pile everything back on this shelf and I'm careful not to knock over any piles of clothes that surround me as I sit cross-legged, but my focus is on the notebook.

God, let it have what I need.

The notebook is blue and slim. There's some gold on the edges of the pages but a lot of it has worn off like Evan has flipped through it every single night. I haven't opened it yet but I'm still hopeful that it's going to have the answers I need. I just need one passage to show his guilt.

Surely you can't kill your spouse and then continue on with life as you know it. Surely there has to be some guilt, and it's that guilt I'm hoping will have led him to write a confession, or at least to discuss how terrible that night was.

All I need is something I can give to the police to prove what Evan did, and it's in here. I know it is. If not, then I'll take matters into my own hands.

Evan will go to jail. Or I'll kill him. Either way, this will finally be over.

"Okay, Evan, let's see what terrible things you wrote in here about my sister." I hate that my fingers tremble as I open the cover. Part of it is nerves, part of it is because I'm getting hungry. I don't think it's that late though. I was too nervous to eat much before I came over and now I'm feeling the effects of it.

"Dear Diary," I mock, reading the top of the first page, but then I stop.

This isn't Evan's handwriting. I'd know Lola's anywhere, the way she loops her Ds and how she tends to scrawl all of her letters together when she's in a hurry. I *want* this to be Evan's. I need it to be his, to be some proof of what really happened here in this house.

But this is Lola's diary. I read the first page, my eyes skimming so quickly I only catch every other word, but what I really want to see is the end, where she would have signed her name, where she would have written a big loopy *L*.

There it is.

It's hers.

"No," I whisper, closing my eyes and shutting the diary at the same time. I feel like I just sprinted around the block. My heart hurts it's thudding so hard. My blood feels like sludge being forced through my arteries and I take a deep breath, then another, before I open my eyes again.

"This has to be it," I say, lightly stroking the diary. "I need this to be it." Tears spring to my eyes. Without some proof of what Evan did, I don't know how I will trap him. I have no idea how I can save Jessica from this nightmare.

Shaking my head clears that thought. No, I'm not going there right now. I need to save my daughter and that means I need to find something incriminating in this closet. The coroner said Lola hit her head on the sidewalk and that's what killed her, but maybe not. Maybe Evan bashed her head in. Maybe there's a weapon in here somewhere. Maybe he hit her with his gun.

If I get it from where it's tucked in the drawer, there might be blood on it. Her hair. The thought is grotesque, but I cling to it, willing myself to go look, to see if the proof I needed was right there all along.

But when I move to put Lola's diary down, it's like I can't let it go. I don't want to put it down. I want to read it, want to know what my sister was thinking and going through.

It's stupid, to sit here and read it, but I can't help myself. I've always been terrible at keeping track of time, but I'll be careful. I know I should stop, but I can't.

"Just a few pages." Every reader in the world knows those are famous last words, that no matter how much we might like to think it's true, *just a few pages* always turns into *just one more chapter,* which turns into finishing the entire book.

But I can't stop myself. This diary will have to stay here when I leave, as much as I hate the thought of leaving it behind. If I put it away now, then I might not have any time to read some of it later. But if I read some... I might find proof that Lola was afraid of Evan. There might be something here that would convince the police to reopen the case.

I don't know that for sure, but I have to try.

Or maybe this is just how I talk myself into doing something I wanted to do anyway.

It's stupid, but I settle back down, knocking over a pile of pants as I do.

"I'll get that in a few minutes," I mutter.

And then I start reading.

Reading my dead sister's thoughts should feel like snooping, but it doesn't. She's not here to tell me that I'm wrong—not here to get mad at me for poking through her diary—and that's why I can't stop.

That, and I see the end of her marriage and her life coming from the beginning. She didn't see it, didn't have time to analyze what was going on, but Evan was leaving her a long time before she learned about his affair.

"Oh, Lola," I murmur. "This is so sad. You loved him, you loved your family, and he had to go throw it all away." I've learned how upset Jessica was about the thought of moving out of the house. I've learned how lost Lola felt, like she was all alone and didn't have anyone to help her think things through.

And even though my sister was screaming for help, writing her pain into these pages, Evan never knew.

Or he just didn't care.

"He deserves everything he's going to get," I mutter, closing the diary. My legs are cramped from sitting this long and I stand, carefully stretching my hands over my head before I bend over and reach down like I'm going to touch my toes. Everything hurts and there's a rush of blood from my head that makes me a little dizzy, like I was just out for a run.

The diary falls from my hand and lands on the wood floor with a *thunk*.

There's an answering one from the first floor.

"What the hell?" Now I don't feel like I sprinted around the block—I feel like I sprinted around the block with something chasing me. I crouch, grabbing the diary and holding it to my chest like it's a baby I need to protect. My ears strain, the silence of the closet almost painful as I try to moderate my breathing.

What did I hear?

Slowly, so I can keep listening, I stand and walk to the closet door. Each footstep, no matter how quiet I'm trying to be, sounds like a gunshot to me. If someone is downstairs, they'll be able to hear me, I'm sure of it.

But nobody should be home. I've been so careful with my

timing and making sure that nobody was in the house when I got here that it doesn't make sense that I would have messed up now.

I move carefully, creeping from the bedroom out onto the landing to look down the stairs.

Slowly, like I'll be able to hide the truth from myself if I don't look quickly at my watch, I raise my wrist to check it. My heart drops.

It's a quarter after five.

FORTY-SEVEN

EVAN

"Are you always high?" I spit the words at my daughter, hoping to get some sort of a reaction from her, but all she does is smile and shake her head.

"Not always."

Her backpack is on the kitchen table between us. I *knew* I'd smelled something when we both got home. She was at Britt's, and I was at the office. Her friend dropped her off right as I was opening the front door. Even though she tried to scoot by me so I wouldn't be able to smell her, she reeks.

"But how often?" I slam my hand down on the table, but Jessica doesn't flinch. Either her senses are so dulled that the loud sound didn't really register with her or she just doesn't care.

I'd like to guess which one I think it is, but I have no idea. Do I even know my own daughter? Not the way I thought I did, I guess, not after...

Not after Lola.

"Does it matter? I'm careful; I'm not going to get caught. Nobody knows I'm smoking except you."

"And Britt." Running my hand through my hair, I turn away from my daughter. This is like a punch to the gut after such a shitty day. The more I try to dig into who Ariel really is, the less I realize I know about her. It was my own fault, letting her into the house like I did.

She's not in AFIS. There's no record of her fingerprints ever being taken, which means I did all that hard work this morning for nothing. She's a ghost, slipping in our house and then back out, and I have no clue who she is.

What she wants.

But I need to know what the hell I've gotten us into.

"You don't really care about the pot." Jessica sounds so confident that I turn to look at her. "You don't—I know you don't. You're worried about something else. What is it?"

I take in her red eyes and how relaxed she looks. It's stupid to unload your concerns on your daughter, but she's the reason we're in this mess.

"I don't know who Ariel really is."

"What?" The word comes out like a laugh, and I glare at her. "What do you mean by that? I thought Miriam helped you find her, and I know how much you love Miriam." Her lips curl up and I rip my gaze away from her face.

When did Jessica get so cruel? Was it me, stepping out on Lola, that pushed her to become this person? Would her mother even recognize her now if she knew what kind of person Jessica had turned into?

I try to think back to before Lola died. Jessica was good then, right? Was she stealing and doing drugs? I don't remember, although I'd give a lot of money for someone to tell me if she was. I want to know when things changed so I can possibly change them back.

But there's no going back, and I know that.

"I thought you just looooved Miriam." Jessica has found a button and she's pushing it. "Or is it just that you love any woman who isn't Mom?"

"Enough." My voice comes out sharper than I mean it to. Maybe it will get her attention.

It doesn't.

"You were just so busy always finding other women, you know that? And you left us here. Mom was going to take me away!" She looks surprised at how loud she's gotten.

"It's in the past." I walk around the table and reach for her. She pulls back.

"Whatever, Dad. The past, the present, the future? It's all the same. You did this to our family and now you want me to stop coping with it the only way I know how?"

"Drugs aren't the answer." This is something I can talk about. I feel like I'm on solid ground now, telling my daughter to lay off the drugs, to be kinder to her body. She might hate me for everything that's happened, but I can talk about how dangerous drugs are.

"What does it matter? Mom's dead. There's no bringing her back."

"It was an accident." I say the words, hoping I can get her to agree with me. She doesn't respond and I search her face for an answer, for some kind of guarantee that I haven't lost my mind.

"It wasn't." She's barely speaking above a whisper now. The entire house feels frozen, like we're trapped in ice, or time has stopped. I can't stop staring at Jessica.

"You were ruining everything. You cheated on her; you started it." Her finger slams into my chest. "But Mom was going to finish it. She was going to take me away." There are tears streaming down her face. She doesn't bother to wipe them away.

"Jessica, I'm sorry. I didn't mean to hurt you. Or your mother. Really, I didn't."

"Then what the hell did you mean to do? Did you think you could just sleep around with someone else and not have any consequences? *You're the reason she's dead.*"

"What?" It feels like someone has punched me in the stomach and I take a step back from her. Before, I wanted to be close to my daughter. I wanted to be able to comfort her if she needed it, but I need space now. I need fresh air, away from her.

"You don't get to stand there and—"

"You drove her to leave." She's still coming. Her face twists in anger. She hasn't touched me since she poked me in the chest, but I keep looking at her hands, waiting for them to form into fists, waiting for her to attack me.

She's going to, isn't she? It's the only thing that makes sense.

"You made this happen, Dad. Are you happy about it? Are you happy about who you made us become?"

"This isn't who you are. It's not who we are." I need to find my footing with her, need to figure out how I'm going to get her to calm down and see reason.

But she just keeps coming.

"Not who we are? Yes, it is. You're a cheater. You pushed Mom to leave. She was a quitter. She wasn't strong enough to handle what was really happening in life."

"Jessica, no." I need her to stop. I have to make her stop.

But she won't.

"And now you want to know about Ariel, huh? You want to know what role she's playing in all of this? I bet I can find out. I'm the only one in the family who knows who we all are."

Her mouth is an angry slit, and she takes a breath, ready to say something else, when we both hear a beep from upstairs.

For a moment, we both freeze. Jessica's eyes are wide, her breath coming in tortured gasps, her chest rising and falling quickly.

I know what we're both thinking.

There's no way I can beat her to the stairs.

We lock eyes and, in my mind, I'm begging her not to go. I'm begging her to stay here with me, let the two of us figure it out without going upstairs. I'm begging her to be the child I know she can be, the little girl who used to hold my hand and squeeze my fingers when she was excited.

I don't want Jessica to turn and run for the stairs.

But she does.

But first she grabs a knife.

FORTY-EIGHT

ARIEL

WEDNESDAY, SEPTEMBER 13

You know the cold wave that washes over you when you jump into a pool for the first time in the summer as a kid? It's like you turn into one giant goosebump, like your skin shrivels to try to protect you from how cold you're about to be, but it doesn't matter. You won't be warm again until you're out of the water, wrapped in a towel, drying in the sun.

I feel the cold drench of fear wash over me but I'm nowhere near a pool. When it hits me what I've just done, my mouth drops open in horror, but try as I might, there's no way to undo what just happened.

My phone is still lit up. I stare at it in my hand.

I texted Miriam for help, telling her I was in Evan's house, telling her I needed her to create a distraction so I could get out because I was honestly afraid for my life. Then I forgot to turn the ringer off.

She texted back. The entire thing lit up in my hand like a Christmas party, the sound of my text echoing through the house. As much as I'd like to hope that nobody else heard it, there's no way I can believe that.

The notification was loud.

Worse, *the arguing from downstairs stopped.*

The sound of footsteps racing toward me makes me look up from my phone. I'm not fast enough to move out of the way, and when Jessica runs out of the kitchen, she stares right up at me.

"Jessica." Can she even hear me? I don't know, don't know if my voice was loud enough, don't know if she'd even listen to me right now. Clearing my throat, I try again. "Jessica."

"You." Her hand is on the railing, her foot on the first stair. "You. What are you doing here?"

"I can explain." Holding my hands up, I try to look as non-threatening as possible. The expression on Jessica's face terrifies me. Her mouth is pulled open in a grimace, making her look more like The Joker than a teenage girl. Even though she's all the way down a flight of stairs, I'm not that far away from her. She's locked eyes on me and isn't going to look away.

But it's not her face that's the most terrifying thing about her; my heart does a little flip in my chest when I see what she has in her hand.

"Jessica," I repeat, finally stepping back from the top of the stairs. There's nowhere to run, nowhere to hide. She knows this house better than I ever will and even though fear drives adrenaline through my body, trying to get me to move, I feel like I'm walking through molasses.

She's moving like she's on fast-forward. She tears up the stairs, not even panting, then faces me. The knife she has looks sharp and deadly, and my eyes lock on it like a magnet.

I was wrong. This entire time I was wrong. That little voice in the back of my head telling me that something was deeply wrong here—I should have listened to it.

"Please," I say, tearing my eyes away to look at her. "Please.

I forgot something here. I came back for it. I'm sorry. Just let me go."

"You were eavesdropping." Her words are a hiss.

"No." I shake my head, trying to look like I'm telling her the truth. It's impossible when my legs feel like jelly and I'm fighting the urge to sink to the floor. "No, I didn't hear anything. I was just here because I forgot something. I needed to get something, but I'll go."

Hoping she'll let me by, I take a step toward the top of the stairs.

Quick as a flash, she's in front of me. Her knife is out between the two of us, the blade pointed right at my stomach. When she catches me looking at it again, she jabs it at me. Her laughter fills the air.

"Jessica, please." I don't want to beg. The last thing I want is for her to know she's won and that she can do whatever she wants to me, but I don't know how to get out of this. "I just want to go home."

"*I just want to go home.*" She sings the words back at me. "Tough shit, Ariel. Why are you really here?"

Movement at the bottom of the stairs catches my eye. Evan stands there, his mouth open, staring up at the two of us. My stomach sinks.

"I knew your mom," I finally say, watching Jessica for any reaction. Maybe it's stupid to play all my cards right now with Evan just a flight of stairs away but what choice do I have? Jessica looks like she's out for blood.

I can't believe how badly I've messed up.

"You knew my mom?" The tip of her knife drops just a little. It's almost imperceptible, but I'll take it as a win.

"Yes. That's why I'm here, Jessica. I want to protect you. I don't want your dad to hurt you too." I'm lying through my teeth, hoping I'll get her to calm down. If I can make her think

I'm on her side, then I might just walk away from this in one piece.

She terrifies me but I can't let her know that.

But she gives me no response. Just a grin, slow and dangerous, spreading across her face. My stomach drops, but before I can backtrack, before I can tell her how much it would mean to me to be able to take care of her, she shakes her head.

"You really think my dad killed my mom?"

I don't want to play mind games with her, but I need to get out of here in one piece. I know I made a terrible mistake, that much is obvious now, but if I can get her to think I'm on her side, then I might make it out of here.

As long as Evan stays on the first floor so I can talk to his daughter. And as long as I can get her to believe my lies.

There are a lot of things I need to go right so I can get out of here.

"Honey, I know it's hard to believe, but yes. That's why I'm here. I just want to keep you safe."

She smiles. "And who the hell are you?"

The way she's looking at me right now terrifies me. There's only one thing I can tell her that will hopefully keep her calm. It's going to be upsetting at first, sure, but my other option is to try to talk her down without catching her off guard.

I just have to hope what I'm about to tell her is enough to give her pause. To make her rethink killing me. To hopefully get her to drop the knife.

"I'm... I'm your mom." God, it's a relief to tell her the truth. I see the look of shock on her face. Her mouth drops open a little bit and the tip of the knife drops even more.

I'm going to make it out of here in one piece.

I'm banking on it. Banking on the fact that her learning the truth will be enough to push her to let me go. She'll want to know more, and for that to happen, I have to stay alive.

"Bullshit."

"I'm serious." Sweat pours down my back. "I'm your biological mom. Lola and Evan, they adopted you—they took you in. Lola was my sister. I'm here because she died, and I promised her I was going to take care of her. I was waiting on you two to come live with me, but Lola didn't make it. I can still keep you safe though." I want to reach out for her, but the blade is still right there between the two of us.

Instead, I take another step toward the top of the stairs.

The knife goes right back up and I freeze.

"So you abandoned me."

No, God, no. I shake my head. "It wasn't like that, believe me. I couldn't take care of you myself, but I wanted to be a part of your life, Jessica, I really did, but Lola wouldn't let me."

I don't want to throw Lola under the bus and upset Jessica, but I need to make her see that I'm here for her.

"You were always the most important thing to me even though I couldn't be around, Jessica. But I'm here now. I came for you. To protect you. Keep you safe."

Yet another step.

"That's your little secret?"

I nod. She smiles, closing the gap between the two of us. I stiffen as she reaches out and wraps her arm around my shoulders. Her head dips toward mine, like she's going to whisper something in my ear.

"Do you want to know my little secret?"

I don't. There are a million things I want right now, but to know Jessica's secret is not one of them. I want to shake my head but my mouth answers for me. "Of course I do."

Her breath is warm on my cheek. "My mom didn't trip and fall."

"Honey, I know. I found your mom's journal. She called me before she died when she was planning on leaving. She was going to bring you to my house. She was terrified of your dad, and he killed her. He pushed her down the stairs. Let me go. Let me save us from him."

Please believe me. Please let me go.

My heart hurts, it's hammering so hard. I can't seem to catch my breath and I'm beginning to feel dizzy.

It hits me that I'm standing at the top of a flight of stairs much like Lola had been when she died. Vertigo washes over me. Bracing my hand on the wall, I wait for Jessica to say something.

Anything.

Does she believe me?

I just want her to do anything other than look at me like that. Like she's enjoying this.

"Jessica," I begin.

The doorbell rings.

Evan still hasn't tried to interrupt us. He's probably shocked to hear me tell Jessica the truth.

It rings again.

"Let me tell you something," Jessica says. She pulls away enough to look me in the eyes. I half-wonder if Evan is going to open the door but I'm much more interested in hearing what she has to say.

I hear the front door open. It slams into the wall, just like Jessica always slams it, but I don't turn to look at who it could be. Miriam, maybe, come to save me.

"Tell me." She's paused, her eyes glazed and unfocused. "Jessica, tell me." I reach out and grab her shoulder, giving it a little squeeze to get her attention. "Jessica, you know I'm right. I'm here to save you. Let me help you. We can leave tonight. I'll make sure Evan pays for what he did to Lola.

He might not die, but he'll be a cop in prison. That's a death sentence in itself. I'm counting on it now.

Her eyes snap back into focus and she locks them on me, shaking her head.

"Dad didn't kill my mom." She leans back close to me again, so close I can feel the heat coming off her. I can smell the pot she smoked, see the pores on her face. "I did."

No.

I would scream but I can't. Her knife slips into my stomach. I feel it, hot and sharp, like a bee sting on a summer day.

For a moment I fight back.

I don't want to die, and I certainly don't want to die without trying to save myself. Instead of grabbing where she cut me, I reach out and grip her shoulders. She's thin. My fingers sink through the clothes she has on and hit bone.

"Jessica," I cry, the pain of the knife wound catching up with me. Colors swirl in front of my eyes and I try hard to catch my breath. It's impossible. Standing this close to her, all I can do is breathe her in.

I could sweep her leg. I could try to push her down the stairs first. *But she's stronger.* Even high, she's stronger.

"I killed her. She was going to ruin my family." Jessica grins as I stare at her.

No. There was part of me that knew this, if I had only listened to it. My mouth drops open. I want to scream but her hands are on my shoulders. Is she going to pull me into a hug?

No. She shoves me. For just a moment I teeter. It feels like the world is spinning underneath my feet and if I could just get it to stop then I'd be fine.

But it doesn't stop.

My heel slips over the top stair and that's when I know exactly what my sister felt before she died.

FORTY-NINE

JESSICA'S DIARY

I shouldn't have ever worried about Ariel being in the house to help out. She hasn't moved in and I kinda wish she would. Instead, she drives here every morning before Dad goes to work and I go to school. She makes us each breakfast and then talks to me about my day.

She's amazing. I trust her and I wonder if she knows what my dad is really like. I thought for sure that she was under his spell just like everyone else in our lives, but now I'm not so sure. There have been a few times where I thought she might be onto him. She watches him sometimes, but not in a good way.

It took me a while to figure out what the expression on her face was like and where I'd seen it before. Maybe it sounds silly if you don't see it, but I know exactly what she reminds me of.

Back when Mom was still alive and I was younger, she would take me all the time to the zoo. It was our special place, and we'd take a picnic and eat it right by the lion enclosure before she'd shuttle me off to get me ice cream. Even on really hot days I used to love going to the zoo to see the animals and spend time with her.

But there was always something about the lions that set me on edge. When it was really hot out or they had just been fed then they would generally just lie around, being lazy. I liked that about them. They reminded me of our neighbor's cat who would sometimes stretch out on the hood of our car when Dad parked it in the driveway.

They just looked like oversized house cats, and it always made me laugh to think about them killing a mouse and bringing it to the zookeeper for a scratch under the chin.

But they weren't always so happy and so calm, and when it was feeding time, it was almost scary to watch. Instead of looking relaxed and sunbathing, they would pace. They walked up and down the side of their enclosure, their heads swinging from left to right, their huge paws thudding against the ground. My heart always beat faster when my mom would lean down to me and whisper.

"They're going to feed them. Make sure to look!"

I didn't want to look. I didn't want to see the way they watched the keepers. It wasn't that they were just watching the dead animals or raw meat the keepers brought; they were watching the *people*. They didn't just want to eat a dead chicken or goat. They wanted to bite the hand that fed them.

And Ariel looks at my dad the same way.

He doesn't notice it, I'm sure of it. It's not friendly. It's not the expression of someone who's happy with another person. It's not the way an employee should look at their boss.

Sometimes... And maybe this is stupid. Maybe I shouldn't even write it down, because I can't imagine what he might do or say if he were to ever find my diary. If he ever saw these words I'd written and how I really felt about him...

Or maybe he'd see that I'm on his side—that even though I'm scared sometimes just being in the same house with him, that I'm still not going to tell anyone else what's going on. I don't know what he would do if he found my diary, but I have to let it out. Even though it would be so much better to talk to a person, I don't have anyone I can be this honest with.

So I'm going to write it all down. And I'm going to hope he never finds this. But if he does, then, Dad, I'm sorry. I never told anyone. Don't be mad.

I just needed to get this all out of me because sometimes I feel like I'm going to explode. I feel like I'm going to fall to pieces or that my head is going to break because of all the thoughts I keep in it.

Don't be mad.

But sometimes Ariel looks feral. Like a lion. Her eyes are wide, and she stares at you, watching you, waiting to see what you're going to do next. And you look at her like she's trapped, Dad, like you think you're in control. But what control can you really have over a lion in a cage? They're still wild.

You two don't see it, the way you interact, but I do. You let her into the house, put her in this cage with us. Sometimes you scare me. Sometimes I'm terrified of what you're thinking when you look at her, like you don't even want her in our house, but you're the one who hired her. You're the one who brought her here.

She's made our lives so much better, but I don't think you like it.

That feels insane to write. Why wouldn't anyone like it when another person makes their life easier? When another person makes their child feel better about who they are and what's going on in their life?

I don't know.

All I know is that I really like Ariel.

I don't want anything to happen to her.

FIFTY

EVAN

WEDNESDAY, SEPTEMBER 13

It takes me longer than I'd like to admit to tear my eyes away from Ariel and Jessica standing at the top of the stairs.

I just heard it all, heard what Ariel said, and there's no way to take it back, to make her unsay it, to keep Jessica from knowing the truth.

And as much as I'd like to keep watching and listening, I have to get rid of whoever's at the door.

But I'm not going to open it. I'll just get rid of whoever's out there. Letting them in is a terrible idea, but I can yell at them through the wood. I can make them leave and protect my daughter.

Again.

Then I can try to deal with Ariel. She just told Jessica the truth, that she's her mom, and even though she *knows* things only Jessica's mom would know, I can't believe it.

I don't remember Lola's sister, but I wasn't paying attention that time we met.

But that doesn't mean she's lying.

Shock jolts through me as I think about how much Ariel reminded me of Lola.

Oh God.

And all I'd done was ignore that feeling.

It's her.

I just stood there, watching, too afraid to intervene with Jessica because I know how things go when someone stops her from doing what she wants, and now the truth hangs between us all, ugly and dangerous, and I have to get rid of whoever stopped by before I can handle Ariel.

Before I can try to handle Jessica.

I don't have to look up the stairs to know things are bad. I saw it all over Jessica's face. She has a knife. She's angry.

Someone is going to die.

I should intervene, but I'm on autopilot. Someone is at the door and I need to get rid of them. The worst thing that could happen would be them getting in and seeing what's going on. Jessica has this under control, right? She wouldn't really hurt Ariel.

But then why would she take a knife with her when she went upstairs? I thought she and Ariel were getting close, but maybe there was more to how they were acting. Maybe I should have been more worried.

But not for my daughter. She can handle herself.

Who the hell is at the door?

My stomach twists hard as I hurry to it. What if it's one of my officers just stopping by to bring me something? They did that all the time after Lola died. Jessica and I couldn't make it through an entire day without an officer bringing by something to eat, or a book they thought I'd like. Flowers. Chocolate. Liquor. Anything they thought would help to take my mind off what just happened.

The doorbell rings again.

I have to make sure whoever is out there will leave us alone.

I won't open it. I'll just get rid of them, make sure they leave our front door, keep them from hearing what's going on in here. After all, the last thing we want is for our visitor to cause a scene and make our neighbors notice something might be wrong. If they didn't already hear the shouting. I'll just speak to them through the door and get them to leave.

I'm reaching for it when it happens.

The door slams open. I haven't even touched it, let alone unlocked it, but it flies into the wall, the sudden movement knocking me off balance. I stumble back. "What the hell?"

Behind me, I hear scuffling. I want to look. I just can't.

My eyes are locked on who's walking in the door.

Dakota. With her blonde hair swirling around her face, her gorgeous mouth pursed. Her eyes flick over to me, and I feel my heart stop, which probably has to do with how she makes me feel but also because of what's going on behind me.

"Dakota," I say, trying to step in front of her. I have to block her view of the stairs. I have to make sure she doesn't see what's going on. She looks at me but then back down at her phone.

Her phone. I hadn't noticed it at first but now it's all I can look at. She has it clutched in one hand. In the other, a key. *My house key.*

Where did she get that? There's only one person I've ever given a house key to so she could get in if there was an emergency.

Miriam.

That's how she got a key. That's how she opened the door. But as concerning as that is, the key isn't the problem. It's her cell phone. She has it out in front of her like she's taking a picture.

But she's not. She's doing something far worse.

She's *recording.*

Miriam pushes into the house behind her. Her eyes are

wide, her car keys hanging from her hand. I watch as her mouth falls open as she takes in the scene behind me.

I don't have to look to know what she sees. I can crane my neck a little and watch on Dakota's phone. That's how I see Ariel fight back against Jessica. It's how I see my daughter push my housekeeper and send her tumbling down the stairs.

We all see it.

"Oh my God!" Miriam's voice breaks the spell.

I have to get them out of here.

There's a sickening thud behind me, then silence, heavy and oppressive. I want to shake it off, want to break that silence so what just happened will be undone, but there's no way to do that.

"You need to leave!" I snatch for Dakota's phone, trying to grab it from her, but the girl is too fast. She pulls it away from me, tapping on the screen.

Behind me, Jessica thunders down the stairs. I whip round as she runs up to the three of us, her knife raised.

"Jessica, no!" It's going to hurt. I know that. But I step in front of her anyway, my arms out, stopping her from hurting Dakota. I have to save her. I have to stop Jessica.

"She saw!" My daughter is wild. Some of her hair is stuck to the side of her face with sweat. Her eyes, still rimmed with red, are wide. I see blood on the blade in her hand and I have to tear my eyes away from it.

She skids to a stop by me, the knife still up. I wince, then stare at her. She's breathing hard, her chest rising and falling rapidly. Her nostrils flare and her eyes, narrowed and dark, don't dart away from Dakota.

"You can't hurt her!" My voice is loud and I wince, realizing that anyone walking by the house will be able to hear me. Turning, I look at Miriam and Dakota. My assistant has her hand on Dakota's shoulder and is trying to pull her out of the house.

"Dakota, Miriam, please. You have to give us a chance to

explain." How many times have I heard criminals say the exact same thing? My stomach twists with the words but they might have worked. Dakota pauses. Miriam still yanks on her shoulder.

"I filmed it all." When Dakota speaks, her voice is high and tight with stress. "All of it. You can't hide from that. You can't hurt us."

My heart drops when I hear her words. How could she possibly think I would ever do anything to hurt her? But then I see her eyes are locked on my daughter.

My daughter. With a knife. Who just killed another woman.

"You filmed me," Jessica snarls. "You'll never show it to anyone. I'll stop you."

Another step and I grab her, wrapping my arm around her stomach to hold her back.

She's thin and bony but stronger than I would have thought. She strains against my arm, and I stare over her shoulder at Dakota.

"I'll kill you!" My daughter sounds unfamiliar to me. Her voice is hard and brittle, like glass that will shatter if you touch it. Even though I want to let her go, even though just touching her makes my skin crawl, I'm afraid of what might happen if I do.

"We need to go. Jessica, please!" Miriam sounds terrified, her voice tight, like she can't get enough air to speak any louder.

Jessica turns on her, her knife out. I'm still holding my daughter back, but it feels like I don't have any control over her.

"Dakota, we need to go!"

She's slipping from my grasp.

"You're not going anywhere. Why are you here?" My daughter screams the words. It's clear Jessica isn't going to drop this, and I can tell Dakota has had enough. She squares her shoulders and thrusts her phone back at Miriam.

"Hold that, Grandma."

Grandma? My mouth drops open as the full realization of what she just said hits me. *No. This can't be true.*

"You're her grandmother?" I manage, staring at Miriam. My arms relax just a little bit as I speak, and Jessica twists her way out of my grasp.

"I am." Miriam lifts her chin. She looks up at me for just a moment then starts tapping on Dakota's phone. "You would know that if you ever asked about my life and weren't busy screwing around."

"Evan, look at me. I love you. I don't know what's happening here, but I can fix this! We can be together!" Dakota's voice pulls my attention from Miriam. My assistant is still fiddling with Dakota's phone, and while I want to ask her what the hell she's doing, my attention is drawn to Dakota.

I loved her. But why is she here? I can't let her see this.

When I don't answer, she continues. "This is crazy! Jessica is crazy! But I know you! Please, leave with me. Go away with me and we'll take care of this, okay? We'll figure something out!"

"You don't love him." Jessica interjects, stepping between the two of us. "You just wanted to ruin my family."

"No." Dakota shakes her head, her blonde hair flying out around her like a halo. "I love him." She looks at me, her eyes begging. "I love you, Evan. Don't you see that? I don't care about any of this. It's Jessica that's the problem, not you. We can be together."

"You can't love him," Miriam snaps at her. She has the phone back up, pointing it at me. It hits me that she must be taking another video. "You're just a kid. He was using you."

The phone is right in my face.

I have to destroy it.

"Why are you here?" I'm desperate for answers. Desperate

to figure out how I can get them out of my house without anyone else getting hurt.

This was apparently the right question to ask. Miriam squares her shoulders to speak. "Ariel confided in me that she thought you killed Lola. I promised her I'd help her get revenge. Not just for your wife but for my granddaughter. Look at what you did to her! You ruined her! She thinks you love her, but you don't. You used her and discarded her after you killed Lola."

Her voice climbs higher and higher, and Dakota whips around. "Grandma! You told me you needed me to come with my key because you were going to help me get him back. You told me he *loved* me."

Miriam curls her lips. "He only loves himself, darling. I came here with you to stop him. To save Ariel." She looks past me and I know what she sees.

Ariel's body, broken and on the ground. Blood. My daughter, the murderer. *Again.* But they don't know that, do they?

"You two have to listen to me," I say, but before I can try to get them to understand, try to get them to leave so this nightmare can be over, Jessica slips from my grasp, her knife out, her body quivering with excitement. I want to scream at her to stop but I can't.

"You can't hurt me!" Dakota throws her arms up like she's surrendering to the police. "You can't! We filmed it all. We have video that proves you killed Ariel." She points at Jessica, her finger shaking. "I saved it. What, did you think we'd come unprepared?"

She laughs. The sound is funhouse, terrifying, distorted. I want to clap my hand over my ears, but I don't.

And that's why I hear what my daughter says next.

FIFTY-ONE

"I don't give a shit about a video." Jessica lunges forward and I cry out, grabbing at her to try to stop her, but she's strong and thin and she slips through my fingers. There's no way for me to hold on to her, not when she's throwing herself forward like this. My hands close on empty air and the only thing I hear is Dakota scream.

"Jessica, no!" It's too late. I know it's too late, but I still call for my daughter, still try to get her to stop. When she stabbed Ariel, she was so far away that I didn't hear the sound of the knife cutting into her flesh, but I do now. I hear it slice into Dakota, smell the hot copper of her blood as it spills out of her.

Jessica won't stop. She's savage, and even though I should try to pull her off Dakota, I'm useless. Never in my life have I felt this unable to do anything. This is why I'm not great on the road. This is why I was destined for working in an office. I've never been one to get involved with suspects when they're really violent.

I've never been one who could step in between two people and pull them apart.

The last time I was called to a fight on the road, I stood

back. I watched it all play out in front of me, and while I was hoping for there to be a good outcome, it wasn't like I could get involved to do anything about it. I remember the sound of more sirens filling the air as backup made their way to me. I remember turning and looking at the officer's face as he realized what was going on.

He was horrified. I should have been horrified too.

But I couldn't manage to feel anything. I remember him shoving me out of the way, throwing himself into the melee. I saw how he threw punches and took punches, how he finally managed to separate the two. Then he looked over his shoulder at me and I saw written there on his face his disgust.

I couldn't even do my job. I was pathetic. I should have been written up. Should have been fired. There were a lot of things that should have happened to me, but I somehow made it out unscathed. He didn't say anything, not to the lieutenant or captain, anyway, and nothing happened to me.

And so what did I learn? That I can stand uselessly by when there's a fight going on. That someone else will take care of it for me.

I need to stop Jessica. *I just can't.*

I want to scream at my daughter and get her to let Dakota go, but the only thing I can do is watch and what I'm seeing terrifies me.

Jessica still has the knife in her hand. It has to be slippery covered in so much blood, but she doesn't seem to be bothered. Her grip is tight as she swings it forward. The blade slips into Dakota's stomach again and again, and I hear the sound of someone screaming.

Me. I'm screaming. My daughter, the child I raised, whose skinned knees I kissed, is killing someone again. She's killing *Dakota.*

And I'm not stopping her.

"No!" Miriam screams, stumbling backwards. Her eyes are wide, the phone still out.

I have to get the phone.

Jessica and Dakota fall to the ground. My daughter is on top, her arm still swinging up and down, the knife stabbing, stabbing. There's so much blood. It flows from the cuts on Dakota's stomach and chest, already pooling around her on the floor. When I breathe, I want to throw up.

I gag, bending over to grab my thighs. When my head finishes spinning, I look up.

Jessica is crouched over Dakota. She has blood splattered all the way down her shirt. It soaks into her jeans, leaving dark spots behind. Still, though, she has her knife.

"No! You're a murderer! Ariel was wrong. She was wrong. Oh God. She thought Evan, but you... you killed Lola!" Miriam's trying to run. If she would just put down the damn phone, she could make it, but she seems determined to keep it trained on the scene. On Jessica. On Dakota.

She keeps backing up, her eyes wide, her mouth open in an O. Her hands tremble but stay steady enough to keep the camera trained on Jessica.

I can't look away.

Miriam is out on the deck now. She has to turn around to work her way down the stairs or she'll fall. I'm in the doorway. Grabbing the frame, I lean against it. When did I get here? How did I manage to walk out of the house? It's all a blur, Jessica the only thing I can really focus on.

I can't take my eyes off her.

She's so beautiful. So dangerous. She runs up behind Miriam. The knife clatters to the deck, droplets of blood flying off it and splattering like wet paint. I watch my daughter raise her hands.

Miriam's made it down one step. She's holding on to the handrail with one hand, clinging to Dakota's phone with the other. How did I not pick up on the fact that Miriam is Dakota's grandmother?

I missed so many things.

Miriam turns, her eyes wide. They lock on my daughter, and I can only imagine what she sees.

Jessica looks wild. Her arms are outstretched. The curve of her lips is the same that I saw when I hurried home from work after she'd pushed Lola.

Instead of running, Miriam taps on the screen. She's frantic, her eyes wide, her finger tapping incessantly, then the phone is tilted up, pointed too high to catch Jessica or me—*if she would just put it down, stop tapping, stop holding the phone up, then maybe*—but she's too focused on what she's doing.

And then Jessica does the unthinkable.

Miriam screams. Once. She only manages to scream once and then I hear the sound of her body tumbling down the stairs, thudding harder and harder until she finally comes to rest on the walkway.

FIFTY-TWO

"Daddy?" Jessica's voice breaks me from my stupor. I can't see Miriam from here, can't see her spread out like she's making snow angels on the ground, but I'm sure that's what she looks like. I don't have to see her to remember how Lola looked when Jessica pushed her.

And she just did it again.

"Daddy, what do I do?" Jessica calls for me again, and just like any father, I turn to her. It doesn't matter what she's done. It doesn't matter that I just watched her kill three people.

I wonder for a moment if there are more she's killed. If I've just missed all of the signs and she killed more people than just her mother and the three tonight. But I can't think that. I can't let myself go down that path or I'm going to drive myself nuts.

"I'll take care of it."

Jessica sinks against my chest as I wrap my arms around her. She turns her face against my shoulder, and I hug her closer.

"I promise you, Jessica, I'm going to take care of it. I did before, right?"

She nods.

My daughter is a monster.

"There are three of them." Her voice is a gasp. "Three of them, Daddy."

She hasn't called me *Daddy* in years. The last time... When was the last time? Probably when she needed me—really needed me—to take care of something. Skinned knees? A bike with a slipped chain? A little boy who was mean to her?

Now my baby girl is all grown up and I wouldn't want to be any little boy who was ever mean to her. I've seen what Jessica can do. It's not pretty.

"It's okay." I exhale through the lie. *It's not okay and nothing will ever be okay again.* "We have to take care of Miriam first. We have to make sure nobody sees her." I risk a glance down the stairs to where she lies, just like I thought she would, spread out like she's sleeping. Her neck looks snapped, her head twisted to the side. There's blood on her mouth.

"What do I do?" Jessica grabs at my shirt, clawing at me like she's trying to climb inside my body. It's the same panicked way she acted after she killed Lola. "Daddy, what do I do?"

"I have to move her body," I tell her, looking down the street. How are we so lucky that none of our neighbors have come outside to see what all the commotion is? It's dinnertime, and that's the only reason why I can think nobody is looking out their windows.

Still, I look at each house in turn.

Nothing. No movement behind any of the windows. We're lucky right now but there's no way that I think our luck is going to hold. We can't just stand here and pretend that everything is going to continue to be fine when I know it's not. This can all fall apart without any warning, and we need to get a move on.

"Move Miriam," Jessica parrots, nodding. "Right. I'll help."

"Good." Miriam's not a big woman, not by any means, but she's larger than Lola was. I was able to pick my wife up by myself, I hugged her body to my chest and carried her like I had when we got married, moving her closer to the bottom of the stairs to ensure it looked like she really fell and wasn't pushed. But Miriam is different. One of us will have to get her feet; the other will have to get her head.

It's all so familiar to me and I feel like I'm outside my body, watching myself move.

I remember the phone call, the panic in her voice when Jessica said that Lola had fallen down the stairs. She'd been almost hysterical, sobbing for me to come home, her words coming in little snatches that I could barely understand.

And then I got home, and I hugged her, and I told her it was going to be okay. I walked right past my wife's body, right past her gorgeous face now covered with rain, and ran up the stairs. I remember pulling Jessica into a hug and holding her tight. She'd been shaking, barely able to take a deep enough breath to tell me what happened, but she tried.

And I ended up stopping her.

"Dad, I push—"

And I'd stopped her. That was enough—it was *more than* enough—to make it clear to me that she'd done something she shouldn't have, and while I'd like to think she wasn't about to say what I think she was, I'm not stupid.

I've heard a lot of confessions in my years as a police officer. When I worked my way up through the ranks as a detective, then a lieutenant, then a captain, I heard it all. Deathbed confessions, ones that brought relief, even ones under duress when we had them in the interrogation room for hours on end. My daughter is the first person I've ever had confess with her face pressed up against my chest.

I still get chills when I think about it.

Jessica and I hurry down the stairs. We sound like a bunch of cattle pounding through a barn and I wince.

Pause. Check the neighbor's windows.

Still nothing.

"Okay." I rub my hands together to warm up. It's not chilly

outside, not by a long shot, but I feel cold to the bone. It honestly feels like I'm never going to be able to get warm again and I blow on my hands. "Okay," I repeat. "I'll get her under the arms. You can just get her feet, alright?"

Jessica doesn't respond. I shouldn't have to ask my teenage daughter to help me move dead bodies.

But she shouldn't have killed these people.

She's violent. Dangerous. But she's my baby girl. How in the world could I ever send her away?

I can't.

Bracing my feet, I squat down and grab Miriam under the armpits. She's still warm but her body has a heaviness to it that doesn't seem normal. Tugging back on her to see if I could move her without Jessica's help, I'm not surprised when she doesn't budge.

I'm strong but not strong enough to do this. She's stuck here, right in our front yard, until Jessica stops staring at the ground and helps me.

"Jessica. Quit looking at your feet. We need to do this."

Why is it that teenagers can always move quickly when they want to, but not when you need them to? I need her to get her butt in gear and she's looking at her feet like she's never seen them before.

"Jessica." My voice is sharp. She doesn't look up.

I stare again at her. It hits me. She's not looking at her feet. She's looking at a phone on the ground. I can't see what's on the screen because the last bit of the dying sun is reflecting off the glass, but it's pointed right up at Jessica. She's looking down at it like she's taking some artsy selfie or something, but it's not her phone.

Jessica's phone is in a black case. This one is in a pink case.

It's Dakota's.

My stomach lurches with the thought of the young woman I cared so much for dead in my house. I'll have to figure out what to do with her phone, how to dispose of it. Actually, I need to destroy it now, stop it from pinging off any towers. It may be too late, but I'll take care of it. Jessica seems entranced by it, and I need to move it, destroy it, get back on track.

There are so many things to do, so many things I have to do to cover my tracks, to cover Jessica's, and I can't seem to think straight.

"Give me the phone." I lower Miriam's shoulders back down to the ground. Walking over to Jessica, I bend down to pick up the phone, but she beats me to it. Her jaw is slack. Tears spring to her eyes.

"Daddy?"

"Jessica. Give it to me." I'm nervous now, the feeling prickling at the back of my neck. "We need to get rid of it."

"Daddy!" Her voice breaks on the word and she shoves the phone into my hands. I almost fumble and drop it, I'm so surprised that she's giving it to me without a fight. "Look at it!"

"It's a phone," I say, but whatever else I was going to say falls away when I look down at the screen. For a moment, I can't figure out what I'm seeing. There's grass. Our path. Feet. *Miriam's feet.*

Jessica's sobbing.

"Was she still recording?" I remember Miriam tapping on the phone like her life depended on it. She's never been entirely computer savvy, but she told me a month or so ago that her granddaughter was teaching her how to use her phone. *Her granddaughter, Dakota.*

"It's a livestream." Jessica sounds choked. She reaches out to snatch the phone from me but then pulls her hand back. "It's a livestream. Look."

I don't know what to make of what I'm seeing on the screen. There's a counter in the upper right-hand corner and the little number there keeps going up, up, up.

"What is this?" I point to the number. My finger trembles.

"Viewers."

"Viewers?" I might make fun of Miriam for not really knowing her way around technology, but I'm honestly not much better. *Viewers.* The phone slips from my hand and lands with a *thunk* in the grass.

Jessica doesn't move to pick it up.

I can't make sense of what's going on. "Jessica," I say, glancing at my daughter out of the corner of my eye. "Are you telling me Miriam was livestreaming when she fell?"

She nods. When she swallows it's so loud I hear it.

"Those people are watching?"

Another nod. This time she looks away from the phone on the ground and over to me. "Yes."

The phone landed on its back, the screen facing up toward us. Whoever might be watching now is only getting to see grass but as soon as one of us picks the phone back up, they'll get a great view of everything.

We need to move away from the phone. We need to destroy it or rewind or somehow undo everything that just happened here, but we can't.

"Daddy? What do we do?"

I open my mouth to respond. Even though I don't know what to tell her, I know there has to be something we can do. There has to be some way we can make it out of this. Nothing is coming to me, but I have to hope that I'm going to have some sort of an answer for my little girl when I finally do speak.

But nothing comes out.

"We need to run," she says, grabbing my hand. It's sticky and when I look down at it, I'm not surprised to see blood. She doesn't seem to notice as she tugs me to the stairs. "We need to get out of here. They're going to come for us."

She's right. We can stand here and wait for whatever is going to happen to us to happen or we can try to take some control over our lives and get the hell out of here, the phone be damned.

"Leave her," I say to Jessica, when she pauses to look at Miriam. She quickly turns away from me, but I still see the expression on her face.

It's not sorrow, like I thought it would be. There's glee there. I see it in the way her lips curl up, at how her brow furrows just a little bit and then smooths. Jessica doesn't feel bad about killing Miriam.

She enjoyed it.

"Are you coming?" At the base of the stairs, she turns to look at me. Her face is a mask now, impossible for me to read. As I watch, it changes. She frowns, now looking more upset.

But I know what I saw.

"I'll be right there," I tell her. "Pack a bag. Do it quickly. We leave in ten minutes."

"Okay." A pause. She has one hand on the railing, her foot on the first step. She's full of potential energy, just like a sprinter in the blocks waiting for the starting gun to go off. "Thank you."

"You're welcome." My tongue feels fat in my mouth as it fumbles around the words. She sprints up the stairs. Even though I can't see Dakota's body in the door, I see how she jumps over it. I imagine her doing the same at the base of the stairs where Ariel's body waits for me to clean it up.

Then I swallow.

My daughter is a monster.

We can run. I can try to keep her safe, but keeping her safe will always mean cleaning up after her.

Dakota's screen is smashed, but her phone still works. I carefully pick it up, not wanting to cut myself on the glass. It's difficult, but I make sure to keep my feet out of the shot.

I'm not here. I was never here. That plays as a refrain in my mind like I can make it happen by hoping it's true. I don't want to admit that I was here. I want to still be at work. I want to have never heard the sound of a knife slipping into someone's body, the sound of a body smashing down the stairs.

How much did everyone really see?

All I see on the screen is the grass in our yard and Miriam's feet. For all the viewers know, it could be Jessica holding the phone right now. *I'm not here.*

There's a small box on the right side of the screen and I tap it. My fingers are sweaty, but a box pops up, covering up part of the video. I don't know a lot about how these things work, but I'm pretty sure everyone can still see what's being livestreamed, so I make sure to keep the phone steady and off my feet. *I'm not here.*

Inside the box, comments fill the lower part of the screen and I skim through them, using my finger to scroll to the beginning.

Jaxbites 92: where's the sound

BigCity: Sound, please!

Jaxbites 92: I can't hear anything

xxx9847xx: what just happened? did you see anyone?

I pause. Did they just say that they didn't see anyone?

BigCity: Man, it's like someone fell. Dropped the phone.

22loverrr69: then who picked it up? someone is there

BigCity: Why would someone livestream something like that? It's so weird.

They didn't see anything. I can't believe it.

22loverrr69: who's there? i'm looking to see something

xx9847xx: obviously someone got hurt

Jaxbites 92: if we had sound we'd be able to tell what was going on

BigCity: I hate this app. What's the point of starting a livestream if you're not going to show anything?

xx9847xx: this is crap

It hits me. *I'm safe.* The pounding in my chest is almost unbearable and I take a few deep breaths to try to calm down. There's no way this can be true, no way Miriam didn't really get me on video. Dakota did, but that wasn't livestreamed. I can get rid of that. I can delete the video, destroy the phone, make sure it never goes into evidence. I can make sure nobody ever finds the phone and no crack team at the FBI can work their magic to pull the deleted file back off the phone.

I can make it seem like I was never here. They don't know anything. The last thing I want is for people to realize I didn't even do anything to try to stop Jessica. They can't know how I froze.

But the livestream doesn't show me at all, if these comments are to be believed. I can delete the videos. Destroy the memory card. Carefully, so I don't drop the phone, I close out of the livestream app.

Nobody will ever know the truth.

They'll only know what I tell them.

My head feels stuffed full of cotton like I was out drinking all night long. Even though I don't want to do this, I don't know that I have a choice.

I can try to save my daughter. Or I can try to save everyone else she's going to come in contact with in the future. My hand trembles as I pull my phone from my pocket.

Jessica, the daughter Lola and I wanted so badly, the baby we thought we'd never have. And we finally got her, and even though I know Lola missed having her sister in her life sometimes, we had a baby, and it was enough.

At least, it was for a while.

I *knew* there was something familiar about Ariel and I just kept writing it off because I was so happy to have someone in the house to help out. I was thrilled not to have to worry about cooking or cleaning or any of that, so I missed all the little signs that would have pointed straight to the truth—that Ariel wasn't here by accident.

That she knew Lola. Knew Jessica. That even though Lola and I had raised Jessica, even though we were the ones to get up in the middle of the night when she was crying or help her when she was sick, even though we were the ones who suffered through her bad grades and attitude, Ariel has always been more Jessica's family than I was.

I raised her. But Ariel was her mom.

I feel myself sink to my knees in the grass. My head spins with the truth about Ariel and Jessica. I thought Lola and I did our best to raise Jessica, to keep her safe, to make her into a good person.

But we obviously failed.

And now what do I do? Protect Jessica? Keep standing by her and cleaning up her messes even though I know it's going to be too much eventually, that it's going to wear me out and I won't be able to do it forever?

Or do I stop it?

The phone is heavy in my hand. I weigh it, bouncing it up and down, the wet from the grass soaking through my pants to my skin. Finally, though, I know what I have to do.

I make the call.

FIFTY-THREE

JESSICA'S DIARY

I can't stop crying. Even though I know tears aren't going to do anything to help me out, even though I know I'm on a path that I'm not going to be able to get off, I can't stop crying.

I wish things were different. I wish...

Well, it doesn't matter what I wish, does it? All that matters is that I have to do what my dad tells me to do. I have to listen to him.

If I don't, he'll kill me. He's already covered me in bruises. Of course, as the police, he knows where to hurt me so nobody will ever see them. I cover the marks on my hips and legs with long pants. My arms are a little trickier, but it's chilly out in the mornings so I wear long sleeves and I make sure to sit next to the air conditioner in class every day.

Who cares how sweaty I get? All that matters is that nobody knows what's really going on at home.

Nobody needs to see the proof of where he's pushed me into the counter, how he's pinched my arms, what my legs look like from him shoving me into chairs.

Would anyone believe me? Would anyone see that he's dangerous and that I just want out of the house, or would they all take his side? I think I know the answer to that question. I know how much people in town love and admire him. He's the chief of police, for God's sake.

Nobody is going to believe that he pushes me around when he's unhappy with me. Just yesterday I was getting ready to come downstairs and he grabbed me, pulling me back from the top step. One hand was around my arm, his fingers pressing into old bruises, the other grabbed my hip.

"Be careful," he'd whispered into my ear. His breath was warm on my cheek, but there wasn't any way I could twist away from him. "Be careful—you don't want to end up like your mother."

And now he wants me to do the worst thing ever. He thinks Ariel is dangerous. He thinks she knows something that she's not supposed to.

I've never seen him this paranoid in my life. He's supposed to be this great guy and is supposed to always have his head on straight, but he's gone off the rails, I swear he has. I don't know what to do about it and I don't know that I have a choice in the matter.

I have to do what he told me to.

And he told me to kill Ariel.

God, just writing those words makes me want to throw up. Just the thought of hurting her, of being so cruel to the one person who's been kind to me this entire time, makes me sick. How in the world could I ever do that?

How could I kill someone who I think could help me get out of this living hell?

"Please no." I didn't want to beg him. This is my *dad*. This man is supposed to protect me and now he wants me to do the worst possible thing I can think of, and I don't know anyone who can help me stand up to him.

"You're going to kill her," he told me. "I'll get it all set up. You need to stop her, Jessica, or she's going to find out the truth. She's going to learn that you were the one who helped me cover up Lola's death. There's no way in hell the police will look the other way. If you want to have any kind of a life, you need to do this."

But I don't know how. There's just no way I can live with myself if I do this, but I don't see any way my dad will let me live if I don't. He wouldn't kill me, right?

But then I remember that he killed Mom. He's been pushing me around, hitting me, covering me with bruises. I don't know why he went off the deep end, but I do know there isn't really anything I can do to stop this. If I want to make it out of this house alive, then I need to play by his rules even though those rules are going to push me to do something I don't want to.

I can't do it. But I have to.

He told me he'd set it all up. He told me he'd make sure Ariel was upstairs and not paying attention to anything going on around her. He told me I had to hide in my room with a knife and then kill her.

It's Ariel or me.

FIFTY-FOUR

EVAN

It's one of the best response times our department has ever had. I hear the sirens filling the air as the officers speed toward our quiet little neighborhood and, even though it's crazy, I can't help but feel a flash of pride.

Look at how quickly they're getting here when someone calls in to report a murder.

They need to hurry though. I have the keys to our car, so Jessica can't drive away. Still, she could get Ariel's. She could come down here and try to take Miriam's from her pocket. I don't know if I'd have the strength to stop her.

Resting my head in my hands, I sit on the bottom stair. My muscles ache and even my joints feel tired, like I just ran a marathon. I want to curl up into a little ball and go to sleep. I want to let someone else take care of all of this for me, the way I took care of Lola's body when Jessica killed her.

I did what I had to then.

I moved my wife, just enough, just to make it look like an accident. I covered up the fact that there been a fight, called off my affair with Dakota. I got Jessica calmed down, made sure everyone would believe Lola accidentally slipped and fell to her death.

All because I wanted to believe my daughter hadn't meant to push her mother. But now I know I'm wrong. Jessica didn't push Lola by accident. She pushed her on purpose, to stop our lives from being torn apart. I thought she felt terrible about it and nothing like that would ever happen again.

I was wrong on both accounts.

"Daddy!" Jessica calls me from the deck, but I barely have the energy to turn and look at her. The sirens are getting louder now, and she has to hear them. "We need to go!"

I have to force myself to turn and look up at her. She's so gorgeous standing there, her mannerisms so much like Lola. I can't look at my daughter without remembering my wife.

My stomach turns. Lola wasn't her mom. I knew that, but how I missed the truth about Ariel, I'll never know. I thought I was doing the right thing trusting her, but I was wrong.

I should have seen the truth about who Ariel was in the way she laughed, how her mouth quirked up more on one side the way Lola's did. Or how she would push the oven door shut with her hip. How she'd roll her eyes just a little and then catch herself like she knew what she was doing was wrong.

She felt familiar and I'd ignored it. I'd told myself that it was just because I knew so many people that she felt familiar. Just because I was so grateful to her for coming into the house to help out.

And because I was wrong, three more people had died.

I stand up so I can look at her. "Honey, we're not going anywhere."

The sirens are so loud now. I can tell they're on our street without even having to turn to look for them. The officers driving can probably see me standing at the bottom of the stairs.

They can probably see Jessica bending over the railing, her face twisted in anger.

"What do you mean?" The words explode out of her. "What do you mean *we're not going anywhere*? They're right there!" She points and I turn to look.

It's a caravan. I knew it would be. There wasn't any other response I could have expected when the chief of police calls and reports his daughter for murder. I'd already broken Dakota's phone. It was easy to shut off the live feed and delete the video since I know all of her passwords. I'd also taken out her SIM card and smashed it, then carried the tiny pieces to our back shed and buried them deep in a half-empty bag of potting soil.

Later, I'll go out and get rid of them. I'll take everything off our property and dispose of it in the river or a nearby lake. But for now, I have to hope that the potting soil is safe.

But I know it is. The officers will come. They'll arrest Jessica. She'll argue, of course, tell them I was here, tell them I helped cover up Lola's death. There will be questions and I'll have to come up with answers. I'm not looking forward to the time I'm going to spend in the interrogation room.

I've been on the other side of the table. I've dealt with suspects who claimed they were innocent, but the difference there is that I am. I actually am innocent. I didn't kill anyone, not really, and I'm not going to go on the run only to die in a shootout so my daughter can try to avoid going to jail.

"Dad!" She's screaming now and I turn around to look up at her. Her face is purple. Her hands grip the railing so hard that her fingers are sinking into the wood. I can still see blood on her hands and I'm sure the officers will see that as soon as they pull up.

I have to make sure this goes perfectly.

Her fingerprints are on the knife.

Blood is on her hands.

There's no proof I was home.

I can claim that Jessica went insane.

At this point, it's not just about me. Of course I don't want to go to jail. Of course I don't want to go down for a triple murder that my daughter committed. She's out of control. I can't handle her. There's no way I'm going to take the fall for her.

Not a chance.

"Hands up!" The first two police cars are already parked out in front of our driveway. They completely block the road.

Again I scan the neighbor's windows.

Curtains twitch.

I don't know if Jessica is going to put her hands up, but I do, moving slowly, not wanting to spook them. I know the officers who have their guns trained on the two of us. I've had coffee with them, even taken one of them a box of diapers when his wife had a kid. Right now though, none of that matters. The only thing that matters to them is three dead bodies.

I called it in. I'll be fine.

But Jessica?

Turning slowly, I look up at my daughter. Her hands are on her head, just like mine. She's not staring at the officers as they slowly approach. She's staring right at me, hatred written all over her face.

I'll kill you.

She mouths the words, but they hit me with the same impact as if she'd just screamed them in my face. I take a step back, wanting more space between the two of us. It doesn't matter that she can't get to me right now. In this moment, I'm honestly afraid of what she might do.

"Chief." An officer lightly touches me on the shoulder. "You can put your hands down. Are you okay? Did she hurt you?"

"No." I shake my head. "I mean, yes, I'm fine. She didn't hurt me. I just got home and saw..." My voice cracks and tears spring to my eyes. I don't know if they're real or just from stress, but it doesn't matter. "She killed them all," I finish, my voice a hoarse whisper.

There's compassion in his eyes when he looks at me. I can see it. It's obvious.

This is going to work.

FIFTY-FIVE

EVAN

Mike Maroni, the man who helped me put myself back together after Lola died, sits across from me. He's got some gray scruff growing in, which tells me that he hasn't slept since I called last night about Jessica.

To be completely honest, neither have I. Even if I were at home in my own bed, I don't think I would have been able to get any sleep. Here at the precinct, stuck in a small interview room, the chance of getting any rest decreases exponentially.

Keeping my hands folded in front of me on the table, I take another deep breath. Just an hour ago another detective sat here and told me that I was almost free to go. He'd thanked me for being so willing to sit here through the night as they tried to figure out exactly what had happened with Jessica and told me I'd be home before the sun came up.

Now, there aren't any windows in this godforsaken box of a room, but I'd bet anything that the sun is up and I'm still here. Turning my head a little bit, I catch a glimpse of Mike's watch—

7:15 a.m. Yep, the sun is up, I'm dead on my feet, and I'm still here even though I was told hours ago I'd be home by now.

But that was before the SBI showed up. Of course the State Bureau of Investigation would get involved. My department isn't going to be allowed to handle this case, not when it involves the chief's daughter. I knew an outside agency would be called in, but I didn't think that would mean I'd still be here this morning.

There's a knock on the door. I start, my head heavy and thick with exhaustion, and turn to look at it. An SBI agent leans in, all bluster and frowns. Unlike my officers, who usually have a smile on their faces when they're in the office, he wears a grimace that only deepens when he looks at me. "Keep him here a bit longer," is all he says to Detective Maroni, who still sits across from me like he's terrified to do differently.

The door slams shut.

The two of us are silent for a moment. Being awake right now, thinking about Jessica and what she did, it's enough to make me go crazy. I need sleep, need to shut off my brain so I don't keep replaying what happened.

Over and over. Jessica killing Ariel. Killing Dakota. Killing Miriam.

My throat hurts when I swallow, and I shift on the chair. The edge of it cuts into the back of my legs. Mike doesn't look at me.

I clear my throat. "Mike, do you think there's any way I can get out of here soon? I just want to get home, get some rest. I'm sure you understand."

Mike shifts position in his seat. It's obvious he's uncomfortable with the request. He clears his throat. "Listen, Chief, you know I'd love to let you go home now, but the house is still an active crime scene."

"I can get a hotel room." Planting my hands on the table, I start to stand up. My legs are numb from sitting for so long and I move slowly, letting blood flow back down to my feet. "That's not a problem. I just need sleep."

"Yeah, I don't think you can do that." Mike clears his throat and stands up too. He moves a lot faster than I do, whether that's because his legs aren't going numb from sitting for so long or because he's just in a huge hurry to make sure I don't get out of this room.

"What? What do you mean?"

"I mean, Chief, you can't leave."

Mike scrubs his hand down his cheeks like he's really upset about what he's saying to me. All I can do is stare at him. He clears his throat again.

"I need rest. I need to go home. What, you don't think I'm guilty of hurting those three women, do you?"

Anxiety eats at me. My heart hurts from throbbing so hard in my chest and I reach up, rubbing it. I need to get out of here and not only get some fresh air but get some space to think. It's difficult to have a coherent thought on this side of the interview room. This little desk, the hot light over my head, the way the chair rocks a little bit every single time I move... It's all cliché as hell but it works, and I feel like I'm coming out of my skin.

"Oh, hell, Chief." Mike stares at me. "Please just wait, okay?"

"Am I under arrest?"

There's a beat. Another moment of silence then Mike shakes his head. "Don't make me say it, Chief."

"Arrest me." Holding my hands out in front of me, I press my wrists together and hold them up for him to see them. I want to make my point. "If you're going to hold me here, Mike, then you need to arrest me. Man up. Do it."

I'm being stupid and I know that. What I need to do is shut up, sit down, and ask for a lawyer. I've never had to call one before, but I know who the good ones in town are. I know who I can rely on to make sure this doesn't go south.

Well, any more south than it already has.

Mike opens his mouth like he's going to argue with me, but before he can so much as squeak out a sound, the door flies open. In walks the SBI agent. He swaggers, two slim volumes tucked under his arm. When he looks at me, he grins.

My stomach drops. I sit back down. I have no idea what this man just found but I have a feeling I'm not leaving here anytime soon.

"Chief Warner," the SBI agent says, grinning at me. "I've just had the most delightful chat with your daughter."

Just thinking about Jessica makes me sick. Of course I knew she was going to be questioned. She was there, covered in blood, when the police arrived. It's a terrible thing to throw your own daughter under the bus, but I don't have a choice.

I have to save people from her. Getting her locked up is the only way to protect people.

He's waiting on me to respond but I keep my lips pressed tightly together. Whatever he's fishing for, I'm not giving it to him.

"She told me everything."

Still no response. Mike is looking back and forth between the two of us like he's watching a tennis match. The SBI agent towers over me, and while I'd love to stand up and show him that I'm not scared of him, I can't move. Truth is, I need this chair's support so I don't just sink to the floor.

"Recognize these?" He moves quickly, slapping the two notebooks he had tucked under his arm onto the table. They land with a loud smack, and I wince.

He doesn't.

"I don't think I've ever seen these before." It's a lie. I know exactly what one of them is. The other, though, I've never seen before, so that's not a lie. Still, he thinks he has me.

"Your wife's diary," he says, nudging the blue volume toward me. "Our officers found it in the hall at the top of the stairs. I think your housekeeper was doing a little snooping and found it. I think maybe she got scared of what you might do to her since she knew you offed your wife."

"I didn't." My lips are dry, and I lick them, but my tongue feels like a desert. I kept the diary—why did I do that? I should have destroyed it, I should have—"I didn't kill Lola. It was an accident. She fell to her death; she—"

"She was pushed. And then you covered it up."

"No." How did he find this out? He's not acting like he's guessing. The expression on his face combined with his tone of voice tells me he's entirely confident about what happened. "No, she fell."

"No. She was pushed. You covered it up, you made it look like an accident. Then, when Ariel found out the truth, you forced Jessica to attack her to keep her from telling anyone else. Miriam and Dakota were unfortunate, weren't they? Did you tell Jessica to kill them too? Or did you do them yourself? You got tired of Lola and killed her, then you got tired of Dakota and killed her too. Was Miriam just collateral damage for you?"

"What? No! You're wrong! I didn't kill any of them. This was all Jessica." I slam my palm on the table next to the other notebook. He hasn't told me what it is and, at this point, I'm afraid to ask. What has my daughter been telling them? This was supposed to be easy. It was supposed to be a way to protect Jessica from herself and keep her from hurting other people.

But what did she say to them? And how do they know about Dakota? I thought we were so careful, that nobody knew the truth. But I must have been sloppy.

Groaning, I close my eyes. When I open them, I can't look away from the books in front of me.

He catches me looking at the second notebook. "Your daughter's diary," he says, pushing it closer to me. "Jessica was relieved to tell us about it."

Jessica has a diary?

"She told me how you killed Lola, how you threatened to kill her if she didn't help you cover it up. She could barely hold it together, the poor thing. And she's just a kid. What kind of a sick fu—" He pauses, catching himself. "What kind of a monster do you have to be to kill your wife then make your daughter help you cover it up? What kind of a monster tells his daughter she has to kill the housekeeper?"

"No." My voice is a whisper. "No, you've got it all wrong. That's not how it went. Jessica pushed Lola—she was angry and she pushed her!"

Mike makes a disgusted noise in the back of his throat. I glance at him, but he won't meet my eyes.

"Come on, Evan." The SBI agent sits on the corner of the table. "You don't want to read what your wife and daughter really thought about you? You don't want to know how terrified Jessica was of you? And Lola too? How scared they were to live in the same house with you? That's sick. You're sick, you know that? Hitting your daughter? Covering her in bruises? You're a monster."

I can't catch my breath. I want to argue with him and tell him he's got it all wrong, but from the expression on his face, it's obvious he doesn't think he does. When I risk a glance at Mike, I instantly wish I hadn't. He's staring at me, a look of pure disgust on his face.

"Bruises? No. You don't know what you're talking about. I've never laid a hand on her. Never would I—"

"She's covered in them!" He slams his hand down on the table and I jump. "Quit lying to me!"

I'm silent. He's never going to believe me, not without a video of Jessica killing everyone. And I took care of that, didn't I? When I speak, my voice is quiet. "What's going to happen to Jessica?" This is what really matters. I'll get a lawyer, I'll fight this. I'll make sure I don't go to prison.

I hope.

I just need to make sure she isn't going to be able to hurt anyone ever again.

They don't answer right away.

I drop my head into my hands and exhale hard, trying to keep my swirling thoughts from dragging me under. It's difficult for me to think straight right now.

"Jessica won't be going home, if that's what you're worried about. We'll take care of her; get her the help she needs. She's safe. She'll get counseling. We'll make sure she has someone in her life who will love her and protect her."

"She's the one who killed Lola." My head snaps up so I can look at him. "She pushed Lola down the stairs then called me, freaking out, needing me to fix it. I didn't tell her to hurt anyone. I wouldn't!" My voice is too loud. I see it in both men's expressions and I take a deep breath, forcing myself to settle back down.

"Quit blaming your daughter for everything you did wrong. You're disgusting." The SBI agent gathers up the two diaries and turns to leave. Before he does though, he looks at Mike. "Book him. Lock him up. This asshole doesn't deserve to see the light of day."

"There's a video!" I hit the table, triumphant. Both men turn to look at me. Mike's eyebrows are raised, and I feel a flash of hope. "A video. Of Jessica."

"A video?" The agent sounds interested. "Where?"

"Dakota's phone. I deleted it, but you can still get it, right?"

The two men look at each other. Mike gives his head a small shake, his mouth pressed into a firm line. It feels like the floor drops out from under me.

He doesn't believe me.

"It's on the phone. She saved it. I deleted it but you can still get to it, right? I promise you: you'll see the video and you'll know I'm telling the truth!"

The agent laughs. "Right. You sound really convincing, you

know that? Almost like your training as an officer is helping you lie. We found the phone where you told us it was. It's completely destroyed. You did a great job breaking it. There's nothing left."

"I want my lawyer," I say, standing up. My legs shake a little bit but I'm not taking this sitting down. "I want my phone call; I want my lawyer." I pause, trying to decide if this next demand is going to work or just get me in more trouble. "And I want to speak to my daughter."

The SBI agent pauses at the door then slowly turns around. "You can have your phone call. And get a lawyer—you're going to need one. But there's no way in hell I'm letting you harass that poor girl. You stopped being a father when you convinced her to help you clean up her mother's murder."

He leaves, slamming the door behind him. Immediately, I turn to Mike, but he won't look at me.

"Mike. Please. You know I didn't do this."

He pauses. "It's all written in the diaries." Another pause. "I wish I could help you, Chief, I really do, but you screwed up. You're on your own on this one. Turn around—I need to take you to a cell."

I turn, putting my wrists behind my back. My legs wobble but I refuse to come across as weak in front of Mike. A shiver shoots through me when the handcuffs click shut on my wrists. Mike turns me back around, his hand on my shoulder to guide me, then he clears his throat.

"Evan Warner, you have the right..."

I'm not listening, not really. I'm going to get out of these handcuffs.

And then I've got to stop my daughter.

FIFTY-SIX

JESSICA

THURSDAY, SEPTEMBER 21

I did what I had to do. There may be some people who don't agree with me, who think I might have had another option, but I didn't.

Ariel was going to find out the truth. *She was going to ruin everything.* And then when my dad was so willing to throw me under the bus, well, there wasn't any way I was going to let him.

He told me to run inside and pack, but I already knew what he was going to do. I saw the expression on his face—that of a trapped animal who's willing to chew off their own leg to escape. He was going to chew off his leg to save himself, and that meant I was going to take the fall.

But I refused.

Now I roll over, pulling a blanket up around my shoulders. It's not really cold in the juvenile detention facility but I like being comfortable and I want my bruises covered up. On the weekends I can sleep in, and I really don't want to do much of anything today. I could really use a shot of vodka, but I guess I can't complain.

Honestly, I can't believe it all worked out as well as it has so far. Even though I'd been planning ahead for when the police got involved, I didn't think it would be this perfect.

I'd been keeping a diary, making sure it looked like my dad was really as terrible as I needed him to be to cover my ass when all hell broke loose. Sure, hitting myself and running into things to give myself bruises hurt, but when I got high or drank something first then I barely noticed the pain. I needed to be covered in them and I needed to keep them hidden from him.

The loud music in my room kept him from hearing me slam into things. He didn't hear me punch myself, the sick sound of flesh on flesh making my stomach turn. I had to make sure he didn't know.

It was important that he not have any way to explain them away when the police asked him about them.

And then I needed to make sure they would find my diary. During my interview, when they were treating me like a common murderer, I broke down. I showed them my bruises. Some were fresh, some faded and green, backing up my story that he'd been abusing me for a while. I told them how I saw him kill my mom, how he made me help him cover it up.

I told them he made me do these horrible things and finally I told them where to find my diary.

My diary. The one I'd been carefully writing in. I've always loved creative writing, and what better way to use my skills than to make sure my dad ends up where he belongs? No parent who's willing to turn their back on their child deserves to walk free.

The last entry was hurried. I had to make sure I didn't get any blood on the pages so nobody would suspect that I wrote it after I'd already killed three people. Dad thought I was packing to leave, but I was making my own little insurance policy. Yes, I threw a few things in a bag to make him think I was doing what he asked, but I'd seen the truth of what he was going to do on his face. He was going to call the police and turn me in.

And there wasn't any way I was going to let that happen. If he hadn't called the police, if he'd really wanted to help me, then I would have destroyed the diary.

Maybe.

Or maybe not. If there's one thing my dad has taught me, it's to always look out for number one. He's never been afraid of making sure that he was protected, no matter what he was doing, so why should I? Why should he be able to throw other people under the bus just so he doesn't get in trouble but I can't?

He shouldn't. Even though my dad has always been the best at taking advantage of other people and making them do whatever he wants, I won this time.

And this time was really the only time that mattered.

Grabbing my earbuds, I'm about to slip them in and turn on some music when there's a soft knock on my bedroom door.

"Come in." I keep my voice quiet. My dad will be in jail for a long time and I'm in juvie while my lawyer figures out how to best handle this. Even though he told me he can't promise any results, he thinks I've got a good chance of getting out of here, of living my life.

Of course, my life won't really start until I'm eighteen. But I'm patient. I can wait.

"Hey, how are you doing?" This woman is named Gail. She has thick white hair and wears small gold hoops every day. Her constant smile irritates me, but at least she hasn't tried to be my best friend.

"I'm good." I'm antsy to get out of here, but I have to bide my time.

"That's great. Hey, I just talked to your lawyer. You have a phone call. Why don't you come to the front office and you can take it?" She's waiting for me in the door, making it clear to me that I don't have much of a choice in the matter.

Who in the world could be calling me? Besides my lawyer, I haven't had any calls. Sure, there have been some reporters who've tried to interview me, but the staff here won't let them talk to me.

Curiosity more than anything else makes me swing my legs out of bed and head down the hall. I follow right behind Gail, ignoring the looks other girls give me as we pass through the recreation room. None of them have approached me after my first night here when word got around I'd just killed three people. Besides, they just sit around reading and doing puzzles, and I want no part in that.

"Here you go." Gail holds a door for me, waiting until I pass her to speak again. "Talk as long as you need, okay? I'll be right here if you need me." She gives me an encouraging smile and then closes the door.

I'm in a small room with a desk, chair, and phone. There's a pad of paper and pencil on the desk. Behind me are windows so Gail can keep an eye on me and get to me if needed. The door to this room doesn't lock from the inside.

I sit down. My palms are sweaty. Not knowing who's on the other end of the phone makes me nervous. Finally, unable to stand it any longer, I pick it up.

"This is Jessica."

"Jessica." The woman on the other end of the line sounds exhausted. Her voice is weak, like just saying my name was almost too much for her. I recognize it, I swear I do, but the connection isn't great and my heart's beating hard enough to make it difficult for me to hear.

I switch the phone to my other hand, wipe my sweaty palm on my pants. Switch it back.

"Who is this?" Does my voice tremble a little bit? If so, I hate it. "Who are you?"

"It's your mother."

No. I can't breathe. I feel like I'm choking. For a moment, I close my eyes, try to focus.

"Jessica?"

"I'm here. But you're dead. I stabbed you."

She chuckles. The sound makes the hair on my arms stand up. Nervously, I turn and look behind me, fully expecting to see Gail watching me through the window. Her back is to me, and she throws her head back and laughs as I watch.

I can't hear her.

So she can't hear me.

"You tried to kill me, but I made it through. You should be glad, darling."

"And why's that?" I feel a tension headache coming on. Reaching up, I rub between my eyebrows to try to relieve the pressure.

"Because I know what you wrote in your diary was a lie. I know Evan didn't want you to hurt anyone. You lied about that, just like you lied about the bruises on your body."

I'm sweating harder now. "What are you going to do?" I have to force myself to relax my grip on the phone. My fingers cramp and I exhale hard, trying to wrap my mind around what's happening.

"I'm your mother, Jessica, what do you think I'm going to do?"

Oh God, I have no idea. She knows the truth, which means she could do anything to me. She could tell the police, tell my lawyer, get Dad out of jail. I'd never see the light of day again.

"Just tell me what you want." My teeth are gritted, my eyes squeezed shut. This is unbelievable. She can't be alive—I stabbed her and then she fell down the stairs and then—

"I'm getting out of the hospital soon. I'll tell everyone how terrible Evan was, that he abused you."

What? I'm holding my breath.

"I'll save you. You're my daughter. I just wanted you back, and now you're mine. We'll get to be a family."

"And if I don't want to be a family?" The words explode out of me.

There's a pause. I think for a moment about hanging up just so I don't have to hear what she's going to say.

"Then I have something very different to tell the police." Her voice is cold. "All I've ever wanted was a family, Jessica. Your mother took that from me, made it impossible for me to have a life with you. But I can have it now."

Chills race up and down my spine. I'm glad I'm sitting down because I don't think I'd be able to stand. Once again, I turn and look out the window for Gail. This time, I'm not looking to make sure she's not eavesdropping; I'm looking because I want her to interrupt me.

She's still there, her back to me, still laughing.

I feel cold. My skin is clammy; I'm horribly aware of my heart beating.

"Did you hear me, Jessica?"

I turn back to the desk, spread my free hand out on the top of it. The wood is cool under my hot skin. "I heard you." I croak out the words. "So you're saying, what, that you're going to lie for me but I have to be your daughter?"

"That's exactly what I'm saying. You're a smart girl, Jessica. We can both get what we want. You get freedom, I get you in my life."

"My lawyer will get me out of here. I won't be here for long, so I don't need you." I hope I'm coming across more confident than I'm feeling right now.

She laughs. "Do you know what the statute of limitations is for murder?"

"No." I pick up the pencil and tap it against the desk before dropping it again. My entire body screams for me to stop this conversation and get out of here but there's nowhere for me to go.

"There isn't one. I can turn you in today, Jessica. I could turn you in to the cops in a week, in a year, in a decade. You want to stay out of jail? You need me to do it."

I can't escape from juvie. Ariel knows where I am, and if she's to be believed, she can either free me or ensure I'm stuck here forever.

"There has to be another way." I don't like begging, but she's me backed into a corner.

"The only way out of there is with me, darling. You want a life? I want you in mine. It's your decision what I tell the police."

"If you tell them one thing now and then change your story later, you'll get in trouble too. You know that, right?" I'm finding my footing. She might think she's in control, but I can still fend for myself. "You'll go to jail for lying or obstruction or something."

"You think I care about that?" Her voice is louder now. Stronger. "I lost everything when I lost you! It's you and me, Jessica. We can live our lives together outside of jail or we'll both suffer the consequences of your actions. Your choice."

I don't speak. I *can't* speak.

"I'll come see you when I get out of here in a few days. You better have made your decision about the type of life you want by then. I love you, Jessica. I shouldn't have given you up so many years ago, but I didn't feel like I had a choice. Lola said she would take care of you and protect you. She promised me that she and Evan were the best people to raise you. But I never stopped loving you and now we'll be together. Think about what you want, okay? Everything I've ever done has been to protect you, to ensure you'll be safe and happy. That's not going to change now."

"I'm going to be in here until after the trial." It almost feels good to spit the words at her. "Until Dad is found guilty. Until they know I'm not a danger to anyone."

There. Let her deal with *that*.

She laughs. My fingers clamp down on the receiver. Hard.

"Jessica, I just got off the phone with the DA. You're young. You get good grades. It's obvious you were abused by your father and that he pushed you to do these horrible things. You've shown remorse."

I don't interrupt. I can't seem to speak.

"He doesn't want to press charges. There are going to be some conditions to your release of course. Therapy. You'll be living with me. But you don't have to worry about staying in juvie forever. Just until everything gets sorted out. Trust me, darling, I'm not going to leave you there. I love you. I'm never going to leave you again."

Rather than responding, I hang up. It feels good to slam the receiver down and so I do it again, harder this time, fully expecting the molded plastic to crack. It doesn't, and I sit back in my chair, breathing harder.

God, I need a drink.

The walls in here feel like they're closing in on me.

Planting my elbows on the table, I drop my head to my hands and massage my temples. She thinks she's won, but I'm not playing this game. I don't want her in my life, don't want that threat of being turned in to the police hanging over my head every single day.

If there's one thing I'm good at though, it's playing the game. I played it with my dad and won. I can play it with Ariel.

She threatened me. There's only one thing I can do in response.

Satisfied, I push back from the desk and leave the room.

Gail turns to me, still mid-laugh, her cheeks bright. "Everything okay, Jessica?"

It's nice how much she cares. Gail is one of the good ones. She turns to me, putting her coffee cup down so she can give me her full attention.

"Things are looking up," I tell her, giving her a thumbs-up. The terrible pit in my stomach I felt when talking to my mother is gone. It's been replaced by a sense of calm. "I'd like to call my lawyer. Can you make that happen?"

"Of course." She beams at me, probably surprised I'm not making a beeline right back to my room. "Yes, definitely. Let me get his number and we'll make sure you can connect with him. Why don't you stay right here?"

I lean against the counter and watch as she walks off to her office. The woman next to me glances up at me but then resumes working on her computer. That's fine. I don't want to talk to her. I need just a moment to gather my thoughts and figure out what I'm going to say to my lawyer.

I'll ask him to call my mom, to make sure the DA wasn't lying about me getting out of here. I'll tell him how excited I am to have her in my life, how much I'm looking forward to starting a life with her, how she mentioned therapy and that I think it's a great idea. I'll say and do whatever I have to just to get out of here.

If she comes through on her promise and tells the police that my dad forced me to do these terrible things, then it should all work out in my favor. I'll have counseling and will probably have to stay here for a while, but I can be good. I can bide my time. Dad is taking the fall.

As he should. He's the one who ruined our family to begin with.

This will all work out—I know it will. It's only four years until I'm eighteen and I won't have to worry about the state trying to tell me I'm not an adult. Ariel wants to hold this over my head for the rest of my life, but I'm not going to let her.

Four years.

And then I can end this.

Accidents tend to happen when people are around me. I don't trust her to keep a secret, not when she wants to hold it over my head like this. But I will trust her when she's dead.

A LETTER FROM EMILY

Dear reader,

Thank you so much for reading *The Wife in the Photo*. I really hope you enjoyed it! If you want to make sure you don't miss out on my new releases, just sign up at the following link. Your email address will never be shared, and you can unsubscribe at any time.

www.bookouture.com/emily-shiner

The Wife in the Photo is my first book with Bookouture and I hope you enjoyed reading it just as much as I enjoyed writing it! It's been an adventure from day one, and now I'm thrilled it's in your hands. If you enjoyed *The Wife in the Photo*, I would be very grateful if you would write a review. Not only do I love to hear what my readers think, but reviews make a huge difference and can help new readers discover my books.

I love hearing from my readers and learning what they thought about my books! If you want to share your thoughts or ask questions, do get in touch. I always respond to readers who reach out, so feel free to shoot me an email at emily@authoremilyshiner.com. You can also find me on Facebook or reach me via my website.

Thanks, Emily

KEEP IN TOUCH WITH EMILY

www.authoremilyshiner.com

facebook.com/authoremilyshiner

twitter.com/authoreshiner

instagram.com/authoremilyshiner

ACKNOWLEDGMENTS

It takes more talented people than I ever realized to bring a book to life. Thank you to the entire Bookouture team for an incredible experience and for trusting me to write for you and your audience.

A very special thanks to Kelsie Marsden, my editor extraordinaire, who is attentive, insightful and keeps me on track! Without her vision and gentle prodding, this book wouldn't be half as incredible as I believe it is.

Thank you to Bruce for the advice about police matters and Claire for being a shining light when I was ensconced in the drudgery of edits. There's always time for tea and a board game, even when facing a deadline.

The biggest thank you is to my readers for being supportive and kind, for reading what I write and connecting with me online, and for giving me a reason to crawl out of bed at 4:30 a.m. to craft stories!